CRIME FAMILY, A BUCK TAYLOR NOVEL

Crime Family, A Buck Taylor Novel

CHUCK MORGAN

Charles E Morgan

COPYRIGHT

First printing 2023

ISBN 978-1-0881-3172-5 (Paperback)

LIBRARY OF CONGRESS CONTROL NUMBER
2023906444

DEDICATION

To all those folks who work in secret to protect us from the next terrorist attack. We owe you a debt of gratitude.

| 1 |

Chapter One

Brian Cole slid his six-foot-four-inch frame onto the barstool and slapped Tucker Clark on the arm.

"Hey, bro, what's eatin' you?" he asked.

Brian was stocky, with short hair and a thin mustache. Today he wore jeans and a faded red T-shirt. His voice was deep and raspy.

Lacy Marks sat a tall, frosted glass of beer in front of him and nodded as she made her way down the bar. Cole followed her as she went, noting the tight jeans she was wearing. He thought about that night behind the gym, senior year, when he had tapped that ass. His cheeks got red, and he turned back to Tucker Clark.

"You look like someone killed your dog. What's going on?"

Tucker Clark took a sip from his glass and looked at his old friend. Tucker was a shade over six feet tall and was lean and fit. His muscular build didn't come from a gym, but from years of hard work on the ranch. He had a bald head, no facial hair and penetrating dark eyes. The kind that could intimidate the hell out of you. They had graduated high school twenty years ago and had been friends since first grade. Where Tucker Clark had stayed in the county and went to work for his dad, Brian Cole had gone off to the Colorado School of Mines, and when he was finished, he graduated with a PhD in biochemical engineering.

They had lost touch for several years while Brian Cole worked somewhere back east, doing something he couldn't talk about. But they reconnected a couple of years back when Brian Cole showed up at the Longhorn Lounge and told his friend he was back in town. Tucker Clark was glad, and he had learned a long time ago not to ask what his friend was doing, so he just accepted him back in and restarted their friendship. They could be found most nights sitting on the same two barstools.

"Fuck, man," said Tucker Clark. "My old man is busting my ass."

"That's not new," said Brian Cole. "Your old man or your grandpa have been doing that since we were kids. I remember your old man getting pissed because we got caught stealing candy from the grocery store. We were six or seven. He tanned both our hides. Not because we stole, but because we stole something stupid like candy. He had old man Teller, the owner, shaking in his boots when he suggested to Teller that he not call the sheriff. Man, those were some fun times we had." He slapped Tucker Clark on the arm, and his friend just looked at him. He never cracked a smile.

"This is more serious than that," said Tucker Clark. "He's blowing a gasket this time."

"So, what's got him all twisted up now?"

Tucker Clark looked at his friend. "Nah. Let's drink. There's nothing you can do to help, anyway."

They sipped their beers for a while, and Brian Cole ordered another round. Mostly so he could watch Lacy Marks walk away again after she set the beers on the bar.

Brian Cole spun on his barstool and looked around. The Longhorn was crowded, but it was Friday night, and there wasn't much to do in Fairplay, Colorado, on a Friday night. So, he spun back around and faced his friend.

"Come on, man. How long have we been friends? There isn't anything we can't solve together, so fill me in, and maybe I can help."

Tucker Clark took a long drink from his glass, set the glass on the bar, and leaned in closer to his friend.

"I was supposed to get Gunther Halverson to agree to sell us something for a low price that Dad and Gramps would turn right around and resell and make a fortune on, but I can't get the old goat to give in. And we're running out of time. So, we have to settle this thing by the end of next week, or we could stand to lose millions."

"What the hell could old Halverson have that would be worth millions? He lives in a shithole house and has been driving that same old truck since the nineteen fifties."

"I can't get into the details, but what he has, you can't see. Just believe me when I say this is a big deal, and all I've done is fuck it up."

"Why doesn't your old man just threaten him? That works on everyone else in the county."

Tucker Clark smiled. "I tried that. The old man just

laughed in my face." He leaned closer. "I set his barn on fire. I even threatened his old lady if she didn't help. She laughed in my face too."

Brian Cole thought for a minute. "I assume that whatever this is, Halverson needs to be alive to make the deal, right?"

Tucker Clark nodded. He wasn't shocked by the unspoken suggestion.

"So, you need some leverage, right?"

Tucker Clark nodded again and took a sip from his beer. "What are you thinking?"

Brian Cole was quiet for a minute. "How many cows is the old guy running on his place this year?"

Tucker Clark looked at him, not comprehending. "I don't know," he slurred. "Maybe a hundred head. Why?"

"What would happen to him if he lost a significant portion of his herd? Would it bankrupt him?"

"I don't know. I guess. Are you suggesting we rustle his cows? Where the hell would we hide them? You're crazy, man."

"Not rustle them," said Brian Cole. "What would happen if all his cows suddenly died from a mysterious disease or chemical? Something that couldn't be easily detected. He'd need money fast to cover his loss. Then your old man could clean up."

Tucker looked bewildered. "Where the fuck are we supposed to get some disease? You're just funning me, right?"

Brian Cole laughed and then lowered his head so no one could hear. "You let me worry about the product. You think about where we could do it without getting caught." He sipped his beer and stared at Tucker Clark.

Tucker finished his beer and waved to Lacy Marks to bring two more; he leaned closer to Brian Cole. "Are you serious?"

Brian Cole smiled. "I've been working on something that might do the trick, but it will take both of us."

"How much risk are we talking about? Can whatever you've got up your sleeve hurt Halverson or us?"

"Nah. It's harmless to people, just animals, especially cows and horses."

"And it can't be detected?"

"Nope. You have to know what you are looking for. The routine tests that a vet would run would never detect this. It's clean, and it's fast acting. Once we spray it over the cows, they'll be dead in minutes, and then you can negotiate with Halverson and get him to cooperate. He'll be devastated, emotionally and financially."

"What do we need to do?" asked Tucker Clark.

"You don't have to do anything except show up and find the cattle. You leave the rest to me."

Tucker Clark looked serious. "What's in it for you?"

His friend smiled. "Not a thing. I've been working with this stuff for a long time in the lab, and this will give me a chance to see if it works in a real-world application."

"But what if it doesn't work?"

Brian Cole sipped his beer and set the glass on the counter. "Nothing happens. The only two people who know about this are you and me. You have to swear not to tell anyone, ever. If it doesn't work, it should still make the cows too sick to sell for food. Either way, you win, and you get your old man off your back. So, are you in or what?"

Tucker Clark took a big gulp from his beer glass and looked at Brian over the top of the glass. "You think you can pull this off?"

Brian looked serious when he responded. "Have I ever lied to you in all the time we've known each other? I'm telling you right now, I can make this happen if you want me to, but you must be totally committed—no wishy-washy bullshit. You say no, right now, and we'll never talk about it again, but you say yes, and we are in this all the way. No matter what happens."

"Okay. I'm in. Halverson has his herd up on the mountain in the good grass. No one ever goes near that range, so we should be able to do it without anyone noticing."

Brian Cole reached out his hand, and they shook. "Let's meet at your place tomorrow at dusk. It's better to spray this stuff after dark when the wind is quiet. Remember. Tell no one."

They finished their beers, ordered two more and Tucker Clark headed over to the pool table. Brian Cole smiled and looked at the mirror behind the bar. "That was almost too easy," he said to himself. He laughed and headed for the pool table.

Chapter Two

Dan Pearson stood up and moved from his desk chair to the Park County, Colorado, map on the wall. He was a fireplug of a man, five foot seven, and he weighed about one hundred and ninety pounds, with curly dark brown hair and a brown handlebar mustache. At fifty-five years old, he was in great shape, which helped him climb around the mountains in Park County.

Dan Pearson was a man on a mission and felt that this was the year he would find what he was looking for. Of course, he had believed that same thing every year for the last ten years. Dan Pearson was a treasure hunter; at least, that's what he did in his spare time when he wasn't helping his wife around the little ranch just north of Como or working at his day job.

Dan's wife stepped into the small, cluttered office and set a large coffee cup on Dan's desk. She stepped over to the map, and Dan pointed to a small forest service road on the east side of Tarryall Creek.

His wife smiled. "Do you think that's where it is?" she asked.

"I know I've been wrong about the last six or seven places, but I have a good feeling about this one, Barb."

Barb Pearson was a heavyset woman with grayish-blond hair and a warm disposition. She had tolerated Dan's treasure-hunting obsession since he first got involved with the quest, but this past year, she had put her foot down. They had agreed that Dan could search for his treasure all day on Saturday, but Sunday was the day they would spend together, either driving to the city to visit their grandchildren or spending time together on the ranch. She had mixed feelings about the treasure hunt. For Dan's sake, she hoped it would end with some small success, but she also secretly hoped he would grow tired of the continuous disappointment and quit. So far, it hadn't worked out either way.

She stood next to him and half listened to what he was telling her about some new information he had discovered on the internet and that several of his friends from the treasure-hunting websites had agreed with his assertions.

Dan picked up the cup of coffee off his desk and took a big gulp. "I should be back sometime after dark," he said.

"Make sure you take your rain gear. They're calling for storms this afternoon. I don't want you coming home looking like a drowned rat. Be careful."

She kissed him on the cheek and walked out of the office. Dan smiled as she walked away. Barb was a good woman, and he owed it to her to find the treasure so she could live in grand style instead of just making do, paycheck to paycheck.

He left his laptop on the desk, folded a smaller map and

stuck it in his shirt pocket. He slung his backpack over his right shoulder, drank the remaining coffee and carried the cup into the kitchen, where he placed it in the sink. He looked at the counter next to the door, and there was his small Yeti cooler. Barb had packed him a nice, hearty lunch and a snack for later. He loved that woman beyond belief and was amazed at how much she was willing to put up with.

He picked up the cooler, opened the door and entered the garage. He had loaded everything he needed in his truck the night before. He had checked to ensure his metal detector was charged, and that he had his toolbox and a couple of shovels. The last thing he checked before he started the truck and backed out of the garage was the Glock semiautomatic pistol he always kept in the glove box. Satisfied he had everything he needed, he pulled out of the garage and headed south just as the morning sun crested the hills to the east.

Dan Pearson drove north on Highway 285, then turned south onto Packer Lane, which merged into Tarryall Road, just west of Michigan Creek. He followed Tarryall Road south until he came to County Road 140, which took him east until he ran out of road. He found the old two-track fire road, turned between two old fence posts, and continued east. His destination was North Tarryall Peak.

Four miles up the almost nonexistent road, he noticed a large herd of cows grazing on what looked like new grass in a large field. He had to stop for a minute as several cows moved across the road in front of his truck. This was open range, and cows walking on the road was not an uncommon sight. He wondered who was running cattle this far off the beaten path and made a mental note to return on Monday and check the brands.

Dan Pearson worked for the Colorado Department of Agriculture as a brand inspector, a job he had been doing since graduating from Colorado State University. The Brand Inspection Division had been around since before Colorado was a state. It was formed by members of the cattle industry in 1865, became a state agency in 1903, and joined the Department of Agriculture in the 1970s.

Dan Pearson and the sixty-seven other men and women who made up the division protected and monitored the livestock industry in 104,000 square miles of Colorado. Dan's area included Park County and the five counties surrounding it. He worked alone, which was how he liked it, and could spend as many as 250 days a year away from home. Dan was on his tenth new truck since joining the agency twenty-five years ago.

With the cows safely off the road, Dan continued until there was nothing left to drive on and parked his truck. He exited the cab, stretched and took a long-overdue piss in the trees. He grabbed his backpack, his GPS, a shovel and a metal detector and headed deeper into the woods, climbing uphill until his GPS alerted him that he had arrived.

Dan set down his gear, took a break to eat the roast beef and cheddar cheese sandwich and washed it down with a bottle of water. Fed and rested, he started searching for an opening in the mountain wall that he knew was there. The opening had to be there. All his research said it should be there. He tried several promising spots but could not find what he was looking for. Even his metal detector drew a blank, and as the sun began to set behind the mountains on the other side of the valley, Dan sat down, finished his bottle of water and, saddened by his lack of discovery, decided it was time to head down the mountain. He knew he had stayed too long past dark and was concerned about driving down the trail this late, but he had promised Barb he would be home.

After loading his gear back in his truck and taking one last look , he turned his truck around and began the long slog home. He was coming up on the field where he had seen the cattle when he noticed a black pickup truck blocking the road. He slowed to a stop and looked around. Not seeing anyone, he took his pistol out of the glove box, grabbed his big Maglite from the holder next to his seat and slid out of the truck, softly closing the door.

He knew something was wrong right away. There were no sounds. He should have heard the cattle making noise as they moved about the field, but he heard nothing. He stepped to the edge of the road and shined his light across the field. Every cow his light landed on was lying down. This was not good, he thought to himself. Keeping his pistol at his side, he jumped across a small ditch and stepped into the field.

He approached the first cow and noticed it wasn't breathing. As he made his way through the field, he saw more dead cows. From what he could see, he figured there were a couple of dozen dead cows in the field and nothing visible to indicate how they died. He couldn't understand how this was possible. When he passed the field earlier in the day, the cows all appeared healthy. What the hell could have happened in a couple of hours?

He turned to walk back to his truck, and the bright beam

of a flashlight hit him right in the eyes. He was temporarily blinded and brought his hands up to cover his eyes. His eyes may not have seen the sight in front of him, but his brain had recorded it, and he thought the person standing in front of him was wearing a space suit. Too late, he realized it wasn't a space suit but a rubber hazmat suit, and too late, he realized this person was pointing a pistol at him.

He started to raise his pistol when he heard the first shot and felt a piercing pain in his lower abdomen. He staggered backward and fell to his knees. He tried to see through the blinding light and caught a glimpse of the person raising the black pistol. His brain registered the pain as another bullet entered his skull, and then the blinding light went away, and there was nothing but darkness.

| 3 |

Chapter Three

Brian Cole and Tucker Clark finished loading the gear from Brian's SUV into Tucker's pickup truck. Tucker had mentioned that where they were heading was rough terrain, and they would do better in his truck. Tucker's twelve-year-old son and his friend Marcus Wells stood off to the side and watched with interest.

Billy Clark was tall for his age, with a muscular build. He had shoulder-length hair and an attitude that said: I can do whatever I want, and no one can touch me. Marcus Wells was just the opposite. Short, skinny, with short hair and glasses. He was timid by nature, but when he was with Billy, he was invincible. He looked up to Billy in every way, and Billy made sure that none of the kids in school bothered Marcus.

"Dad, why do you need all that bleach?"

"Just stay out of the way, Billy, and don't touch anything," said Tucker.

Brian Cole went to lift a blanket that was covering

something in the back of the SUV when he nodded at Tucker and tipped his head towards Billy Clark.

"Billy, see if your mother needs help cleaning up from dinner."

"Aw, Dad. I want to help. Can't we go with you? We'll stay out of the way, promise."

"Go help your mother."

With Billy's long face leading the way, Billy and Marcus headed for the house, but stopped at the door and headed around the corner, where they could keep watching what was happening. They crouched next to the corner of the front deck and watched as Billy's dad and Brian loaded two large cylinders into the back of the truck and secured them to the cargo rail.

Tucker Clark pulled back the truck bed cover, and they looked around and slid into the truck. They headed out of the drive and turned north on Highway 285 then south onto Packer Lane, which merged into Tarryall Road, just west of Michigan Creek. They followed Tarryall Road south until they came to County Road 140, which took them east until they ran out of road. They found the old two-track fire road, turned between two old fence posts, and continued east. Their destination was a field near North Tarryall Peak.

Tucker Clark hadn't noticed that his son and friend Marcus had jumped on their dirt bikes as soon as the pickup truck left the yard and headed cross-country. They had overheard when Billy's dad told Brian where they were going, and Billy knew how to get there faster. He figured if they cut through a couple of other ranches, they could get there before his father did. Then they could find a good spot to hide and watch to see what his father and friend were into.

There was little talking during the first half of the drive, both men lost in their thoughts. As they drew closer to the turnoff that would take them to the field, Tucker Clark asked, "So you're sure this stuff won't hurt people, right?"

"Stop worrying, Tuck. All we will do is kill a few cows; no one else will get hurt. Once this stuff gets into the air, it will dissipate in a few minutes. There's nothing to worry about."

"All right. Are you gonna tell me what this stuff is?"

Brian Cole looked sideways at him. "If I tell you, I'll have to kill you." He laughed. "Even if I told you, you wouldn't know any more than you know now. If it makes you feel any better, there is also a kill switch built into the stuff. Once in the air, it will die within a couple of hours. It doesn't like oxygen."

They spotted the cattle field up ahead and parked in the middle of the road. This far up in the mountains and this late in the evening, he wasn't worried about someone coming either up or down the so-called road. They slid out of the truck and looked over the field.

"There must be a hundred cows," said Tucker Clark. "Are we gonna kill them all? Seems like kind of a waste."

"We'll kill as many as you think it will take to hurt Halverson. This is your party. You tell me what you want to do."

Tucker Clark looked pensive for a minute. "Let's get it done before I change my mind."

They walked to the back of the truck, pulled back the bed cover, and started pulling out the equipment. Tucker Clark looked at the hazmat suits Brian Cole had laid on the tailgate.

"These don't look like the suits the cops wear on TV. Why so heavy, and why the oxygen tanks? This looks serious."

Brian Cole slipped on his suit. "This is just for protection. You don't want to get any of this stuff on you. Now suit up before it gets too dark to see."

They put on their suits. The boots and gloves were a part of the suit, so they didn't have to use duct tape to seal the suits. Brian Cole checked the flow from the oxygen tanks and connected the first tank to Tucker's suit. He slung the tank over his shoulder. He did the same for his suit.

He pulled out the small bottles and checked to ensure the pressure gauges were full and the bottles were pressurized. He showed Tucker Clark how to turn the bottle on and spray the aerosol. He gave Tucker a thumbs-up, and they headed into the field, stepping over a small ditch on the side of the road.

Tucker watched as Brian Cole waded through the sea of cows and was amazed that within minutes the animals started to fall over. He stepped away from Brian Cole, walked to the other end of the herd, and started spraying the noses of the cattle. The cattle never had a chance to move out of the way. They started dropping like flies, and Brian and Tucker moved farther into the herd.

The sun had long set over the mountains on the other side of the valley by the time they were finished, and they walked back to where they had begun. Tucker checked several of the nearest cows, and none seemed to be breathing. He gave Brian Cole a thumbs-up.

Just then, they saw headlights coming down the road and heard another truck approaching. They moved away from the road and out of the range of the lights. The truck pulled to a stop, and the driver climbed out of the truck and lit up the area with a large flashlight. Tucker spotted the pistol in the driver's hand as he stepped over the ditch and into the field, crouching next to the first cow. He stood up, shook his head and moved deeper into the field.

Tucker looked around and didn't see Brian. He wondered where he had disappeared to. He didn't have to wait long as he spotted Brian move from behind the pickup truck, step over the ditch and follow the driver. Brian turned on an incredibly bright flashlight and Tucker saw the driver turn around and shield his eyes, the pistol still in his hand. He heard the gunshot as it echoed across the mountains and down into the valley, and he saw the driver fall to his knees and wrap his arms around his abdomen. He saw the driver look up and raise his hands as the second bullet hit him in the face. The driver fell to the ground.

Brian Cole turned around and walked to the back of the truck. Tucker Clark caught up with him.

"What the fuck did you do?" he screamed through the hood. "Why did you have to kill him?"

Brian Cole placed the pistol into the side pocket of his backpack and looked through the clear plastic that covered his face. "We need to get out of here. Let's get cleaned up."

He pulled out a small kids' plastic pool and set it on the ground. He pulled another spray bottle out of the bed, filled it with bleach, and pushed the pump to pressurize the tank. He told Tucker to stand in the pool, which he did—looking over his shoulder at where the driver had fallen.

Brian Cole sprayed Tucker Clark from head to toe with

the bleach, stopping to refill the bottle several times to make sure he covered his entire body. They repeated the process, this time with Brian Cole standing in the pool, and then they removed the air tanks and the hazmat suits. Everything went into thick black trash bags. They dumped the bleach from the pool into several large containers and secured the lids. Then they loaded everything back into the truck.

"What the fuck were you thinking?" asked Tucker Clark. "No one was supposed to die but the cattle. We are seriously fucked."

Brian Cole grabbed him by the front of his T-shirt and pulled him close. "Get your head out of your ass and get in the truck. This guy could have ruined everything. It will be days before anyone finds him. Now move it."

"We had an agreement. What the hell is wrong with you? We were going to kill the animals, not people. I didn't even know you had a gun with you."

Brian Cole had heard enough. "The guy had a gun. You think he would have hesitated using it if he spotted us first? And besides, when did you get queasy about killing people? Do you think your old man would have hesitated? Fuck no, he wouldn't. Your old man would do whatever it took to protect his family. You need to grow the fuck up."

Tucker Clark grabbed him by the arm and swung him around. He started to get in his face when Brian spun around and slammed Tucker into the side of the truck. Before Tucker knew what was happening, there was a knife up against his throat. He could see the fire in Brian's eyes.

"You bought into this whole plan, whatever may come, so don't get all self-righteous on me. It's a damn good thing

I was prepared for the unexpected because you weren't. We did what we needed to get your old man off your back, and we can't change that, so pull up your big girl panties and let's go. And Tucker, if you ever touch me again like that, I will kill you."

He slid the knife back into his pocket, pushed him out of the way and climbed into the passenger seat. Tucker Clark had never seen this side of his friend, and it scared him. He shook his head, walked around the truck, took one more look into the field and slid into the truck. He didn't notice Brian Cole unclip the small camera from the passenger's side window.

Tucker Clark was not happy, and the drive back home was completed in silence. He had no idea what had gotten into his friend, but he was certain they were in deep trouble.

| 4 |

Chapter Four

Buck Taylor stood in the water behind his five-year-old granddaughter Rosie, looking out over the Gunnison River. He had his finger through the small D ring on the back of her fishing vest, which had once belonged to Buck's daughter, Cassie. Rosie held the tip of the fly rod up and kept the loop of fly line in her hand, ready to cast to wherever Buck told her to cast. She was ready.

They had spent an hour in the park next to the river, practicing casting into an old Hula-Hoop that Buck set on the ground twenty-five feet from where Rosie stood. It was a beautiful morning, sunny and warm, with a little breeze. A perfect day to learn to cast.

Buck could tell from the first cast she made at the Hula-Hoop that she had the same skills he had seen in Cassie when she was the same age as Rosie.

Cassie was known all over the county for her skills on the water. While all her friends from high school were wasting time over the summers, Cassie was leading fishing trips down the rivers and creeks of the area for her grandfather Fernando's guide service. By the time she was eighteen, she was in high demand and making a lot more money than her friends, who were working for minimum wage at the local fast-food places.

Cassie was Buck and Lucy's middle child and was every bit a middle child. In high school, she played soccer, ran track and played volleyball. She lettered in all three sports. She was also the one who got in trouble for violating curfew, drinking and whatever other mischief she could find to get into. Buck was surprised when she was accepted to the University of Arizona with a full scholarship for volleyball. He was even more surprised when she was accepted into law school. Cassie was never much for regimented education.

She dropped out of law school several years ago, and her career path took a different track. She joined the Forest Service and was now working as a wildland firefighter with the Helena Hotshots. The Helena Hotshots were one of the elite firefighting teams based out of Helena, Montana. Buck was not surprised. He never saw her sitting behind a desk as a lawyer. She loved the outdoors, and she was as tough as they came. Lucy wasn't pleased that she quit school without any discussion, and she worried whenever Cassie was called out on a fire, but she also knew her daughter, and if this was where she was happy, then so was her mom.

Buck helped Rosie into the new waders he had ordered from Amazon and snapped the connector on the shoulder straps. The waders were the smallest size he could find, and the straps were still too long, even cinched up tight. He reached into his backpack, pulled out two large binder clips, rolled up the extra material on the straps and clipped them.

Rosie examined the assortment of flies attached to the felt pad over one pocket and pushed a couple of them with her finger. The vest was the first vest her Aunt Cassie had worn, and she was excited to follow in her footsteps. She looked at Buck and smiled. With the vest in place, she looked ready to go. Buck put on his waders and fly vest, grabbed his net and closed the back hatch of his Jeep.

"You ready?" he asked her.

"Yes, sir," she said, and they headed for the footbridge that led from the park to the Lucy Taylor Memorial Riverwalk that ran along a mile of the Gunnison River. The trail had been a gift to the town from Rachel and Hardy Braxton, Lucy's sister and brother-in-law, to honor Lucy after she passed away following a five-year battle with metastatic breast cancer.

Hardy Braxton and Buck had been on-again, off-again friends since kindergarten. They'd played football together for the Gunnison High School Cowboys. They were the team's defensive backfield and were called the "Wrecking Crew" during senior year. Between them, they broke every defensive high school football record in the state, many of which still stand.

Buck had passed up several full-ride scholarships and instead joined the army and later the Gunnison County Sheriff's Department. On the other hand, Hardy had accepted a full-ride scholarship to Stanford and spent the next four years as an all-American football player. He then played in the

National Football League until a knee injury sidelined him for good.

Hardy left the NFL and took over the reins of his father's small livestock company. Over the years, he turned that small company out of Gunnison County into the world's premier bucking stock and livestock company. A rodeo didn't happen anywhere in the country that didn't have numerous animals from Braxton Bucking Stock in its corrals. He also invested heavily in energy exploration companies and owned the largest private fracking company in the country. By all measures, Hardy Braxton was hugely successful.

Hardy had married Lucy's younger sister, Rachel, the year after Lucy and Buck got married. Their marriage was blessed with four children, who were now involved in numerous family businesses. Businesses that now numbered at least a dozen and stretched from Gunnison to California and even dipped down into South America. Hardy was the big dog in Gunnison County, and he was not afraid to use that power to his family's advantage.

The Braxtons were the wealthiest family in Gunnison County and one of the wealthiest families in the state. As such, Hardy had been able to purchase a mile of riverfront along the Gunnison River. They created a mile-long walkway with picnic areas and an open-air amphitheater for concerts and other events. The walkway was a huge hit with the townspeople, and Buck was proud of how it represented Lucy.

During the past year and a half, Jason, Buck and Lucy's youngest son, worked as both architect and project manager on the Riverwalk. Jason was a partner at an architectural firm in Boulder, Colorado. He was a devout Catholic, which he got from his mom. He was also the one member of the family that took everything to heart, and he worried about Buck and his job.

Buck pointed to a small eddy behind a large boulder about twenty feet from shore. Rosie flipped the rod tip back, creating a decent loop in the fly line, and aimed the fly towards the rock. Unfortunately, it landed short of the spot Buck had indicated, and she looked up at him with concern.

"Try it again; this time let out a little more line with your free hand," he said softly. She flipped the tip back, releasing the line as she made two false casts and dropped the fly on top of the eddy.

"Let the fly sink for a second and then slowly start pulling in line."

She did as instructed; the rod tip jerked, and she gently pulled the tip up. Her face lit up like a thousand lights.

"Fish on," she yelled, her excitement getting the better of her. Several fishermen on either side of them stopped to watch the tiny fisher person. Buck held her vest tight as she worked the fish towards shore, and when it got close enough, he handed her the net, and she scooped up the fish, keeping the net in the water. The fishermen up and down the river applauded, and Rosie waved at them. She handed her grandfather the rod and reached into the net; keeping the fish submerged, she removed the hook from its mouth.

She spotted her father standing next to her great-grandmother on the opposite bank and raised the fish slightly out of the water so her dad could take a picture with his cell phone. She held the fish under the belly and faced it upstream. After a minute, the fish swam out of her hand. She stood up, and Buck gave her a huge hug.

Rosie stepped out of the water and ran along the trail to the footbridge. She ran across the bridge and hugged her dad.

David was Buck's oldest son and was a sergeant and night shift supervisor with the Gunnison Police Department. He looked like his dad when Buck was his age, slightly taller at six foot two and a little heavier, but the resemblance was almost scary. He also played guitar in a local bluegrass/country band.

"Did you see that, Dad?"

"I did, baby. You were great," he said.

"As good as you?"

"Maybe even better. Maybe as good as your aunt."

Rosie's smile got even bigger, and then she hugged her grandmother, Rosalie. Rosalie Torres was one of the elders of the community. Pushing seventy-eight and five foot two, she was a force to be reckoned with. What she lacked in stature this still-active Latina more than made up for with drive. She was still on the organizing committee for the Labor Day picnic, and she served on almost every volunteer committee that functioned within the county. Nothing went on in Gunnison that Rosalie was not a part of.

Fernando Torres, Rosalie's husband and Lucy's father, had run a small horse ranch outside the city border. He had also been an outfitter and hunting guide. His love of the outdoors was something he was proud to have passed on to his two daughters, Lucinda and Rachel, and his son, Michael. Life was not always easy for Fernando and Rosalie, but they did the best they could and made sure that their children never wanted for anything.

It was a sad day five years ago when Fernando suffered a heart attack while guiding several hunters up near Monarch Pass. Although the hunters had made a valiant effort to revive him and had succeeded several times, by the time search and rescue reached them, Fernando was gone. The family still missed Fernando every day, but it was okay. His daughter Lucy was with him.

On the opposite shore, Buck stepped from the water as his cell phone rang. He pulled it out of the front pocket of his waders and looked at the number.

"Yes, sir," Buck said.

"Sorry to call on your day off, Buck. Hope I'm not interrupting anything important?" asked Kevin Jackson.

Kevin Jackson, the director of the Colorado Bureau of Investigation, had been the youngest person to run the bureau when he was appointed by Governor Richard J. Kennedy. He'd had a stellar career with the Colorado Springs Police Department before being tapped for the top post at CBI. He was more bureaucrat than cop, having spent most of his career on the administrative side at CSPD, but he was well respected in the law enforcement community, and Buck was impressed with him.

"No, sir. What's up?" asked Buck.

"I just got a call from the Park County sheriff. Earlier today, they found the body of a state brand inspector. All indications are he was murdered. Odd thing is, they found him in a field surrounded by a bunch of dead cows. Since brand inspectors are state employees, the investigation is ours," said Kevin Jackson.

Kevin Jackson didn't go into too much detail, even with

what little he knew. He knew Buck liked to view the crime scene with his own eyes before listening to anyone else's narrative or opinions, so he kept the information to a minimum.

"Dead cows, sir?"

"Yeah. Dead cows. And before you ask, there is no preliminary cause of death on the cows."

"Okay, sir. I'll head over as soon as I can get changed. Can you call Bax and see if she can meet me there and have Franklin roll the forensic team?"

"Forensics is on the way. Bax will get there as soon as she can, and I left a message for Paul to check in and see if you need him. Anything else?"

"No, sir. I'll let you know what we find and if we'll need any other resources," said Buck.

He hung up, looked to where David, Rosie and Rosalie stood and pointed to his phone. David nodded and leaned down to let Rosie know that they would have to go to lunch without her grandfather. Buck headed for the bridge, and Rosie waved to him and made a heart shape with her fingers. Buck did the same thing as he crossed the bridge and headed towards his Jeep.

| 5 |

Chapter Five

Buck Taylor was six feet tall and weighed in at one hundred eighty-five pounds—very little of it flab for a sixty-two-year-old man. Buck's hair was salt-and-pepper, with what seemed like a lot more salt than pepper, and he wore it longer than was typically the fashion of the day. Buck was always pleased when he looked in the mirror since, other than getting older, he was in as good a shape as he had been when he played defensive linebacker for the Gunnison High School Cowboys, what seemed like a long time ago. He still tried to jog five miles every day when he could, and he tried to ride his mountain bike every weekend, weather permitting. Except for a couple of sore knees coming from age, Buck was in good shape, which was important in his line of work.

Buck Taylor was an investigative agent for the Colorado Bureau of Investigation. He was currently assigned to the CBI field office in Grand Junction, Colorado, but he hadn't been in the office much during the past year. Somehow, he had become the favorite "go-to" guy for the governor of Colorado, Richard J. Kennedy, who was, in fact, one of "those" Kennedys. The governor had been in office more than four years, and Buck had been instrumental in closing several high-profile investigations during that period, which made the governor look good. As a result, when a situation came up that might get a little hairy, the governor always asked to have Buck assigned.

Buck had been married for thirty-four years before breast cancer stole the one person he cared about most in the world. He missed Lucy every day, even after all this time.

If you asked Buck, he would tell you that he fell in love with Lucinda Torres on the first day of their senior year in high school. On the other hand, Lucy always told people that Buck stalked her the entire senior year before she gave in to shut her friends up and agreed to go to the movies with him. She had always considered him just another jock, another football player who was too full of himself. What she found on that first date was a shy, unassuming gentleman, for lack of a better word, who, it seemed, cared more about pleasing her than bragging about his prowess on the football field. She would tell people it was love at first sight that had taken a year to accomplish. From that day forward, they were inseparable.

During senior year Buck had been approached by several college football scouts who wanted to sign him to play for their schools. Gunnison High School was a small school back in 1978, and Buck and his family were amazed at how many schools had recruited him, but for Buck, college wasn't in the cards.

Buck hated school and spent a lot of time getting himself out of trouble instead of getting an education. When he found something that interested him, he had no problem learning all he could about the subject, but regular schoolwork just bored him. After several long heartfelt discussions, first with Lucy and then with his parents, he decided to join the army after graduation. Surprisingly, no one was surprised.

Buck spent four years after high school in the army, and by the time his enlistment was up, he had been promoted to first sergeant. He spent three years of his enlistment in the military police and really took to police work. That was when he decided to apply for a position with the Gunnison County Sheriff's Office.

Since he was already well known in the county, he had no trouble getting a job as a deputy. He proposed to Lucy the night he received the call that he had gotten the position. His life and career were set. He made the most of his time with the Gunnison County Sheriff's Office, becoming the under-sheriff in charge of the Investigation Division and coming to the attention of the Colorado Bureau of Investigation.

Buck had worked with the Colorado Bureau of Investigation on several cases inside the county and had earned the respect of the investigators he had worked with.

As twilight started to fall on Buck's career, he knew that unless he wanted to go into politics and run for sheriff, he had reached the highest position in the sheriff's office that he could obtain. He loved his job, but when the first offer came in from CBI, he sat down with Lucy and had a long heart-to-heart talk.

He'd spent seventeen years in the sheriff's office and had

always figured he would retire from that job. They had three children, two in high school and one not far behind, and he was a well-respected member of the community. Did he have the right to disrupt their lives, pick up, move someplace else and start all over? The kids had friends, Lucy owned a small deli/ice cream parlor, and they had a nice life.

He could stick it out for another ten years and retire, and they could travel and see the world as they had always planned. Twice he turned down the offer from CBI, although more and more, he felt like he was trapped behind a desk instead of doing what he loved, which was investigating crime.

The final offer came directly from Tom Cole, then-director of the Colorado Bureau of Investigation. Buck always remembered that day. The Denver Broncos had just lost another game, the third one in a row, and his friends had all packed up and headed home when there was a knock at the front door.

Now, anyone who lives in a small community knows that no one ever uses the front door, and no one ever knocks. So, who could this possibly be this late on a Sunday evening?

Buck answered the door and was surprised to see the director of the Colorado Bureau of Investigation standing on his front porch. The director smiled and said, "Before you close the door in my face, please listen to my offer."

Buck invited him in, and he and Lucy sat on the couch and listened as the director laid out his plan. He was opening a new branch office in Grand Junction, Colorado, that would house five agents and a small forensic unit. Buck could continue to live in Gunnison but would have to report to the office in Grand Junction twice a month. Otherwise, he would be free to work from his house. There would be no disruption in his life other than spending time on the road as his investigations warranted. He would work alone, but he would have all the branch office's resources at his disposal.

Before Buck could say a word, Lucy said, "Buck, this is what you have been waiting for, a chance to be a real investigator again. You have to take this." That was one of the things that made him love Lucy every day. She always knew what he was thinking and understood what drove him. She had nailed it this time. Buck looked at the director and replied, "Well, I guess it's settled; looks like you have a new investigator on your team."

That was twenty-six years ago, and Buck had never looked back. He had made the most of those years and was one of the most respected and feared investigators in the state, but all that work couldn't make up for the loss he suffered.

Lucy was diagnosed with metastatic breast cancer following a routine mammogram, and they set off together on their next adventure: the quest to beat the dreaded disease. After a double mastectomy and five years of chemo, they knew their time was drawing to a close when the cancer returned several times to her brain and was no longer controlled by the radiation.

Together, they decided to stop all treatment, even though they had always told the family that the decision was Lucy's alone to make. Lucy spent the last couple of months of her life taking care of her small business and spending as much time as she could with her children and grandchildren.

The end came quietly one spring night. Lucy had been sleeping on and off for twenty or so hours a day in the end.

The night she died, Buck had been lying in bed next to her, reading a report, when she snuggled into his arms and rested her head on his shoulder. Sometime during the night, Buck had fallen asleep. When he woke up, Lucy was gone, and his world was shattered.

They say that time heals all wounds, but Buck wasn't sure that was the case when you lost your closest friend. And even now, all these years later, he missed her more and more each day.

Buck always thought back to that Sunday morning when the family had gathered for a private ceremony at the little dock along the Gunnison River to scatter Lucy's ashes. Each family member got to say a few words about Lucy, and when they finished and turned to go, they were stunned to see several hundred of their neighbors and friends standing silently behind them in the park. Word had gotten out about their private service, and everyone turned out to pay tribute to Lucy. The affair turned into a huge party, with plenty of food and drinks. Lucy never wanted any kind of service, but Buck figured she would have loved this spontaneous outpouring of love.

| 6 |

Chapter Six

Buck traveled north on Highway 285 and passed through the town of Fairplay, following the directions the Park County sheriff had texted him. The county seat of Park County hadn't changed much since the last time he had been there. Sitting at almost ten thousand feet and with a population of 724, Fairplay was the largest municipality in a county with a rich history of agriculture, mining and recreation. One of Buck's favorite places to fish, the South Platte River, passes through the South Park Valley, which comprises a significant portion of the county and is home to one of the state's most productive gold medal fishing areas.

He turned his Jeep Grand Cherokee onto the two-track dirt road, traveled a few miles and spotted the emergency vehicles parked along the road. He pulled in behind a Park County Sheriff's Office SUV, grabbed his backpack off the passenger seat, slid out and stretched. He looked across the field and saw the black lumps littering the area. Spotting a group of people farther up the road, he headed that way.

Sheriff John Toomey stepped away from the group and walked up to Buck, his hand extended. Sheriff Toomey had worked for Park County for more than twenty-four years, the last fourteen as sheriff. He was six feet tall and had a slight beer belly hanging over his duty belt. He had short gray hair and was clean-shaven. His tan pants and dark brown shirt were pressed with sharp creases. John Toomey took pride in his appearance and the way he carried himself.

"Buck, good to see you. Wish it was under better circumstances."

They shook hands. "Good to see you too, John."

He looked at the group standing on the side of the road. "What's going on?" asked Buck.

"We may have a problem," said Sheriff Toomey. "We received a missing person call from the wife of the victim, Dan Pearson. He's a state brand inspector. His wife had the coordinates of where he was going, so we were able to send a deputy up here to check on him. Found his truck just up the road. The deputy spotted the body in the field and went in to check it. As you can see, there is a shitload of dead cows in the field. As soon as the deputy saw the bullet hole in his head, he backtracked out of the field and called for backup. Another deputy arrived on the scene and found Deputy Carmichael, the first responder, lying next to his SUV. He was unconscious and had shallow breathing. Deputy Rivers called for an ambulance and called me."

Buck looked concerned. "How is the deputy doing?"

"The ambulance is taking him over the pass to Centura Hospital in Frisco."

"So, besides your deputy, no one has been in the field?" asked Buck.

"Dr. Jess said we shouldn't take a chance until we know if the deputy's health issue is related to the dead cows."

"Who is Dr. Jess?" asked Buck.

"Come on. I'll introduce you."

They approached the group, and Sheriff Toomey introduced Buck to Dr. Jessica Rivera. Dr. Jess was a local large animal vet. She was fresh out of veterinary school after having worked for a vet clinic out on the eastern plains near Fort Morgan. She was tall and stocky, her brown hair tied in a French braid.

"I called her on the way up here when dispatch told me about the cows."

Buck and Dr. Jess shook hands. He also shook hands with Deputy Rivers. Deputy Katrina Rivers was a four-year veteran of the sheriff's office after serving two tours with the army in Afghanistan. She was about five foot four and muscular. She had short black hair and brown eyes. Buck noticed that both women had strong handshakes and calloused hands.

"Doctor, John says you think we should be cautious about entering the field."

"Yes, sir. We have no idea what killed the cows, but since the deputy was found unconscious, I suggested we get the state police hazmat team out here before we take the risk."

Buck looked at Sheriff Toomey.

"Already called your office, Buck. Director Jackson said he

would call them out. He called me just before you arrived and told me they should be here within the hour."

"Doctor, any thoughts on what we might be dealing with? Just brainstorming; I won't hold you to it."

"From here, it's difficult to tell what caused the deaths. The sheriff lent me his binoculars, and I couldn't see any outward signs of violence. No blood, no physical damage as we might see from a lightning strike, nothing evident. We have a couple of options. Since there were no storms in the area last night, we can rule out a lightning strike. That leaves chemical or biological. There's also no animal predation, which tells me that this happened sometime during the night."

"Chemical or biological," said Buck. "Could this be an act of terrorism?"

Dr. Jess looked nervous. "At this point, I wouldn't go quite that far, but there is very little in nature that could cause a problem like this. There could be clover in the field, which can cause severe complications in cattle, even death, but the effects take days in most cases. I also didn't see anything near the road indicating any toxic plants. Honestly, it looks like these cows just fell over and died."

"What kind of plants would we be talking about?" asked Sheriff Toomey.

"There are several that grow around here. Lupine, death camas, nightshades, poison hemlock, water hemlock or larkspur. Most of these don't grow up here, but the ones that do, there would be outward signs of ingestion, and death could take hours to days. My guess is that these cows all died together, so I doubt it was something they ate."

Buck thought for a minute. "Ingestion would also not

account for the condition of the deputy. I doubt he stood here and ate plants while waiting for backup. So, if not ingestion, could it be something airborne?"

"That's a strong possibility," said Dr. Jess. "Except there is nothing up here that appears to be toxic. I don't know at this point. It's got me baffled."

"John, do you know who owns this herd?"

"From what I can see of the brands, it looks like they belong to Gunther Halverson. His family was one of the first families to settle in the county."

"Any reason his herd would have attracted a visit from a brand inspector?"

"No. I was getting ready to inform his wife when you arrived. I should let her know before word gets out."

"I'll go with you," said Buck. "Deputy, please stay here and wait for the hazmat team." He shook the doctor's hand. "Thanks, Doctor. I appreciate the help. I would appreciate it if you could stick around and fill in the hazmat team."

"Happy to help, Agent Taylor."

Buck followed the sheriff to his SUV and slid into the passenger seat, and they headed back towards town.

"Buck, this is the craziest thing I've ever seen, and I've seen a lot in this county. What're your first thoughts, if you don't mind me asking?"

Buck was quiet for a minute. He hated speculating this early in the investigation since he hadn't had a chance to walk the crime scene, but he could tell that the sheriff was troubled and had every right to be.

"I tend to agree with the doctor. The situation with the deputy concerns me, and only inhalation makes sense, but inhalation of what is the question. Have you called for the forensic pathologist?"

Colorado was one of about a dozen states that still used the coroner system instead of the medical examiner system. The coroner for each jurisdiction was an elected official, and that person did not have to have any experience or even be a medical professional. Anyone could run for coroner.

The system was evolving so that the coroner was required to complete a formal training program in death investigations, but it was a slow legislative process. Coroners would contract with a licensed forensic pathologist to handle any investigations that required an autopsy.

These forensic pathologists were highly trained doctors who split their time among several jurisdictions to keep costs down. Many forensic pathologists were current or former medical examiners, and several were retired, working part time to keep their hands in the game.

"Yeah," said the sheriff. "I had dispatch call Dr. Clayton Roberts. He should be there by the time we get back."

| 7 |

Chapter Seven

Sheriff Toomey turned his car onto a dirt road and headed towards a small brick and stucco ranch house. He parked in front of the driveway, and he and Buck slid out of the seats and approached the house. The front door opened before they got to it, and Barb Pearson, looking like she hadn't slept at all the night before, stepped onto the front porch.

"John, did you find that damn fool? I'm guessing he got stuck in a rut somewhere. I told him to . . ."

She stopped talking and looked at Sheriff Toomey and Buck. Tears appeared in her eyes, and she lifted her apron to wipe the tears away.

"No," she said. "No. Where is he, John? Is he all right?" She started to shake, and Buck grabbed her arm and held her up.

"Mrs. Pearson, I'm Buck Taylor. Can we step inside?"

He led Barb Pearson into the neat house and helped her sit on the couch. Sheriff Toomey kneeled in front of her and took her hands in his.

"Barb, I'm so sorry. We found a body we believe is Dan. I am so terribly sorry."

Barb sat still as tears rolled down her face. It was like she heard the sheriff but wasn't comprehending what he was telling her. She looked into his eyes.

"Dan's dead. No, that can't be. He told me he would be careful and be home after dark. He never came home. There must be some mistake. It can't be him. He was in great shape, he just had a physical a month ago, and everything was fine."

Buck had entered the kitchen and returned with a glass of water, which he handed to Barb Pearson. This was one part of the job, even after all these years, that he hated.

"Barb, Dan didn't have a medical problem." He hesitated for a minute. Barb looked at him, confused.

"Dan was shot. We found him in a field up near North Tarryall Peak. Do you know what he was working on up there?"

Barb looked even more confused as she wiped her eyes. "Dan was murdered?" she asked. "No, that can't be. Dan wasn't working yesterday. Maybe it's not Dan."

Buck sat on the couch next to her. "Mrs. Pearson, are you sure your husband wasn't working yesterday? We found him in a field full of cows."

She looked at Buck. "No, he was off yesterday and today. We were planning to drive over to the city and visit the grandkids. Oh my god, I need to call the kids."

"Mrs. Pearson," asked Buck, "if your husband wasn't working yesterday, what was he doing in the mountains last night?"

"I'm sorry," she said. "I forgot your name."

"Ma'am, I'm Buck Taylor. I'm with the Colorado Bureau of Investigation, and I'm here to help Sheriff Toomey investigate what happened to your husband. I know this is hard, but can you tell us what he was doing in the mountains if he wasn't working?"

"He was looking for treasure," she said nonchalantly.

Buck and Sheriff Toomey looked at each other, and Buck continued. "Ma'am, did you just say he was looking for treasure?"

She nodded her head. "Dan was a treasure hunter. We agreed that he could look for treasure on Saturday, but Sunday he had to spend with me. He left yesterday morning to try an area that he thought might be fruitful and told me he would be back after dark."

Tears flowed like water, and she tried to apologize but got choked up, taking a long sip of water from the glass she had set on the side table. The sheriff stepped away and pulled out his phone. He spoke to someone for a minute and then came back. He kneeled back in front of Barb Pearson.

"Barb, I called my wife, and she is going to come over and stay with you for a bit. She can help you call the kids."

"Mrs. Pearson?" asked Buck. "What kind of treasure was your husband looking for?"

She took a deep breath. "It had something to do with the Incas or the Aztecs. I usually tuned him out once he started rambling. Now he'll never get the chance to ramble again." More tears flowed.

"Ma'am, did your husband have an office here in the house?" asked Buck.

She wiped away the tears and pointed towards a hallway

off the living room. Buck stood up, indicated for the sheriff to stay with her and headed down the hall in search of the office. He found it at the end of the hall.

Dan Pearson's office was not what Buck expected. Buck's office at home was meticulous. Everything had a place, and everything was in its place, and he knew where everything was. This office was the opposite, and Buck shivered.

There were stacks of paper on every flat surface. The walls were covered with maps and printed documents that looked like Dan had printed them off the internet. To Buck's eyes, there was no organization, and Buck wasn't sure where to start looking, so he stepped over to the desk and moved the mouse. The laptop and the second monitor came to life, and Buck sat down and clicked the enter button. The screen came to life, and Buck stopped.

Around the CBI office, Buck was known as a technological dinosaur. He was happiest when he had paper files and his little notebook, but the times were changing, and Buck tried to change with them.

CBI had gone digital a couple of years back, so instead of having a blue binder for each case, Buck just had to open a program on his laptop. The new case was automatically assigned a case number, and Buck would list everyone who needed access to the file and send them email invites. All evidence, lab reports, photos, etc. that were part of the case would be uploaded into the file, and anyone who needed access just had to open the file. That was much better than the old system, where everything had been placed in the binder by hand, and Buck would spend half his time tracking down who had the binder.

For a tech dinosaur like Buck, this made his life so much easier, and he had ready access to anything he needed. Buck just had to click on a file and open the chronology page, which was the first page in the file. Nothing was ever entered into the file without a note entered in the chronology first. The chronology kept track of everything that happened in the investigation.

Buck was meticulous about his case files and had never lost a case in court in all his years in law enforcement because something was missing from his files.

Buck didn't know what to click on first, so he pulled out his phone and speed-dialed a number.

"Hey, Buck. What can we help you with?" asked Melanie Hart.

George Peterman and Melanie Hart were the CBI cyber-security team based out of Grand Junction, Colorado, and they couldn't be more different.

George Peterman had joined CBI after retiring from the navy, where he'd spent his entire career working in cyber-security. As far as Buck was concerned, George and his part-ner, Melanie Hart, were two of the best computer people he knew. Paul Webber was good. Ashley Baxter was better, but these two were world-class.

Melanie was about five foot two, with shoulder-length black hair; she wore black jeans, dark gray hoodies, and had several piercings. Anyone meeting her for the first time would think she was a high school kid, but she had received her doctorate in computer science from MIT about a dozen years before. She'd joined CBI right out of college.

George Peterman, on the other hand, could have passed

for her father. George was about the same height as Buck, a shade under six foot, but where Buck still weighed what he'd weighed when he played football in high school, George had added a few pounds over the years.

Buck heard a click on the line. "Hi, Buck," said George Peterman. "What's up?"

Buck filled them in with what information he had, from the field and dead cows right up to sitting at Dan Pearson's desk.

"That's weird," said Mel. "What do you need us to do?"

"I'm looking at the victim's laptop, but I have no idea where to start. Can you guys get into it?"

"Sure," said George. "Do you still have the USB drive we gave you?"

Buck reached into his pocket and pulled out his keys. He held the drive and inserted it into the laptop. "Done. What's next?"

"Is the laptop password protected?" asked Mel.

"Doesn't seem to be. As soon as I moved the mouse, it opened to a bunch of file folders."

"Awesome," said Mel. "Just sit back and give us a few minutes, and we'll download everything in the hard drive. What are we looking for?"

"Not sure," said Buck. "He's a state employee, so we need to see if anything happened in his job that might have led to him being murdered. He was also a treasure hunter, which I think could also be dangerous depending on what he found. See if you can find some loose ends and give them a tug."

George came back on the line. "Okay, Buck. Pull out the

USB. We've got what we need. We'll take a look and see if anything looks interesting."

Buck thanked them and hung up. He closed the laptop, stood up and moved around the room. He took pictures of the maps and the documents that hung on the wall and then went through the stacks of papers on the side tables. He heard the front door open, and a few minutes later, Sheriff Toomey stepped into the office and looked around.

"Find anything interesting?" He picked up a map off a stack sitting on a chair, looked at it and shook his head. "Where the hell do we start?"

Buck laughed. "Yeah. I had my tech guys download his laptop. They'll start going through it to see what they can find. Let's leave the office for later. Ask Mrs. Pearson to lock this door and make sure no one touches anything until we get back. Let's head back to the site."

They left the office, and Sheriff Toomey introduced Buck to his wife, Mary. They asked Mrs. Pearson to keep everyone out of the office. They offered their condolences once more and left the house. They slid into the sheriff's SUV and returned to the crime scene. It was going to be a long day.

| 8 |

Chapter Eight

The sheriff parked his SUV behind two black Suburbans. The state police hazmat truck was parked a little farther up the dirt road, and three state troopers were standing at the back talking with a tall black man with short gray hair and a gray goatee. Buck and Sheriff Toomey walked up to the group. Franklin Williams introduced Buck and the sheriff to Troopers Delany, Springfield and Truman. They shook hands all around.

"Guys, what do you think?" asked Buck.

Trooper Delany responded for the group. "With what we see and were told about the first deputy on the scene, we will take extreme caution. Franklin and one of his team will suit up with us. We've got level four hazmat suits and air tanks. We will take air samples and soil samples while Franklin and his helper work the area around the body. I've also asked Dr. Jess if she will suit up. We need to get some samples from the cattle."

"Franklin, you good with this?" asked Buck. Franklin had been a crime scene investigator with the Colorado Bureau of Investigation for more than thirty years. Buck didn't like that he couldn't get close to the body, but he trusted Franklin to get everything they needed.

Franklin nodded, and they stepped aside as Trooper Springfield pulled a large black box out of a compartment on the side of the truck and set it down by the group. He opened the box to reveal several black rubber suits. They each grabbed a suit and started to snug their way into them. The suits were not as tight as a wet suit, but they were still bulky and hard to slide into. As each person suited up, Trooper Truman carried six air tanks to the back of the truck. He also checked the communications links in each suit. The last thing he wanted was for someone to have an issue. Satisfied that everything was in working order, he helped each person put on his suit and tank.

Buck walked back to his Jeep and came back with a Nikon digital camera that he handed to Franklin. With one final equipment check, the team stepped over the ditch and into the field. Franklin and his helper headed for the body, and the troopers carried various pieces of monitoring equipment that they positioned around the field.

Dr. Jess, wearing a black level four hazmat suit and tank, stood next to the ditch and waited until Delany waved for her to come over to where they were standing. She stepped over the ditch and headed towards the group, stopping every couple of feet to look at a cow. She pulled a small scalpel and a test tube out of a pocket in the suit, took a sample from the mouth of one of the cows and a skin sample from the nose of another.

Franklin took pictures of the dead body from every possible angle and took some close-up shots of the two bullet holes. His helper, Marsha Thompson, picked up the pistol and flashlight and put them in an evidence bag, which she sealed and labeled with a big black marker.

Buck watched Franklin and his team and periodically used his binoculars to get a closer look. He felt isolated from the investigation, a feeling he was not comfortable with. He turned as he heard a vehicle drive up the road and park beside his Jeep.

Ashley Baxter slid out of the gray Jeep Grand Cherokee and slung her backpack over her shoulder. CBI Agent Ashley Baxter had worked with Buck on many interesting cases over the years besides working on her own cases. At thirty-four years old, she was the youngest agent in the Grand Junction Field Office. She'd joined CBI straight out of college, and, having had no experience in the field, she valued the time she got to spend with Buck because she learned so much about running an investigation.

Bax stood about five foot six with blue eyes and blond hair that she often kept tied in a ponytail that hung through the hole in the back of her CBI cap. Some people would describe her as husky, or what used to be called having a "mountain girl" figure. She wasn't gorgeous, but she was pretty enough to turn men's heads when she entered a room until they spotted the badge and gun clipped to her belt. She had been with the Colorado Bureau of Investigation for eleven years and had earned Buck's respect.

She was also a whiz at doing deep background searches—a talent Buck did not share—so he relied on Bax to help him. They worked well as a team and collaborated more and more as the years rolled by.

"Fuck, Buck," said Bax. "What have we gotten ourselves involved in this time?" She laughed as she walked up and shook hands with Buck and the sheriff. She looked out over the field and studied the area for a minute. Buck handed her the binoculars, and she scanned the area around the body. She handed him back the binoculars.

"No chance we can get near the body?" she asked.

"Not likely," said Buck. He told her about the deputy who ended up on the ground after getting near the body.

"Any thoughts on what this is?" she asked.

"The vet, Dr. Jess, gave us some insight into the kinds of plants that could kill cattle, but none are fast acting. We know Dan Pearson was up here yesterday on a treasure hunt. So, whatever happened took less than twenty-four hours. She also mentioned it could be something airborne."

They watched the troopers and Dr. Jess take more samples from the cattle and samples of several plants. Two of the troopers moved farther into the field towards what looked like a ravine; they disappeared from sight.

"So, do you think this was related to his job? The director mentioned he was a brand inspector," asked Bax.

Just then, Buck's phone rang, and he pulled it from his belt and looked at the number.

"Hey, Paul."

"Hey, Buck. The director said to give you a call. What do you need me to do?"

Paul Webber was over six foot four with a muscular physique. He had joined CBI seven years earlier after spending ten years with the Dallas, Texas, police department. His last post had been as a homicide detective. Paul may have seemed like a giant, but those who knew him knew he was a pussycat. He was one of the most soft-spoken men Buck had ever met.

Buck filled him in while Bax listened in. It would save him from having to repeat himself. He explained about the treasure hunt Dan Pearson was on and gave him a good description of the scene they were all looking at.

"Is this job-related?" asked Paul.

"Bax asked me the same thing. At this point, we have no idea. It could be job-related since they found him in the middle of a lot of dead cows. On the other hand, it could be connected to his treasure hunt, or it could be wrong place wrong time. We'll need a lot more information than we have now to narrow that down."

"Okay. Do you want me to meet you guys at the crime scene?"

Buck thought for a minute. "No. I'd like you to go to the Pearson place and go through the office. I've already downloaded the laptop to George and Mel, but the place is full of maps and internet articles. Start working through it and see if you can determine what he was looking for and if anyone else might be looking for the same thing."

Buck handed his phone to the sheriff, who gave Paul the address and handed the phone back to Buck.

"Okay, Buck. Do I need to stop someplace and get a couple of rooms, or have you already done that?"

Buck hadn't taken the time to think about rooms for the

night. The sheriff reached for Buck's phone. "Paul, there's a nice little hotel called the South Platte Inn, just at the west edge of town. Stop in and tell Marshal I sent you. He'll set you up."

He handed the phone back to Buck, who checked to make sure Paul was good and hit the red button, hooking the phone back on his belt.

"Bax, there's no use us all standing around here. Why don't you go with Deputy Rivers and talk to Mr. Halverson, who owns the cattle, and see if he can tell us anything that will help us? At this point, we have no idea if he knows this has happened to his herd."

Deputy Rivers stepped up and introduced herself to Bax, and they shook hands. They headed to Bax's Jeep, slid in, Bax turned around and they headed for the main road.

Buck looked at the sheriff. "What will this do to Halverson, financially?"

"Halverson is either dirt poor or he is loaded. He never talks about his situation with anyone. I do know this. He drives a shitty old pickup truck, and he and the missus live in a shack that should have fallen down years ago, but I've never seen him with his hand out. His family were the first settlers in the valley, and he owns a lot of land around here. Losing this many cows would crush most people around here. I guess we'll find out."

Buck was looking across the field when he noticed Delany holding his gloved hand up to the side of his head and then walking towards the other trooper. They both climbed down into the ravine.

"Something's going on," said Buck as he lifted his

binoculars and looked towards the ravine. Out of the corner of his eye, he spotted Franklin head in that same direction, and he too disappeared into the ravine. The radio on the back of the hazmat truck crackled, and Buck walked over and picked it up.

"Taylor, go ahead."

"Agent Taylor, this is Delany. We have two more bodies, and they're kids."

| 9 |

Chapter Nine

Bax followed Deputy Rivers's directions and turned off Highway 285 at the beat-up metal mailbox that said halverson in large faded white letters. If the mailbox was any indication of what they would find at the house, then Bax wasn't expecting much. As they rounded a corner, they spotted the old, dilapidated house and an old barn in even worse shape. What caught Bax's eye was the ambulance parked in front of the barn.

Deputy Rivers keyed the mic attached to her shoulder. "Three twelve to dispatch."

"Dispatch, go ahead, three twelve."

"Hi, Jenny, it's Kat. What's going on at the Halverson place?"

"Hi, Kat. Mrs. Halverson called in a medical emergency and asked for an ambulance and EMTs. Whatever's going on, we just called for Life Flight. They're on their way back after dropping Ben at the ER."

"Thanks, Jenny."

Bax pulled her Jeep in behind the ambulance, and they both slid out of the Jeep and walked into the barn.

They found Mrs. Halverson standing behind the EMT, who was hooking up a clear liquid drip line to Mr. Halverson's right arm. He was pale and appeared to be unresponsive. Deputy Rivers walked to the side of the gurney and tapped one of the EMTs on the arm. He looked up, surprised.

"Hey, Kat. What's up?"

The EMT, who was six foot three or four and weighed in at close to three hundred pounds, looked back to make sure the drip line was working and stood up.

"When we got here," he said, "Mr. Halverson was unconscious and unresponsive. Blood pressure is erratic, and his breathing is labored. Not sure what's going on, so we decided to have him flown to the hospital in Frisco."

They heard the helicopter as it landed in the front yard. The two EMTs lowered the gurney and, lifting it from both ends, carried it to the waiting helicopter, where a flight nurse was waiting for them next to the open door. They slid the gurney into the helicopter and took a minute to fill in the nurse on his condition. The nurse climbed into the helicopter next to the gurney and closed the door. The helicopter lifted off in a cloud of dust and headed north. The EMTs stepped back into the barn and cleaned up the supplies they had used to stabilize Mr. Halverson.

Deputy Rivers walked over to Mrs. Halverson, who was standing at the barn door with her arms wrapped around her chest. She looked in shock.

"Mrs. Halverson, I'm Deputy Rivers, and this is Agent

Baxter from the Colorado Bureau of Investigation. I know this is not a great time, but can we ask you some questions about what happened here?"

The gray-haired woman nodded as she pulled her sweater tighter around her chest. She wore a faded floral dress under the sweater and had on rubber muck boots.

She stepped out into the sunshine. "I don't know what happened," she said. "Gun left before dawn and told me he was heading up to the cattle. Instead of taking the truck, he was going to take the ATV."

Bax had spotted the ATV parked haphazardly in the middle of the barn. Mrs. Halverson continued.

"I didn't hear him come back, so I'm not sure how long he was in there. I came out to get some grain for the horses, and I found him slumped over on the front seat. He looked pale, and he seemed to be having a hard time breathing. I couldn't get him to wake up." She started to shake and pulled her sweater tighter.

"Mrs. Halverson," said Bax. "Where does your husband keep the cattle?"

She thought for a minute. "There's some open range up near North Tarryall Peak. It borders our property, and this time of year, there's good grass for grazing. He has them up there."

Bax pulled Deputy Rivers aside. "Call dispatch, use your cell phone and get me the number for the emergency room at the hospital." Deputy Rivers stepped outside and pulled her phone from her utility belt. She spoke for a few minutes and wrote a number in her notebook. She handed the note to Bax.

Bax stepped over to her Jeep, pulled out her phone and dialed the number.

When the phone was answered on the other end, Bax said, "This is Agent Ashley Baxter with the Colorado Bureau of Investigation. I need to talk to the emergency room physician right away. He is working on a deputy, and you have another patient that should be arriving any minute by chopper. Please interrupt him, no matter what he is doing. I have some information that he needs to have now."

The line went to hold music, and a minute later, Dr. James Harrison answered the phone. "Agent Baxter, this is Dr. Harrison. We're a little busy right now. What is this about?"

"Dr. Harrison, you have a patient being airlifted to you right now. He has the same symptoms as the deputy you are working on. We believe they have both been exposed to some kind of biological or chemical toxin. We have about a hundred dead cows that probably died from the same thing. I would suggest you quarantine both the deputy and Mr. Halverson when he arrives until we can get you some answers."

"Agent Baxter, are you serious? We're a small community hospital. We don't see this kind of thing. How can I verify who you are before I send a panic through the hospital and the community?"

"I appreciate your caution, Doctor. Do an internet search and call the Grand Junction office of the Colorado Bureau of Investigation. They will verify I am who I say I am. Please do that quickly. We don't know if this involves a contagion or what, but you need to take precautions."

Dr. Harrison hung up, and Bax speed-dialed a number.

"Hey, Bax," said Buck. "What's up?"

"Buck. They just put Mr. Halverson on a chopper to the hospital in Frisco. His wife found him unconscious in their barn. He appears to have the same symptoms as the deputy. She said he had taken an ATV to a field near North Tarryall Peak to check on his herd. She doesn't know when he returned to the barn, but he never came into the house. I called the hospital and told them to put both Halverson and the deputy into isolation until we know more."

"Good job, Bax. We have another problem. We found two dead kids in a ravine at the south end of the field."

"Oh, shit," said Bax. "Do we know who they are?"

"Yeah. Franklin took a picture and emailed it to my phone. Sheriff Toomey knows both boys. You'd better head back here."

"On our way," said Bax. She hung up and rejoined Deputy Rivers and Mrs. Halverson.

Deputy Rivers was on her phone, and it sounded like she was talking to a relative of Mrs. Halverson. She disconnected the call and looked at Mrs. Halverson.

"June and her husband will be here as soon as they can. Will you be all right until they get here?" she asked.

Mrs. Halverson thanked her, and Bax told her they would be back at some point to talk to her more in depth, but they had to go. She nodded and thanked them.

As they walked to the Jeep, Bax told Rivers about her conversation with Buck. They slid into the Jeep, and Bax headed down the long dirt road.

"Bax," said Deputy Rivers. "What do you think is going on?"

"I don't know, Kat. But whatever it is, it's not good."

She turned onto Highway 285 and hit the gas.

| **10** |

Chapter Ten

Bax pulled in behind a white van with Georgia plates and spotted Buck talking with a young medium-height black man with a shaved head. She slid out of the Jeep, and while Deputy Rivers went to find the sheriff, she walked up to Buck.

"Ashley Baxter, meet Dr. Clayton Roberts. Clay is the new forensic pathologist," said Buck.

Bax reached out and shook his hand. "Doctor, pleased to meet you."

"And you also, Agent Baxter," he said with a soft Southern accent.

"You're obviously not from around here," she said with a smile.

"No, ma'am. Been here about six months. I'm a general surgeon at the hospital, and I donate some spare time to the county health agency. Took over the pathologist position for Park and Summit Counties when Dr. English passed away."

"We were just talking about how to proceed," said Buck.

"We haven't had many cases where we can't get close to the crime scene or the bodies."

"I made some calls on the way over, and there is a level three containment facility in Denver that we can use. I have transport coming to take the bodies as soon as the hazmat team can prepare them," said Dr. Roberts. "I'll do the autopsies there just to be safe."

Buck waved over the sheriff and Deputy Rivers. "John, we're running out of daylight. We should make the death notifications."

Sheriff Toomey shook his head. "Yeah. We received a missing person report from the one kid's mom a little bit ago. I have a deputy there right now. He can make that one. The other one is a little trickier."

"Why's that?" asked Bax.

"One of the kids is Billy Clark." The sheriff hesitated. "His family is kind of notorious around here. They're involved in everything bad that happens in the county and are not fond of me or my deputies. We need to tread lightly."

Buck looked at Bax. "The sheriff and I will handle that one. You stay here and help Dr. Roberts coordinate the removal of the bodies. Also, see what Dr. Jess wants to do. I'd like her to do a necropsy on at least one of the cows. Also, call the secure courier and send the samples she and Franklin have taken to the state lab. I'll let Max know they're on their way."

"No problem," said Bax, and she headed for Franklin, who had just stepped out of the decontamination tent and was stripping off the hazmat suit.

Buck and Sheriff Toomey headed for the sheriff's SUV.

Once inside the SUV, Buck asked, "You said you got one call for a missing person. No one called about the other kid?"

"No," said the sheriff. "I'm not surprised." He didn't elaborate any further.

He started the SUV, backed up to a wide spot in the road and turned around. They headed for the Clark property, and the sheriff looked nervous. "John, what's going on?" asked Buck.

"The Clark family have been around the county for sixty years. They control most of the criminal activity in this area, and I've heard they have branched out to human trafficking. We know they control the drug trade as well as illegal guns, prostitution, and much worse."

Buck looked at him. "Why haven't you put them away?"

"Believe me. We've tried. Even when we catch one of them doing something illegal, no one will testify against them. Everyone in the county is afraid of them."

Buck looked straight ahead. He had run into some scary people in all his years in law enforcement, but that had never stopped him from going after people who broke the law. He decided he would need to look into this situation and see if there was a way he could help out his friend, the sheriff.

They turned off Highway 285 onto a dirt road that led back about a mile off the highway until they came to a barbed wire fence and gate. The sheriff stopped at the gate and slid out of the SUV; Buck followed. Before they stepped up to the gate, an older woman with gray hair, wearing baggy overalls and a black T-shirt, stepped out of a double-wide trailer fifty feet from the gate. She held a shotgun at her waist, pointed in their direction.

"What the hell do you want, Sheriff?" asked the older woman. "You ain't got no right to come on our property and harass us law-abiding folks. I could shoot you where you stand for trespassing on our land. This here is sovereign land, and we don't acknowledge your laws, so you just turn around and git before I forget my manners and shoot you anyway."

She went on with her anti-government tirade for another five minutes, and the sheriff just stood there. She stopped to take a breath, and Buck stepped closer to the gate. He had his hand on his pistol the whole time she was yelling.

Sheriff Toomey stepped up behind him as she raised the shotgun to her shoulder and started another tirade, calling them fascist dupes and fearmongers.

"Edith," said the sheriff when she took another breath. "We need to speak with Tucker and Claire. It's important."

She started screaming again. "You got no right harassing my children. Who do you think you are thinking you can come onto our sovereign property, claiming to just want to talk to my son? Do you think we're that stupid that you can fool us into letting you just waltz in here and attack us for no damn good reason?" And she was off again.

The door to the double-wide opened, and a younger woman stepped onto the porch. She had an assault-style rifle slung over her shoulder and a semiautomatic pistol in her hand. She could have been a younger version of the older woman, except for the long brown hair that hung down the middle of her back.

"Momma," said the young woman.

"Lizzy, go find your dad and tell him we got cops crawling

all over the place," said the older woman, never wavering with the shotgun as she spoke.

The young woman stepped off the front porch and looked around like she was looking for a bunch of cops hidden in the scrub oak. She stopped when she heard the sheriff speak.

"Come on, Edith, lower the shotgun. We just want to talk with Tucker. I'm not here to arrest him."

The young woman looked up at her mom. "Do like I told you, girl. Get your father."

"Should I fetch Tucker too?" asked the young woman.

"Goddamnit, girl. He's here to arrest your brother, and this is just a trick. Now, do like I told you."

She started to launch into another tirade as the young woman ran around the corner of the double-wide, but Buck was finished listening to her. He spoke as loud as he could.

"Ma'am, I'm Buck Taylor with the Colorado Bureau of Investigation. We are here to inform you that a body was found in a field this morning, and we have tentatively identified it as your grandson Billy. If you would like additional information, you can come by the sheriff's office, and we will be happy to discuss the details with you."

He turned and walked back to the SUV, the sheriff following close behind him. The older woman lowered the shotgun and stood on the porch with her mouth hanging open. For the first time in twenty minutes, she had nothing to say. The sheriff backed away from the fence and headed back down the dirt road towards the highway. He stopped at the end of the road and looked at Buck.

"Was that a good idea?" he asked.

Buck was a patient man, but he had reached his limit

listening to the older woman. He had made patience into an art form. There had been a story circulating the CBI offices for years about Buck getting a murderer to confess just by sitting at the table opposite him and not saying a word for four or five hours. Of course, the time got longer or shorter depending on who told the story, but it was always told as a sign of respect.

"No, probably not, but we got her attention. She was getting more agitated the longer we stayed there, and she was never going to listen to you. Since at least four other guns were pointing in our direction, I wanted to avoid her getting pissed off and doing something stupid."

The sheriff looked surprised. "I didn't see any other guns."

"There were two in the barn behind the house, one person with a long gun in the upstairs window of the big house farther into the property and another long gun behind a tractor out in the field. They weren't taking any chances. Let them come to us."

Buck's phone rang, and he looked at the number and answered. "Yes, sir."

"Buck, how are things going?" asked Director Jackson. "I hear things might be a bit complicated."

"Yes, sir," said Buck. "We may have some kind of contagion on our hands."

He gave the director a rundown of everything that had happened since he arrived on the scene—explaining about the treasure-hunting brand inspector and the two kids found in a ravine below the property. He told him about Halverson and the first responding deputy being airlifted to the hospital in Frisco. He ended by telling him about the encounter they had just had with the Clark family.

The director was silent for a moment, and Buck thought he had lost the call. "Sir?"

"I'm here, Buck. This is just a lot to take in. Any thoughts on whether this is chemical or biological?"

"Not yet, sir," said Buck. "Bax is sending the samples that the vet, Franklin and the hazmat team took to the state lab. The forensic pathologist is taking the bodies to Denver to a level three containment lab to do the autopsies. Needless to say, everyone up here is a little nervous."

"Buck, any chance this is domestic terrorism? The encounter you had with the Clark woman sounds like there's a lot of anti-government thinking happening."

Buck looked at the sheriff, who shook his head. "Director Jackson, Sheriff Toomey here. There is some anti-government hatred working its way through the county, and the Clarks are pretty much the center of it, but I can't see an endgame for them, and I sure can't see them hurting one of their family members. Just doesn't make any sense. Nothing to be gained by hurting Halverson or his cattle. I just don't see it."

"Thank you, Sheriff. I appreciate your input," said the director. "Buck, what's your next move?"

"Well, sir. The first thing we need to do is find out what we are dealing with. I'll have Max rush the results on the samples. We need the autopsy and the necropsy results to confirm what Max finds. We are looking through Dan Pearson's treasure-hunting information to see if he stepped on any toes, and I want to pull Halverson's life apart since the bulk of this attack seems to be directed at him."

"Okay, Buck, let me know what you need. The governor is concerned that once this information gets out, you will be buried in government intervention. He's heard rumblings that the CDC is gearing up a team from Denver to send your way. You don't have a lot of time."

Buck thanked the director and disconnected the call.

"Looks like we may have company," he said to the sheriff. "Now, tell me about the rest of the Clark family."

| 11 |

Chapter Eleven

Deputy Brenda Toomey, the sheriff's daughter, sat in the recliner and looked at Mr. and Mrs. Wells, who held each other on the couch. The small living room was almost suffocating. The tiny house on Clark Street had been home to the Wells family for more than twenty years. Mike Wells, about six feet tall and husky with a long black beard, was the foreman with a small mining company up on Hoosier Pass. Tammy Wells was a second-grade teacher at Edith Teter Elementary School. She was a thin woman with sharp, angular features and a hawkish nose. She was crying uncontrollably.

"I am so sorry," said Deputy Toomey. "Is there anything I can do for you?"

"You can tell us who killed our son," said Mike Wells.

Deputy Toomey hesitated. This was her first death notification, and she was uncomfortable, to say the least. "All I can tell you is that Marcus was found in a field up near

North Tarryall Peak, and his death is being investigated as suspicious."

"What the hell does that mean?" said Wells. "Did someone murder my child?"

"Sir, as soon as we have more information, we will let you know what's happening."

"I want to see my son," said Mrs. Wells.

"I'm sorry, ma'am, but that won't be possible yet. I understand the bodies are being sent to Denver for autopsy, and as soon as that is completed, the coroner will let you know what the next steps are."

"Why the hell are they taking the bodies to Denver, and who else was with my son when he died?" asked Wells. His face was getting redder by the second.

"Was that Billy Clark with my son when he died? Is that why we can't get any answers? That little prick can get away with anything he wants in this county, and you people do nothing about it. Did he get my son killed? I want to talk to him."

"I'm sorry, sir, that's not possible. All I can tell you is that there was another victim with your son. I wish I could tell you more at this time."

Mike Wells pushed his wife aside and stood up, his anger building. "You tell your fucking boss that I will get some answers one way or another. Those fucking Clarks don't scare me. Now, get the fuck out of my house."

Deputy Toomey jumped out of the chair and backed towards the door. Mike Wells glared at her, then sat beside his wife and wrapped his arms around her. Deputy Toomey walked out the front door and headed for her SUV. Once she got behind the wheel, she had to sit for a minute to stop her hands from shaking.

***

Edmund Clark sat at his son's kitchen table and looked at his wife, Edith. "What the hell else did the sheriff say?"

Edith, wiping away her tears, looked at her husband through bloodshot eyes. Her daughter-in-law, Claire, tears rolling down her face, sat next to her holding her hands in hers. Tucker Clark paced back and forth behind them. His father looked at him. "God damn it, Tucker, park your ass in a chair. It's hard enough to think around here with all this bawling." He looked at his wife again. "Today, Edith. What did he say?"

"The sheriff didn't say anything except he wanted to speak to Tucker and Claire. It was the old guy who was with him, some guy from CBI. He told me Billy was dead and if we wanted more information, to come to the sheriff's office."

"And he just left after that? Didn't say another word?" asked Edmund Clark. Edith nodded her head.

Tucker Clark jumped up from the chair.

"Sit the fuck down, Tucker, before I knock you down," said Edmund Clark.

Lizzy, who was standing in the kitchen doorway, coughed and looked at her father.

"What?" asked Edmund Clark. "You got something to say?"

"Yeah, Mom was on a tirade. The sheriff and that cop from CBI stood there for at least twenty minutes while mom let them have it with every stupid thing she ever heard on all those stupid conspiracy theory websites. She sounded like a crazy woman."

Edith glared at her. "That's bullshit. They were plain mean and rude to me and wouldn't tell me anything."

"You're unbelievable," said Lizzy. "You were holding a shotgun on them. I kept waiting for them to shoot you."

"You lying bitch," yelled Edith Clark, and she jumped up and smacked Lizzy across the face. Lizzy raised her fist. "Knock it off, both of you," said Edmund. "Edith, sit the fuck down. Lizzy, see if any of your nieces and nephews saw Billy today."

Edmund looked at Tucker. "When was the last time you saw Billy?"

"I don't know. Maybe yesterday afternoon sometime. You know that kid comes and goes as he pleases."

Claire let the tears flow, and Tucker looked embarrassed. Edmund slammed his hand down on the table. "We have too much going on right now to have the sheriff and CBI in our business. I can't believe you have no idea where your kid is or what he is up to."

"We raised him just like you raised us, Dad," said Tucker Clark. The sarcasm was not lost on Edmund, who leaned across the table and punched Tucker in the face, knocking him to the floor.

"What the fuck," said Tucker Clark.

"That's for being a smart-ass," said Edmund Clark, "and for not protecting my grandchild."

The kitchen door opened, and Tom Clark walked in, followed by his wife, Brenda. Tom was Edmund and Edith's oldest son. He was as big as his father, a shade over six feet, and had a muscular physique. His long graying hair was tied back in a ponytail, and he had a thick gray beard. Brenda was five foot four with a large chest and graying blond hair.

"Is it true?" asked Tom Clark. "Billy is dead. What do we know?"

"Not much. It seems your mother didn't get any information from the sheriff."

Tom and Brenda looked at each other. They knew what Edmund was talking about, and Brenda smiled and walked over and sat on the other side of Claire and wrapped her arms around her.

"What are we gonna do, Dad?" asked Tom Clark.

"We're gonna go to the sheriff's office and find out what the hell is going on."

Tucker stood up. "Not you," said Edmund. "You're staying here."

"He's my son," said Tucker Clark. "I have to . . ."

"Sit down and stay here with your mother. Your brother and I will deal with the sheriff."

Tucker Clark tried to argue, but his father reached across the table and grabbed him by his shirt. He had just drawn his fist back when another person entered the room.

"Edmund, you hit him again, and I'll break your arm. Now, let him go."

Edmund Clark looked at the old gray-haired man with the three-day stubble on his weathered face and released his grip on his son.

"He needs to learn to listen, Dad."

James Clark looked at his son. "He just found out his child is dead. What lesson do you think hitting him will teach him?"

James Clark walked up to Claire and wrapped his arms around her. He kissed her on the top of the head and stood up. "We will find out what happened to my great-grandson, and we will make whoever is responsible pay."

He took Edmund by the arm and led him out the door. Tom followed close behind.

"We got too much at risk right now to go off half-cocked. You two go talk to Toomey and find out what the hell is going on. We need to know if this was a one-off or an attack on our family. I'm gonna call our friends to see if they are hearing anything."

"Do we want to pull up the timeline?" asked Tom.

"No," said James Clark. "Everything is in place. Let's not panic yet. Find out what happened, and then we can talk more about it. In the meantime, it's business as usual."

Tom headed into the house. James looked at Edmund. "How are you doing with Halverson? We need to get him off dead center."

"Tucker said he has it all in hand. He thinks we should be able to move in the next couple of days," said Edmund.

James Clark gave his son a sideways glance and nodded. "Don't fuck this up."

James Clark stepped off the back steps and headed towards his house. Tom came out of the back door, and he and Edmund walked towards Tom's F-250 pickup truck. They slid into the cab, and Tom drove around the house and headed for the highway. As they passed through the gate, he looked at Edmund.

"Dad, I'm worried that Tucker is not going to get Halverson to cooperate. We need to move in a different direction."

Edmund was quiet until they turned onto Highway 285 and headed south. After a couple of miles, he took off his hat and wiped his brow.

"We'll give him two more days. If he can't deliver, then do what you need to do."

Tom nodded and headed towards Fairplay.

| 12 |

Chapter Twelve

Buck and Sheriff Toomey arrived back at the crime scene and slid out of the sheriff's SUV. Bax was talking with Dr. Jess next to her Jeep. Buck and the sheriff walked up.

"Where we at?" asked Buck.

"The courier just left with the samples," said Bax. "Everything was double-wrapped, just in case. The troopers think they have everything they need and are heading back to their base. Once we get the sample results back, we can decide if we need them further. Franklin's team just left. He'll upload all his photos to the investigation file, which I just finished setting up on our system. Dr. Jess and I were discussing her next steps."

Buck filled them in on the conversation he'd had with the director and the response they received when they made the death notification at the Clark house.

"She held you at gunpoint?" asked Bax. "What the hell was she thinking?"

Buck laughed. "I don't think she was thinking at all. We were from the government, and she was protecting her family from government intrusion."

"You have to understand, Bax. Her family is at the forefront of the county when it comes to anti-government sentiment. I think her husband is involved to protect his criminal interests, but she has been brainwashed into believing that shit is real."

"Wow," said Bax. "She could have killed you or started a war."

"Yeah," said Sheriff Toomey. He looked at Buck. "If you don't need me for anything else, I need to head back to the office. A lot of people are going to ask a lot of questions once this gets out, and I want to head some of that off. I have deputies scheduled to sit on the scene overnight."

Buck shook his hand. "Thanks, John. We'll wrap up here and head to the hotel. We'll meet in your office in the morning."

The sheriff tipped his hat to the two women and headed for his SUV. He stopped to talk to Deputy Rivers, who would take the first watch, then he slid into his SUV and headed for town.

Buck turned to Dr. Jess. "Doctor, what do you need from us?"

"At this point, we are good. I have a team coming up from Colorado State University to load up one of the bulls and take it to the level four containment lab they have on campus. I have asked the team there to do the autopsy tonight and get us the results ASAP."

She looked up as they saw a white van struggle up the

dirt road and stop next to them. The driver and two help-ers climbed out of the van, introduced themselves, and asked Dr. Jess to show them which bull they were taking. Jess led the driver over as his two helpers started unloading rubber hazmat suits from the van.

The driver, Scott, looked out over the field. "Holy shit." He looked embarrassed. "Sorry about the language, Doc. Just caught me by surprise. That's a lot of dead cows."

"Can you guys get the cow out of there?"

"No problem," said Scott. "We do this all the time."

He walked back to the van and turned it ninety degrees to the ditch, and then they put on the hazmat suits, checked each other's oxygen levels and pulled a large yellow sled out of the back of the van. Scott connected it to the winch on the back, and they carried it and a huge black rubber body bag across the field to the bull Dr. Jess had selected.

Buck, Bax and Dr. Jess watched in awe as the three tech-nicians maneuvered the bull into the body bag and loaded it onto the sled. Scott walked back to the van and engaged the winch, and within fifteen minutes, they had the bull loaded in the back of the van after spraying the outside of the bag and the sled with bleach. They decontaminated each other with bleach, worked their way out of the hazmat suits, and gave Dr. Jess a receipt for the bull. They climbed into the van and headed for the lab in Fort Collins.

Buck looked at his watch. "Bax, give Paul a call and head for the hotel. Meet me at the Azteca Mexican Café in town at six."

"What are you going to do?" she asked.

"I'm going to stick around here for a few minutes and

work through some thoughts. I also need to call Max and let her know what we need."

He thanked Dr. Jess for all her help, and she promised to call him as soon as she heard anything from the lab. She and Bax walked to the SUVs and headed down the road. Buck walked over to Deputy Rivers, who was setting up a lawn chair and a cooler next to her SUV.

"You're in for a long night after a long day," he said.

She smiled. "That's okay. The sooner we figure this out, the better we will all be. Once the people in the county find out, the sheriff is gonna have a lot to deal with."

"What is your impression of what happened here, Deputy?"

Deputy Rivers looked at him with surprise. She knew Buck had a reputation as one of the best investigators in the state and was well respected by everyone, including the sheriff. She was shocked that he would ask her opinion, since she had been a deputy for less than four years and had never been involved in a criminal investigation. She looked at him questioningly.

"I'm serious," said Buck with a smile. "I'd like to know your opinion."

"I don't know, sir. I mean, why go through this much trouble to kill a brand inspector? Seems like a lot of work for very little gain. And who uses chemicals or something like that to kill cows, anyway? Seems like something you wouldn't have a lot of control over once you released it. Just seems dumb, sir."

Buck nodded and walked up the dirt road past the crime scene tape they had spread across the road to keep everyone out. He stopped next to Dan Pearson's truck and the first deputy's SUV, and walked around, pulling out his phone and taking pictures of the shovel and the metal detector in the back of Pearson's truck. He opened the cab and climbed inside. Deputy Rivers watched him. He leafed through the papers sitting on the passenger seat and found another map of the area. He looked at some pictures that were sitting on the center console and had a thought. He pulled out his phone and made a call.

Buck slid out of the truck, stepped across the road and walked into the field. Deputy Rivers spotted him, set down her lunch and ran up the road.

"Sir," she said with panic in her voice. "Is that a good idea?"

Buck waved to her and kept walking. He stopped where Dan Pearson's body had been, looked around and then moved deeper into the field. He stopped, looked at some of the dead cows and headed into the ravine where the two young boys were found.

After a few minutes of not being able to see him, Deputy Rivers reached for her radio. She was about to call the sheriff when Buck climbed out of the ravine and headed towards her. He stepped over the ditch.

"Are you okay, sir?" she asked. "That seemed kind of dangerous."

Buck nodded. "Whatever was sprayed on those cows and made the deputy and Halverson sick is no longer a threat. I noticed on three separate occasions while we were all out here that a light gust of wind blew directly at us, and even though the troopers and my team were walking in the field kicking up dust, none of us got sick. I needed to make sure my conjecture was right before I put anyone else at risk."

"Seems like a big risk, sir, if you were wrong," said Deputy Rivers.

"Luckily, I wasn't wrong," he said. "Call if you need anything, Deputy, and have a quiet evening."

Buck walked to his Jeep, climbed in, and headed towards Fairplay. He pulled out his phone and made another call.

Chapter Thirteen

"Buck Taylor. How's my favorite cop?" asked Max Clinton. "What the hell have you gotten yourself involved with this time?"

Dr. Maxine Clinton was the director of the State Crime Lab and one of Buck's oldest and dearest friends. She was a matronly woman in her late sixties, about five foot five, with short gray hair. She thought she carried around an extra fifteen pounds she didn't need, but she was still a handsome woman. Married for forty years, Max had four children, eleven grandchildren, and six great-grandchildren. She lived in a one-hundred-fifty-year-old farmhouse in Pueblo, where she liked to tend her garden and sit on her porch and drink iced tea. She was also a bourbon girl and could drink most people under the table. She was loud and outspoken, but she knew her job.

Max had received her PhD in biology from the University of Colorado and worked as a biology professor for twenty years before joining CBI. She was the head of the State Crime Lab, which she thoroughly enjoyed. She was a tough taskmaster, but she had a belief system that didn't allow for defeat. Her goal was to give the crime investigator, no matter which department or municipality they worked for, all the information they would need to solve any crime. She held that as a sacred obligation to the victims. She was dedicated to her job and her staff, and the team at the lab practically worshipped her.

Buck would have been included in that group. Many times, during a challenging investigation, it was Max and her team that lit the spark that led to a breakthrough. Max was one of Buck's favorite people, and she felt the same way about him.

"Hey, Max. I've got some samples headed your way," he said.

Buck gave Max a debrief about the case and the possibility that there was a chemical or toxin involved. He explained he was looking for any information she might be able to find on what might have killed the cattle and the human victims. Buck was confident that if Max couldn't get the answer from someone on her staff, she would have an outside source that would know.

The people Buck worked with always joked that there wasn't anyone in Colorado that Buck didn't know. But the truth was, Max was way ahead of him in that department. She had contacts all around the world, and she never failed to get him the answers he needed.

During one recent case, Buck was looking for information on infrasound weapons and what effect they would have on the body. Within a couple of hours, Buck was on the phone with a colleague of Max's who was an expert in those types of weapons.

"Do you think this could be domestic terrorism?" she asked.

"Not sure at this point. Could be anything. We're just getting started."

"Okay, Buck. We have a level three lab here. We'll look at the samples in there and take extra precautions. I will also have the lab staff look at options outside our normal routine. Exotic chemicals and biotoxins. Don't you worry; we'll figure out what's going on."

"Thanks, Max. Let's keep this quiet until we know what we are dealing with. I've already heard that the CDC is gathering its troops. The last thing I need is them mucking up the water, so to speak."

Max laughed. "You know me, Buck. Discretion is my middle name."

Buck laughed as well. "I thought it was Alice."

Max told him she would get her team on it as soon as the samples arrived at the lab, and Buck thanked her. She ended the call the way she always did. "You're a good man, Buck Taylor; God will watch over you."

Buck wasn't much of a religious man. He hadn't been to church in forty years. He had been raised Catholic but left the church right after confirmation. He always had too many questions about the teachings and too many people telling him that he had to have faith. That wasn't the answer he was looking for. He had a lot of friends, Max among them, who had always offered up a prayer when Lucy was dying.

He never once rejected any of those offers, often smiling and thanking them for their kind thoughts.

Buck had realized long ago that it wasn't God and faith he had a problem with; it was organized religion. In his many years in law enforcement, he had seen too many times the aftereffects of someone's religious beliefs. It amazed him that so many people of faith could cause so much hatred and crime. But then, nonbelievers created just as much havoc.

Buck always believed there was a higher power, but he didn't believe that whatever that power was, it cared about one individual over another. His football coach always offered up a prayer before each game, asking for help in defeating the other team. He always suspected the other team's coach was doing the same thing. So how did God decide which team should win?

He knew a lot of people who said a lot of prayers for Lucy over the five years she was sick, but in the end, she still died. And she was the last person who should have gotten cancer. But Buck didn't carry any hatred. Whom could he get mad at? Whom could he blame?

Buck believed that there were spirits or a force all around us, and he always thanked them for allowing him to enjoy the hike or for allowing him to catch fish or see the sunrise and the sunset. It wasn't religion. It was something deeper. Something Buck didn't understand. He just accepted it. But no matter what, he always appreciated it when Max told him that God was watching over him. After all, what could it hurt?

Buck reached over to clip his phone to the holder on his

dashboard when his phone chimed. He looked at the number and connected the call.

"Hey, guys. What have you got?" asked Buck.

"We're still working on your request," said George Peterman, "but we wanted to let you know that the word is out. Social media has exploded with the story, and the conspiracy theorists are all over this like flies on honey."

"Fuck," said Buck. "I hoped we would get a little more time before this exploded. How bad is it?"

"So far, it's mostly on the hard-line conspiracy pages, but the local newspaper in Park County has it, and they are working on it. Our PR team called here to give us a heads-up. It won't be long before the papers and the news channels in Denver get it, and then it's a whole new ball game."

"Okay. Anything on Dan Pearson's computer that we need to look at?" asked Buck.

"Yeah, we're chasing a couple of things that look interesting. Mel will upload some things we've found to the investigation file in a little bit, and we'll keep working on the pictures."

Buck thanked George and disconnected the call. He dropped his phone on the passenger seat. He'd known it would happen sooner than later, but he wished he had something more to feed the legitimate news media. He had a feeling this was going to be a long night. He didn't know yet how true that would be.

| 14 |

Chapter Fourteen

Sheriff Toomey entered his office through the back door and stopped by the dispatcher, who looked frazzled.

"Hi, Sheriff. We've had at least fifty calls from people in the county, and a bunch of online news people have called as well. We may need some help to handle all the calls."

"Okay," said the sheriff. "Call in a couple of the volunteers and have them man the phones." He turned towards his office.

"By the way," said the dispatcher. "Several of those calls are from the mayor and the county commissioners."

He nodded, stepped into his office and closed the door. He had a feeling this would blow up in his face, and he needed to be prepared. He pulled out his cell phone and dialed a number.

Paul Gibson, the oldest serving county commissioner, answered on the second ring.

"Sheriff, how are you doing?"

"Hi, Paul. Wanted to give you a heads-up on where we are. We found Dan Pearson, the brand inspector, dead in a field surrounded by over a hundred dead cows belonging to Halverson. Deputy Carmichael, the first officer on the scene, was airlifted to the hospital in Frisco, unconscious and having trouble breathing. Gunther Halverson was also airlifted to the hospital with the same symptoms. We also found Marcus Wells and Billy Clark dead at the scene. We think it might have been a chemical or biological toxin. CBI is running tests. We should have a clearer picture tomorrow."

"Do the Clarks know?"

"All we told Edith was her grandson was dead. She was on one of her tirades and had us at gunpoint. We couldn't get a word in. With all the calls I'm getting, it sounds like the word is out, but we are keeping the details tight."

"John, was this terrorism, or did something escape from that government lab we don't know anything about?"

"You sound like one of those conspiracy folks, Paul. Right now, it looks to be intentional."

"Can we spin this so CBI takes the heat because we don't know yet what happened?"

"I think that would be a mistake. Buck Taylor is all over this thing, and he's the best they have. He'll figure it out. One other thing, we might end up with some unwanted federal intrusion. Once word gets out, we won't be able to stop them from getting involved."

There was silence on the other end of the line. "Okay, John. Let me know what you need, and I'll call the other commissioners and fill them in."

Sheriff Toomey set his phone on his desk and fired up his

laptop just as a bunch of yelling came from the front desk. He stood up, walked to the door and opened it.

"Don't give me that shit. You get that chickenshit out of his office, or I'll head back there myself and drag his ass out here."

"Mr. Clark, I need you to calm down," said the dispatcher.

"Who the fuck do you think you're talking to. Get that fuck out here now, or there is going to be hell to pay."

Sheriff Toomey opened the door between the lobby and the offices and stepped up to Edmund Clark. He spotted Tom Clark standing behind him, his hand on the backstrap of the pistol hanging off his belt.

"Edmund, calm down," said the sheriff as calmly as he could. He looked at Tom Clark. "Tom, please take your hand off that pistol. I wouldn't want someone to get hurt. Now, what's going on?"

Tom lifted his hand off the pistol, and Edmund got into the sheriff's face.

"I want to know what happened to my grandson, and I want answers now, and I want to know where the fucking cop from CBI is who yelled at Edith. You guys have a lot of fucking nerve," said Edmund Clark.

"Edmund, why don't you follow me? Tom, please wait for us here."

Tom looked pissed and stepped forward, but Edmund Clark raised his hand to stop him. He followed the sheriff into the office and closed the door.

The sheriff sat behind his desk, and Edmund plopped in the guest chair. Edmund glared at the sheriff.

"Here's what we know so far. We found Billy and Marcus

in a ravine out near North Tarryall Peak. From what we can tell, it appears they were exposed to some kind of toxin. We are running lab tests to find the answer to what the exposure was. Because of the exposure, the bodies were transported to a special lab in Denver for autopsy, as a precaution."

"Who the fuck gave you permission to autopsy my grandson?"

"Edmund, you know as well as I do that any unattended death requires an autopsy, especially one with suspicious circumstances."

Edmund was still agitated. "What the hell are you not telling me? Sounds like some kind of cover-up going on. Does this have anything to do with that secret lab the Feds built without our knowledge?"

Sheriff Toomey started to respond, but Edmund Clark interrupted. "Where is this CBI guy? He insulted and yelled at my wife and *that* I will not tolerate from anyone."

"He's still at the crime scene, but I will tell you right now, he is not someone you want to mess with. He also did not insult Edith. I was standing right next to him. Edith was on one of her anti-government tirades and was holding her shotgun on us. She wouldn't let us even talk, so Agent Taylor raised his voice and told her Billy was found dead. No one insulted her."

"That's not how I heard it, but no matter. I will deal with that on my own." He stood up and leaned on the sheriff's desk. "You get my grandson's body back here right away, and you find the son of a bitch who did this, or I will. You got me?"

Edmund Clark turned and stormed out of the office, and

the sheriff heard the door to the lobby slam shut. He knew trouble was coming from a lot of different directions. He had a feeling things were going to get ugly, real fast.

| 15 |

Chapter Fifteen

Buck parked in the small dirt lot next to the Aztec Mexican Café and slid out of his Jeep, grabbing his backpack off the passenger seat. He walked around the building and opened the door. The most incredible fragrances hit him in the face, and he almost drooled on himself. He walked up to the small podium and tapped the short dark-haired Hispanic man behind the podium on the shoulder. The man looked up, smiled and walked around the podium.

"Señor Buck. It is so good to see you. It has been too long, my friend," he said.

"That it has, Carlos, that it has. How have you been? How's the fishing?" asked Buck.

Carlos Marino waved his hand around the packed restaurant. "Business is good," he said. "And the fishing couldn't be better. Maybe we can spend a few minutes before you leave. You will not be disappointed."

"I'd like that," said Buck. "How are Maria and the kids?"

Carlos Marino raised his hands towards the ceiling. "Maria, she keeps me on my toes, and the kids are growing so fast. She will be thrilled that you are here, and I will tell her to make you and your friends something special for dinner."

He pointed towards the back corner. "I have put your friends in your favorite spot where you can keep an eye on the door." Carlos winked, and Buck thanked him and headed towards the back of the restaurant, stopping to talk to a few of the customers along the way. He slid into the seat with his back to the wall. Bax looked at him with a smile.

"You really do know everyone in Colorado. It's amazing."

Buck laughed. "I met Carlos and his family a couple of years back. Carlos is a part-time fishing guide; we've had some awesome trips together. Those other folks I met when I was here a bunch of years back on an investigation. The crowd in this restaurant hasn't changed much over the years."

Carlos stopped by the table and put a large Coke on the table. Buck's Coke drinking was legendary around the CBI office and seemed to spread to wherever he was working.

"Your food will be right out," he said as he turned and walked away.

Paul looked up from his laptop. "We haven't ordered yet."

Buck laughed. "Don't worry. Maria, Carlos's wife, is one of the best cooks around. You won't be disappointed."

Buck liked eating in this restaurant, and even though his badge and gun were obvious to everyone in the place, he was always afforded privacy by the rest of the patrons. He knew the story was out, yet no one questioned him as he walked through the restaurant. Carlos always made sure no one bothered him.

He had just asked Paul to fill him in on what he had learned at the Pearsons' place when he heard the front door slam open, and a loud commotion come from the front door.

"Mr. Clark, I will be happy to clear a space for you and your son if you give me a minute."

"Where the fuck is he? That CBI cop. I know he's here. Where is he?"

Edmund Clark looked around the room and spotted the only white faces in the place sitting at a back table. All eyes in the restaurant were on him. Carlos stepped in front of him, but before he could say anything, Edmund Clark pushed him up against the wall.

"Get out of my way, you fuckin' little wetback, or I'll burn this place to the ground."

Edmund Clark pushed past Carlos, and then Tom stopped and shoved him hard against the wall again, knocking his restaurant license off the wall.

Edmund Clark shoved his way through the restaurant, shoving people out of the way and spilling drinks as he went. He walked up to Buck's table and glared at Buck. Tom Clark took up a position next to his dad.

"You insulted my wife and yelled at her. That may be something you tolerate, but I don't. You also sent my grandson to the city for an autopsy without my permission. Who the fuck do you think you are?"

Buck stayed seated, and Bax shifted in her chair. Buck knew Paul had pulled his pistol and held it next to his leg.

"First, I need you to calm down, Mr. Clark. You're making a big scene."

Buck could see several cell phones pointed in their

direction. No doubt, this would become an internet sensation before the night was over.

"Who the fuck do you think you are telling me to calm down? Do you know who the fuck you're talking to?"

Buck leaned back in his chair. "You know, Mr. Clark. I've figured out over the years that people who ask that question usually find out that they're not as important as they think they are."

Edmund Clark stuttered. Not many people talked to him like that, and the ones who did lived to regret it. He'd started to say something when Tom Clark attempted to step past him and pushed Bax's chair to get by.

Buck had seen Bax move fast before—as a Krav Maga instructor, she had incredible agility—but tonight he never even saw the move. One minute Bax was being pushed into Paul, and the next there was a loud crash, and Tom Clark was lying on his back on the floor, and Bax was holding her pistol under his nose. Tom Clark looked stunned as Bax pulled the pistol from his belt and handed it back to Paul, who now had his pistol pointing at Edmund Clark.

Buck smiled. "Mr. Clark. I'm sure you've already spoken with the sheriff, and he explained about your wife ranting that we were intruding in your lives. I was concerned the more she ranted that she might do something dangerous with that shotgun, so I raised my voice above hers and told her we had found your grandson. It was not meant to be insulting in any way. I was looking out for her safety and the safety of the sheriff and me. As far as your grandson. Yes, his body and the body of the other young man he was found with were sent to Denver for an autopsy because there are no facilities in the county that could do the job safely. His body will be released to his parents as soon as we know it is safe. Right now, that is all I can tell you. I am sorry for your loss."

Edmund Clark wasn't dismissed this easily. "You haven't heard the last from me, Taylor, and if I find out that something that escaped from that secret government lab they built killed my grandson like that Chinese virus did, I will make the government pay in ways you can't imagine."

Edmund Clark turned to walk away and looked at his son lying on the floor. He looked at Buck, who nodded at Bax, and she stood up and holstered her weapon. Buck stood up, reached across the table, picked up Tom's pistol, pulled the magazine and emptied the chamber. He removed all the shells from the magazine, reinserted it and handed it to his father.

"By the way, Mr. Clark. I do know a lot about you, and by the time I leave this county, I will know a lot more. You can trust me on that."

Clark looked at him. "Are you threatening me, cop?"

Buck looked him straight in the eye. "I never make threats, Mr. Clark."

Edmund and Tom Clark pushed back through the restaurant and slammed the front door closed behind them. Tom Clark stared daggers at their table before he followed his dad out the door.

Carlos walked up to the table, and Buck grabbed his arm. "Are you okay, my friend?"

"Sí. I was scared for you and your friends. I hope this does not come back to haunt you. That Mr. Clark and his family, they are not nice people."

Buck and Bax sat, and Maria appeared behind Carlos

with three hot plates of the most incredible burritos any of them had seen. Buck made the introductions, and Maria made small talk until she had to return to the kitchen. Carlos headed for the door to seat a couple of guests, and Buck, Bax and Paul dug into their food. There was silence at the table while they ate.

| 16 |

Chapter Sixteen

Buck pushed his plate to the center of the table, sat back and stretched. He leaned forward. "That was an interesting encounter," he said. "Do we have any idea what he was talking about, a secret government lab?"

Paul pulled out his laptop, pushed his plate aside and opened his internet browser. He looked at several websites, then clicked on the investigation file and opened some of the websites and chat rooms George had flagged.

"I'm not sure where it all started, but there has been speculation, going back a couple of years, regarding the government building a secret lab in the mountains in Park County. The government has always denied it, but we've been there before. The posts have ratcheted up since word got out about the dead cattle. People are pissed, and the rhetoric is heated."

He turned the laptop so Buck could see, and Buck clicked through the Facebook comments. He slid the laptop back to Paul.

"Any way we can find out if there's any truth to this?" asked Bax.

Paul laughed. "Do you think the government will let Buck visit a second secret bunker? I think we already played that card."

Buck smiled. Several years back, Buck had investigated a case involving several dead students hiking along the Continental Divide Trail doing a grizzly bear survey. They never completed the survey because they were mysteriously killed. Through Buck's investigation, it was determined that they most likely died due to exposure to infrasound, which in this case appeared to be naturally occurring. The investigation exposed a long-abandoned military bunker from the Cold War, deep in the mountains, that the government was refurbishing for a new role. The conspiracy theorists were having a field day, so Buck was invited to tour the facility to ensure that nothing nefarious was going on. The information presented to Buck about the original purpose of the bunker was enough to scare the daylights out of anyone, and Buck was sworn to secrecy. He never revealed that information to anyone, including Bax or Paul.

"Okay. Back to reality," said Buck. "George told me that Mel was loading some information into the file they retrieved from Dan Pearson's laptop. Do we know what they found?"

Paul clicked through the file and opened a couple of documents that Mel had uploaded.

"It looks like Pearson was looking for Aztec treasure." Paul opened another document. "He believed that before the Aztecs moved south into Mexico, they left a large stash of gold and jewels hidden in the mountains. Even though researchers believe that the Aztec land was centered in Utah, Pearson and several of his treasure-hunting friends were convinced that the researchers were wrong and that they had located the treasure in an area of Park County. Pearson was attempting to narrow down the search area."

Paul looked up from his laptop. "That would match what I found in his office. After reading some of his notes and looking at the information he had posted on several treasure-hunting forums, I think he might have misinterpreted some of what he was looking at."

Buck reached for the laptop, and Paul turned it so he could see the information on the screen.

"So, all of this could be because of a treasure hunt?" asked Bax.

Buck looked up from the laptop. "I don't think so."

He told them about his stroll through the field after Bax had left.

"That doesn't sound very safe," said Bax.

"I think we are dealing with a couple of unrelated events. First, the dead cattle make no sense in the context of the treasure hunt. Second, I think the dead cattle have something to do with Halverson. I haven't got a clue how Dan Pearson fits into it other than my gut says they are not related."

"What about the two kids? How do they fit into this?"

"I don't know, but we need to find out, or his family will go on the warpath."

The busboy came by and asked if he could clean off the table, and they all sat back for a minute to let him remove the dirty dishes and glasses. Carlos came by with coffee, a Coke for Buck, and some incredible Mexican pastries for dessert.

Buck asked Carlos if he needed the table, and Carlos told him to take as long as they needed. He headed back to the front door, and Buck continued. "We need to do a deep dive on Halverson. The dead cattle are a direct attack on him. Bax, can you call the hospital and see if his and the deputy's conditions have improved and if we can talk to them?"

Bax stepped away from the table and walked to the front door, pulling out her phone.

"Paul, let's also go deep into the Clark family. I don't think anyone around here is going to stop whatever they are involved in, so that leaves it up to us. Once George and Mel have finished their work on Pearson, get them to help. I'd also like to see what else we can find about this secret lab."

"Do you really believe there's a secret lab in Park County?" asked Paul.

Buck laughed. "I wouldn't put anything past the government, but who knows? Let's cover all our bases."

Bax came back to the table. "Bad news. The deputy and Halverson took a turn for the worse and were airlifted to Denver General Hospital. They're in quarantine. I called Denver General, and all they will tell me is that they are still alive."

Buck pulled out his phone and dialed a number.

Director Jackson answered. "Hey, Buck. What's up?"

"Evening, sir. Halverson and the deputy have been flown to Denver General. Can you get one of our people over there to see what's happening? Halverson is the key to this thing, but I don't know why. I'd like to have our people on him round the clock."

"You think he's in danger?" asked the director.

"I'm not sure, sir." Buck told the director about what happened earlier in the evening with Edmund Clark and his son.

"Didn't they lose a family member?" asked Director Jackson. "Do you think they're involved in some way?"

"Not sure, but they were pretty hot under the collar when they approached us. I may be overreacting, but until we know what led to this chain of events, I'd like to err on the side of caution."

"Okay, Buck. I'll set it up. You guys be careful."

Buck disconnected the call and looked at his watch. The restaurant was almost empty, and it was getting late.

"Let's get some sleep and get back to this first thing in the morning. Let's meet here for breakfast at seven."

They gathered their belongings and headed for the door. Buck pushed into the kitchen and found Maria and Carlos in the small office. He thanked them for their hospitality and apologized for the incident with the Clarks. He pulled out his money clip. Carlos shook his head.

"No, no, Señor Buck. Your money is no good here."

Buck pulled three twenties from his money clip and set them on the worktable next to Maria. "Give this to the staff."

He patted Carlos on the shoulder, hugged Maria and walked towards the front door. Once outside in the cool air, he stopped and looked up and down the highway. Fairplay was a small town by anyone's standards, but there were things going on that didn't seem right. He promised himself that he would find out what the Clarks were involved with and why everyone was afraid of them, and he would put an end to whatever it was.

He headed for his Jeep.

| **17** |

Chapter Seventeen

James Clark walked past the empty stalls as he paced through the barn. He stopped and looked at Edmund and Tom.

"I don't know what's worse, Edith pointing a gun at the cops or you two idiots getting into a fight with the CBI folks. Why not just hang a sign over the gate that says, please investigate us? What the hell is wrong with you?"

Tucker laughed. "Fucking stupid."

Tom jumped up from the chair and grabbed for his brother, but Edmund intervened. "Says you, asshole. How about I kick your ass right now," said Tom.

Tucker laughed from behind his father. "You think you can? You got your ass kicked by a woman."

Tom shoved past his father and grabbed Tucker's shirt. His right fist caught Tucker alongside his chin, and Tucker flew backward into the wall and slid onto the floor.

He stood, dusted himself off and sneered at his brother.

"You hit like a girl. No wonder that bitch beat you. Fucking pussy."

Tom charged at Tucker again and tackled him, and they slammed into one of the open stalls. The hay on the ground flew through the air as they rolled around on the dirt floor. James Clark stood in the doorway and watched as Tucker landed as many blows as Tom. He walked over and took a bucket off the wall, filled it with water from the trough and threw it on the two combatants. They both stopped thrashing about and looked at their grandfather.

"If you two jackasses can stop the stupidity long enough, I have some information about how Billy died."

They stood up and brushed themselves off, drying their faces with their hands.

"According to my source, Billy and Marcus were found in a field full of dead cows up near North Tarryall Peak. No one seems to know how the cows died, but it could be a chemical of some kind."

Tucker stared at his grandfather, and his legs started to shake. His mind raced in a thousand different directions. How did Billy and Marcus get to the field? Why did they follow him? Then he started to get angry. Brian said it wouldn't hurt people. He balled up his fists, and his whole body tensed. He turned back to his grandfather.

"What did you say?" he asked.

"The least you could do is listen to me the first time," said James Clark. "I said, they also found that brand inspector that lives over by Como dead in the same field. Heard he'd been shot."

Edmund looked at his father. "What the hell is going on?

We don't need this kind of shit while we are in the middle of our two biggest deals. Do you know whose cows were in that field?"

James took a couple of steps and turned and faced his son. "I heard the cows belonged to Halverson."

Edmund shook his head. "This can't be happening. Is someone out to screw with us? We were this close to getting Halverson to sign, and now this. This makes no sense."

Edmund looked at Tucker and then at James. "We need to get over to Halverson's place and make sure he signs."

A voice behind them stopped them in their tracks. "Halverson's in the hospital in critical condition," said Lizzy, standing in the doorway.

They all turned and looked at her.

"What are you talking about, Liz," said Tucker. "I saw him in town yesterday, and he looked fine."

"Heard they found him in his barn yesterday, unconscious and couldn't breathe."

"We need to figure out who's trying to sabotage our deal," said Edmund. "We've got too much riding on this."

They all turned when they heard someone else enter the barn. James's wife, Connie, stepped through the door. "Thought you'd want to know. I just got a call from a friend who works at the hospital in Frisco. Gunther Halverson was flown by Life Flight to Denver General Hospital. He's in isolation, and they don't think he's going to make it. My friend says a Park County deputy was flown out with him."

Tom Clark slammed his fist into the wood slat wall, and everyone jumped. He glared at his brother.

"This is all your fault. You had one job to do. Get that old man to sign the papers, and you couldn't even do that right."

"Oh, yeah," said Tucker. "What would you have done differently, you moron. Huh? You got a big mouth and a tiny brain. What did I do wrong?"

Tom Clark went after his brother again. This time it was Lizzy who tripped him up, then she grabbed a hayfork from the wall rack and pressed it against his chest.

"You both need to grow up in a hurry. What's done is done, and unless we can get Halverson's wife to sign, there is little we can do before the deadline, so you two better put your heads together and figure out how to fix this." She looked at Tucker. "He's right, you know. You fucked this up good, so now you're off of it. Tom will clean up your mess, and you will help me get our guests ready. We have another shipment coming in two days, and we need to get them all shipped out. Do not let me down."

She lifted the hayfork from Tom's chest, hung it back on the wall and turned to leave. She turned back and faced them all. "We're going to lose a shitload of money if we can't pull these two operations off."

She turned and left the barn, followed by her grandmother and grandfather. Tom stood and dusted himself off. This was the second time today he had been bested by a woman, and he was not happy. He picked up his Stetson, dusted it off and walked out the door at the other end of the barn.

Edmund walked up to Tucker and stared into his eyes. "Did you have anything to do with any of this crap?"

Tucker looked away from his dad. "I swear to god, Dad, I have no idea what's going on, but I will try to find out."

He stormed out the door the same way Tom had gone, and Edmund heard his pickup truck start and tear down the driveway. He stood there for a minute, alone in the barn, and wondered why his son had just lied to him.

| 18 |

Chapter Eighteen

Buck was restless and having trouble getting to sleep. Something about this case was gnawing at him, but he couldn't put his finger on it. The little bug that bounced around in his head during an investigation was silent, which gave Buck an eerie feeling. He couldn't shake the idea that they were missing something important, but then, they were missing a lot of stuff. He couldn't remember going into any investigation with less information than they had at this point.

He had no forensics from the crime scene to work with. A crime scene that was compromised. He had bodies that were being autopsied out of his control. And he had a sheriff, whom he had known for years as a fine man, who allowed a family of criminals to run roughshod all over his county.

He sat up, threw off the covers, took a long drink from the warm bottle of Coke sitting on the nightstand and walked over to the small desk. He opened his laptop to the investigation file, picked up his phone and uploaded the pictures he had taken in the field to the file.

Buck opened the pictures and looked at them again, now on the laptop screen instead of his phone. He put on his reading glasses and blew up several of the pictures, looking for an anomaly. He opened the files Franklin had posted of the three bodies and followed the same process. He stopped at one picture of Dan Pearson's body and enlarged the picture several times.

He noted that in Franklin's narrative, the picture was taken before anyone got close to the body except for Deputy Carmichael, the first deputy on the scene. He looked closely at the picture and found a boot print in the dirt. He compared that picture to one the ambulance crew had taken of the sole of Deputy Carmichael's boots before they took his body to the hospital. They were a match. Buck pulled the magnification back, and he could see where Carmichael had approached the body.

Once again, he magnified the picture. He spotted it right away. There was an impression in the dirt that was smooth and round. He pulled up another picture and looked closely. He could see the prints made by the troopers as they approached the body. These prints were smooth and round.

He leaned back in the chair and put his glasses on the desk. He rubbed his temples. He knew it wasn't much to go on, but it was more than he had ten minutes ago. Whoever shot Dan Pearson was wearing a rubber hazmat suit, just like the ones the troopers wore.

He looked at the pictures of the two boys who had been found in the ravine and noticed that in those pictures, there were no prints on the ground at all. He clicked on a website on his laptop and opened a topographic map of the area where the carnage had taken place. It took a few minutes to orient himself, and once he did, he ran his fingers along the contour lines on the map. He closed his eyes, and a picture started to form in his head. He noticed that the little bug in his brain had started to move around. Not a lot, but enough to notice.

Buck was starting to see a picture emerge of one possible scenario of what happened. He ran it through his head several times, poking holes in it as he went, and when he sat back, he thought he had a good idea of how some of the day's events had happened.

He finished his warm Coke and decided he needed to get some air to clear his head. He knew the best way to clear his head, and even though there was no moon tonight, he decided to head for the South Platte River and do a little fishing. The South Platte River ran through the middle of the South Park valley, and it was one of the top places on Buck's list to fish. It was tough fishing.

The South Platte wasn't very wide through the valley, and the wind blew all the time, or so it seemed. Conditions could be rough, but when a hatch was on, the fishing could be incredible. He dressed, clipped on his badge and gun, grabbed his light jacket from his backpack and headed for his Jeep.

Fly-fishing was Buck's way to escape everything going on around him. After Lucy died, he lost himself to fishing. It became his refuge, a place he could get lost, and it had always been a place where he could focus. Whenever he needed to shake loose an idea about an investigation, he used fly-fishing as his sounding board.

Once you were on the river, and it was just you and the fish, you had to focus. You had to clear your head of everything but the rod, the fly and the fish. Nothing else mattered. He headed to his Jeep and pulled open the door.

"Agent Taylor," came a voice from behind him. Buck turned fast and had his pistol in his hand when he spotted a tall figure standing under the parking lot light, holding up both hands, palms forward.

The figure stood still. "Forgive the intrusion, but I come in peace," said the figure.

The man in front of him was six foot four and thin, not skinny. Trim. He stood ramrod straight. His hair was gray and cut in a style the military called "high and tight." He had an aristocratic bearing and spoke with a soft yet regal Southern accent.

He lowered his right hand and reached into his thin windbreaker. Buck raised his pistol. The tall man pulled out a wallet and held it for Buck to see.

"I apologize for startling you, Agent Taylor. I am unarmed."

"Who are you?" asked Buck.

"General Samuel Culpeper, MD," said the man with the Southern voice. "United States Army."

"Keep your hands where I can see them," said Buck.

He walked towards the man, his gun in the low ready position so as not to be pointed directly at him.

"Slowly," he said, reaching for the man's wallet, never taking his eyes off his face. He stepped back and opened the wallet. A military ID and Virginia driver's license were in two opposing plastic windows. Buck held up the credentials and compared the pictures on the IDs with the man standing in front of him. He holstered his pistol, took out his phone and took a picture of the IDs, which he handed back to the man.

"You're a long way from home, General, and you came close to getting shot."

"I have been standing here a while debating how to approach you. You caught me off guard when you opened the door, so I decided my best course of action would be to stand under the light with my hands raised. I was hoping you would not shoot first."

"Why were you looking to approach me in the middle of the night?" asked Buck.

"As you saw on my ID, I am a medical doctor. I am assigned to USAMRIID, and I am here because people above me on the food chain are worried about some adverse publicity, and I was asked to come here and meet with you."

Buck looked at the general. "If you'll forgive me, General. You are a general. There are not a lot of people above you, and if I had to guess, I would bet you are probably in charge of USAMRIID. Am I getting close, General?"

The general looked at Buck. "Close."

"Then let me continue," said Buck. "You are here in civilian clothes at two in the morning because someone got wind that we have a problem out here and that the internet has gone nuts talking about a secret government lab that was built in Park County. The people who got wind of our problem are so concerned that they ordered you, a general, onto a plane, flew you to Colorado and told you to drive to a little town called Fairplay in the middle of nowhere and convince me that all the conspiracy folks are wrong and that some weird exotic disease didn't escape from said lab and kill a shitload of cows and several people. How am I doing, General?"

The general looked uncomfortable. "You are a keen observer, Agent Taylor. She told me to be careful with you. She told me your bullshit meter worked better than anyone she knew."

"Who is this she you are referring to, General?" asked Buck.

The general smiled for the first time. "Max Clinton called me."

Buck was silent. "Why would Max call you?"

"Max is an old friend. She was concerned with the samples you sent her earlier today, and when she saw the internet explode with conspiracy theories, she thought I might be able to help."

"And you jumped on a plane and flew out here just like that?"

The general laughed. "I don't know if you noticed, Agent Taylor, but Max Clinton can be very persuasive."

Buck laughed. "You are right about that. But how can you help? We don't even know what we are dealing with yet."

"Agent Taylor. There are very few airborne substances, biological or chemical, that work the way you described the scene to Max. Some can be made in your kitchen sink, but some require specialized labs, level four containment facilities, and millions of dollars to produce. The ones you can make in your sink scare us but are difficult to produce in any great quantity and end up killing the people trying to make them. The other ones are even scarier, and if those formulas were to fall into the wrong hands, they could be devastating. After speaking with my bosses, I have been tasked with helping you figure out which one we are dealing with."

"So why the late-night visit?" asked Buck.

"Agent Taylor, I have been told by numerous people today that you are a man who can be trusted. If you are willing, I would like to take you on a drive that hopefully answers your questions."

"Where are we going, General?" Buck asked as he closed and locked his Jeep. He also pulled out his phone, clicked on a number and hit send. He put his phone away and faced the general.

"Have you ever heard of Plum Island, Agent Taylor?"

| 19 |

Chapter Nineteen

After the meeting in the barn, Tucker Clark jumped into his truck and screamed down the driveway. He was pissed, but more than that, he was scared. Scared that he had been part of a horrific accident that right now could be spreading through the county. His actions could kill dozens of people.

He turned onto Highway 285 and headed east, cruised up Kenosha Pass and slowed as he entered the small town of Grant, not much of a town but more of a collection of houses and a couple of small businesses. He drove through Grant and turned right onto an unnamed dirt road. A half mile up the road, he stopped in front of a large log cabin. He could see a light on in the back.

Tucker reached into his glove compartment and pulled out a black semiautomatic pistol. He checked to make sure there was a bullet in the chamber and flicked off the safety. He slid out of the truck, stuck the pistol into the back of his pants, under his sweatshirt, and raced up the front steps.

He didn't wait to knock on the front door; instead, he reared back and kicked it in. The door crashed into a small table that sat behind the door, and pictures and a lamp hit the floor. He walked into the family room at the back of the house, where Brian Cole, awakened by the sudden noise, rubbed his eyes. He looked at Tucker.

"Tucker, what the fuck, man?"

Tucker Clark jumped over the leather couch and landed on Brian Cole. The surprise in Brian's eyes was now replaced by fear. Tucker stood up, grabbed Brian by the collar of his T-shirt and punched him in the face. Brian slammed back into the couch.

"You no-good motherfucker!" said Tucker. "You told me no one would get hurt except the cows." He hit Brian again. Blood from Brian's nose splattered on the couch.

"You told me that shit we sprayed didn't hurt people!"

Tucker hit him again.

"You killed my son, you fuck!" Tears rolled down Tucker's face. "He was twelve years old, and that shit we sprayed ended his life. You promised me it was safe for people. I should have known better when you made me wear that stupid suit. I should have never trusted you, you crazy fuck."

Tucker pulled him up and hit him again. Brian's face was now a raw mess covered with blood. Tucker grabbed Brian's collar, pulled his head up and got right into Brian's face.

"And not only that, the shit is killing old man Halverson, so I didn't even get what I need from him!"

All that built-up fury left Tucker, and he slumped forward, his head down, tears streaming down his face. Brian, barely conscious, saw the sudden change in Tucker and was afraid of what might happen next. He tried to sit up, but the room spun, and he laid his head down on the arm of the couch.

Tucker stood and looked at the mess he had made of his friend. He reached to the table in front of the couch and picked up a half-empty bottle of beer. He downed what was left in the bottle and threw the bottle across the room, where it smashed into the big stone fireplace, sending glass shards everywhere. He pulled the pistol out of his waistband and stared at it for a minute. He had killed before, but never anyone he knew. He looked at Brian, whose left eye was half closed, his right eye tracking Tucker.

"You were my best friend," Tucker said softly. "You've always been there for me, and I trusted you."

Tucker aimed the pistol at Brian Cole.

Brian pushed back into the couch. He tried to speak, but he kept spitting out pieces of teeth. He cleared his mouth enough to speak. "Don't do this, man," said Brian, blood flowing down his chin. "The shit worked." He spit out a glob of blood. "This is going to make us rich. I am working with people who will pay us a fortune. I will cut you in for half. Don't be a fool."

His head fell back on the couch, and Tucker looked at him, the pistol still aimed at Brian's chest. "I don't want your money. You don't get it. You killed my son."

The explosion reverberated off the log walls as it echoed through the great room. The bullet hit Brian in the chest, and he sunk deeper into the couch. Tucker stepped closer to the couch and aimed at Brian's forehead. "This is for my son," he said, and he pulled the trigger a second time.

Tucker put the pistol back in his pants and walked into

the kitchen. He opened the refrigerator, pulled out a cold beer and twisted the cap. He drank the beer in one long gulp and threw the bottle into the trash. He didn't even think about someone finding the bottle. He didn't care. His life was shattered. Once the world found out about what he did, he would be ruined. His wife would most likely never speak to him again, he would be lucky if his father didn't kill him for costing them millions of dollars, and he missed his son with an ache that he wasn't sure would ever go away. He would spend the rest of his life in prison, or worse, he would get the death penalty.

Tucker took three more beers and walked back into the family room. He stood over the dead body, drank and emptied one of the bottles, setting it on the table. He pulled out the pistol and shot Brian Cole five more times. He took the other two beers, opened the sliding glass door and walked out onto the deck. He plopped into a wooden Adirondack chair and looked up at the stars. His thoughts turned to his son. Billy was the best thing he had ever done. It made all the bad things in his life disappear, and the more he thought, the more the tears flowed.

He heard the crickets chirping and a couple of coyotes howling in the distance. Tucker Clark finished the last beer and set it on the floor next to the other empty bottle. He felt at peace. He watched as a shooting star crossed the sky.

"Goodbye, Billy," he said. "I love you."

He lifted the pistol off the small side table, placed the barrel in his mouth and pulled the trigger.

| **20** |

Chapter Twenty

General Culpeper drove through Fairplay, heading east. Buck had noticed that the SUV did not have government plates and wondered if that was intended to limit exposure. His phone chimed, and Buck pulled it from his belt and looked at the message. He opened a file and read what he had been sent.

He had no idea how she did it, but the few times he had contacted Harriet, he always got what he needed. Harriet was a voice with a touch of a Southern accent, who was at the other end of a number he had been given by the U.S. Marshals Service.

A year or so back, Buck had been testifying in federal court in Denver during the murder trial of a survivalist drug dealer who had killed a DEA agent. One day, after court was dismissed, Buck and Jess Gonzales, the special agent in charge of the DEA's Grand Junction Field Office and one of Buck's closest friends, were talking outside the courthouse.

Suddenly all hell broke loose, and people ran for cover. The marshals who were escorting the prisoner were ambushed in the parking garage, and Buck and Jess raced to their rescue.

Once the dust settled, the prisoner, one of the marshals, and the ambushers were dead, but a lot of people in the garage that afternoon survived, thanks to Buck and Jess. To honor Buck, the U.S. Marshals Service made him a full-fledged deputy marshal, and as part of that award, he was given a special number that he could call anytime, day or night, and Harriet would get him whatever he needed. He had used the number twice before, and he often wondered if Harriet was one woman or an entire team of women, but whatever she was, he appreciated the help.

This morning she had come through again, and Buck sat in the SUV and read the file on General Samuel Culpeper. Besides a medical degree, the general had a very storied past and had served in several combat zones, receiving a silver star for gallantry and a purple heart for being wounded in battle. The general also came from a famous Southern family. His ancestors were the first white settlers in what became Culpeper County in Virginia and had fought for the south during the Civil War. His family had a rich history, and he had served his country faithfully for almost forty years.

The general looked over at Buck. "Something interesting?" he asked.

"Yes, General. Just getting to know a little bit about you. I like to know who I'm adventuring with in the dead of night."

"You have my file?" asked General Culpeper, a frown crossing his face. "I never noticed you call anyone to request it."

"No worries, General. Your secrets are safe with me. It's interesting reading, and you should be proud of your service. You've been around."

"That's not what concerns me. My file is supposed to be deeply classified, and I'm concerned that someone was able to gain access so quickly. In my line of work, anonymity is critical. I will need to rectify this."

"It has already been rectified. My source was concerned about how easily she could access your file, given your position and all, so she contacted the Department of Defense to let them know that your file needs to be reclassified. She will make sure that happens."

The general nodded. "You certainly are a resourceful man, Agent Taylor," he said, and focused on the road. The general stayed quiet for the next portion of the drive, and Buck sat back and enjoyed the ride to wherever they were going. The general looked deep in thought, and Buck wondered if he was working out in his head just how much he could tell Buck about where they were going.

As they approached the base of Kenosha Pass, the general looked at Buck. "How much do you know about Plum Island?"

"Only what I've read, and that's not much. I know it was some kind of secret lab on an island near New York, but that's about it. Why?" asked Buck.

"The Plum Island Animal Disease Center, off the coast of Long Island, opened in nineteen fifty-four and operates today under the Department of Homeland Security and the Department of Agriculture. Its primary responsibility is to research infectious diseases in animals. At some point, during the fifties and sixties, it also researched biological weapons that could be used to target livestock. That program supposedly ended in nineteen sixty-nine. During the early fifties, it was also home to the U.S. Army Chemical Corps.

"Its primary research at PIADC was in the study and prevention of foot-and-mouth disease, a disease that is deadly to cloven-footed animals, and even though the disease was eradicated in the U.S. in nineteen twenty-nine, it is still prevalent around the world. In the early two thousands, the facility was interested in working on human diseases, but that would have required a level four biohazard facility. Local activists went crazy and managed to kill that idea, and Congress determined that it would be better to build a new facility elsewhere. They chose to build that facility at the University of Kansas in Manhattan, Kansas, and it is slated to open in late twenty twenty-three, but that's not the entire story.

"Farmers and ranchers thought the Department of Homeland Security was nuts when they proposed building a mainland facility that stored the only U.S. supply of foot-and-mouth disease in the middle of cattle country. Activists fought the proposal for years, but the National Bio and Agro-Defense Facility was built, and the controversies continue to this day. Most people were unaware that the primary purpose of the fight to build this facility was a ruse. While activists and the government clashed over the location and construction, USAMRIID was building a secret biological and chemical weapons facility in a completely different location, without all the controversy."

Buck looked at the general. "You built this new facility here, in Park County, didn't you?"

The general nodded as he turned off Highway 285 onto an

unmarked dirt road. He continued to speak. "This new facility is a state-of-the-art level four biohazard containment facility. More important, only a handful of people, besides those who work there, know it exists. This is one of the most secret and secure weapons development facilities in the world. Because of the access that today's terrorists have to chemical, nuclear and biological weapons, the United States needed a facility where we could secretly work on ways to protect the country from a terrorist attack, and we have been extremely success-ful. Since this facility opened four years ago, we have been instrumental in stopping over fifteen hundred known terror-ist attacks. We are very proud of the work we do here, and the work is vitally important to our survival as a nation."

The general pulled up to a dark gate that practically blended into the trees. He lowered the window, waved his ID card across the face of a metal post and then waited. The gate rolled back, and the general proceeded through, continuing along the dirt road. The road passed through the trees and opened to a large building. Buck wouldn't have even known the building was there except for the small parking lot off to one side that held about a dozen cars.

The building had no windows, and its dark color helped it almost disappear in the darkness. There wasn't a light to be seen in the entire area. The general parked in front of a single metal door and turned off the engine.

"What you are about to see is critical to the U.S. I was told to remind you that at some point, you signed a nondisclosure agreement while visiting another government facility. That NDA is still in force and will remain so for your entire life. Any violation of the NDA will result in a charge of treason, punishable by death. Do you understand what I have just told you?"

Buck nodded his head. He had been through this before at another secret bunker with another general and understood what was expected of him. This was as much a PR visit as anything. The general would prove to Buck that nothing nefarious was going on, and Buck would later be used to deny anything that might be reported on social media. He didn't take his part in this lightly because, as a member of law enforcement, he also understood what was at stake.

The general slid out of the SUV, and Buck did the same. They approached the metal door, and the general, once again, waved his ID card in front of a small metal panel. He then stepped up and looked into a small hole in the panel. Buck heard a click, and the general opened the door into a dark room. Once the door closed behind them, the lights came on, and they followed the same procedure at a second door. A camera on the wall followed their every move.

The door clicked, the general pulled it open and they stepped into a bright, airy reception area. The general presented his credentials to the guard at the desk, and a green light flashed above the door behind the guard. Buck was handed a visitor's badge, and he followed the general through the door and into a long corridor, which Buck had difficulty believing was contained within the building. The building did not look that big from the outside.

For the next two hours, Buck followed the general through the maze of offices, labs and tech areas. Then they stepped onto a secure elevator, the general swiped his ID again and they descended to a lower level. They stepped up to a door that was marked caution, level 4 containment area.

"Now, it goes without saying that we are not going to enter the containment area. This is where we work with the most dangerous toxins and chemicals in the world—sarin, ricin, Ebola, Marburg and anything else that can be weaponized by terrorists. We do not develop weapons of our own except to work out how a bad actor will use the products. This facility is defensive, not offensive."

Buck looked through the window in the wall and watched as two technicians in hazmat suits connected to several hoses moved vials to a table with a large electron microscope attached to it.

"What would happen if one of these viruses escaped?" asked Buck.

"Can't happen," said the general. "The security measures you have seen so far are only the tip of the iceberg. In the event we have an accident or intrusion into the lab, the entire place locks down. The air and exhaust systems are self-contained and can be shut down instantly. Nothing in this building, except that one door we entered, is connected to the outside."

Buck was silent for a minute, still observing the containment lab. "Could someone carry a virus out on their person?"

The general looked at him. "That can never happen. Everyone passes through an X-ray machine to leave this floor. No one ever works in the lab alone, and it takes ID cards to check back in a virus or toxin sample. If a sample is checked out of storage and enters a lab, the lab cannot be reopened if the sample is not accounted for. It can't happen."

Buck thought the general didn't seem convinced of what he was saying. The general looked at his watch and suggested they head out. They passed through the X-ray machine, and the guard on duty wanded them. They stepped back into the elevator. Once on the main floor, Buck turned in his visitor's badge, and he and the general exited the building.

They slid into the general's SUV and left the property the way they had entered. As they turned onto Highway 285 and headed towards Fairplay, the general appeared preoccupied.

"General, what's really going on?" asked Buck. "That's an impressive facility, but good PR was not why you brought me there."

The general reached into his jacket pocket and held out his hand. He placed a USB drive into Buck's hand. Buck looked at the drive. He waited for the general to explain.

"We might have a problem that could be directly related to your case." The general hesitated. "We think someone has been working on a side project, but we haven't found anything. There have been rumblings in the intelligence community." He pointed to the USB drive.

"That drive contains information on everyone with access to the containment lab. Information that you would not have access to without that encrypted drive. If it helps you with your investigation and helps determine that we are not the cause of the internet chatterer and what happened to your victims, then use it as you will."

"What happens if one of your people is dirty, General?" asked Buck.

"Then do what you need to do, and I will give all the support I can. I have no agenda here, Agent Taylor, except to find the truth and to prevent another terrorist attack aimed at this country."

The sun was rising over the peaks to the east as the general pulled into the motel lot. He handed Buck his card. "If you need anything, please reach out."

Buck left the vehicle and watched the general drive away. He could feel the pressure that the general was under, and he felt bad for him. On the other hand, he seemed like a nice guy who might be caught in a bad situation. Buck put the card into his pocket. He passed his car, and the door to Bax's room opened. She looked at the SUV as it exited the parking lot.

"You make a new friend?" she asked.

Buck didn't answer, just looked at her.

"Oh," she said. "I get it. This is one of those if I tell you, I'll have to kill you things? Fair enough. Go get a shower and meet us at the restaurant. George sent us some stuff we need to look at."

Buck walked into his room and closed the door. He was grateful he had people he worked with who understood things and didn't ask questions. He headed for the bathroom and a hot shower; he prepared for another long day.

| 21 |

Chapter Twenty-One

The voice on the other end of the phone was not happy. "You made certain promises, Mr. Clark, and now you tell me you can't deliver. That's unacceptable."

"We've had a problem develop," said Edmund Clark. "We need a little more time."

"You knew the deadline when we entered into this agreement. If we don't get what we need by the end of the day on Thursday, it will jeopardize a billion-dollar development, and that will make our investors extremely unhappy. You need to make this happen, Mr. Clark. Or bad things will happen."

It wasn't the words that bothered Edmund Clark. He had been threatened by far worse. The calmness in the man's voice shook him to his core. There was no emotion in the threat, yet the threat was received loud and clear.

Edmund Clark put his phone in his pocket, walked into the kitchen and sat down for breakfast. Edith was listening to some shock internet program, and the voice on her phone was screaming about the government trying to poison us all by sending toxic trains around the country to be derailed in specific, high-value cities. Edmund tuned the voice out.

He finished his scrambled eggs and bacon and was drinking his coffee when Tom Clark walked into the kitchen.

"Have you seen Tucker?" asked Tom. "He was supposed to help me feed the pregnant women. I can't find him, and Claire hasn't seen him since he tore out of here last night."

Edmund finished his coffee. "I spoke with the developer. He is not happy, and his threat is loud and clear. We are in trouble unless we deliver the documents from Halverson."

"We should have never gotten involved with those people. They make the cartels look like children."

"They fronted us five million dollars, or did you forget that? And we've already used a significant portion of that to secure the product for the next delivery. Those Asians are scary too," said Edmund.

"So, what are we going to do?" asked Tom Clark. "And what do we do about Tucker?"

"Let's send your sister to talk to Mrs. Halverson. Maybe we can work a deal with her, and she can get the papers signed. It's worth a try. And call your contact in New York and see if we can deliver early. We'll have the last of the product under our control tomorrow night, and I'd like to at least keep our Asian friends happy."

"What are you going to do?" asked Tom Clark.

"I'm going to talk to Toomey and see what's happening with the investigation, and then I'm going to try to find your brother."

Tom Clark pulled out his phone and stepped outside.

Edmund walked outside, climbed into his truck and headed down the driveway. He turned onto Highway 285 and headed south towards Fairplay. He pulled into the sheriff's office parking lot and entered the public area. He told the deputy at the desk that he wanted to see the sheriff. The deputy picked up the phone and dialed an extension.

Sheriff Toomey came through the security door three minutes later. "Mr. Clark, what can I do for you?"

"I want to know what you're doing about finding my grandson's killer?" said Edmund Clark.

"The autopsy is underway right now. We should have the results back later today. I will call Tucker and Claire when the results are in and let them know when the body will be released. Understand that the release is still tentative until we know what killed the two boys."

"Tucker is missing," said Edmund Clark. "We haven't seen him since last night."

"Did he take his truck?" asked the sheriff.

Edmund Clark nodded.

"Okay. I'll let all the deputies know, and we'll see if we can find him. Any idea where he was headed last night?"

"No, we were discussing some new information we received about Billy's death, and he tore out the door and left in a hurry. I have no idea what that was about."

"What new information?" asked the sheriff.

"Information you didn't tell us. Like, he was found along with all those dead cows and that dead brand inspector. You want to elaborate?"

"Can't," said the sheriff. "It's an open investigation. When we know more, we'll tell you."

Edmund Clark huffed and turned to leave.

"I heard you had a little run-in with the CBI folks and that Tom got his ass handed to him. Told you not to mess with those folks."

Edmund turned to face him. "If I decide to mess with them, you'll be the first to know."

He turned and walked out the door. The sheriff walked into the dispatcher's room, picked up the microphone and told all the deputies on duty to keep an eye out for Tucker Clark's pickup truck.

He walked into his office, closed the door and shook his head. The Clark family had been a burr in his saddle for as long as he had been with the department. One day, someone would be willing to testify against them, and he would lock them all away for a good, long time. He looked at his watch and decided breakfast was in order, and he was looking forward to one of Maria's breakfast burritos. He left his office and walked across the highway.

| 22 |

Chapter Twenty-Two

Buck pulled into the parking lot of the Azteca Mexican Café and spotted Sheriff Toomey walking across the highway, heading in his direction. Buck slid out of his Jeep and waited.

"Mornin', John," said Buck. "Any word on the autopsies?"

Sheriff Toomey shook his head. "Just got notified that Dan Pearson is underway. The two boys will follow. You look like you didn't get much sleep last night, Buck."

"Yeah, busy night," said Buck.

They headed for the restaurant, and Buck opened the door. Carlos wasn't at the podium, but Buck saw Bax and Paul at the same back booth they had used last night, and they headed over. Buck and the sheriff sat down, and the server came over with coffee for the sheriff and a large Coke for Buck. She took their orders and headed back to the kitchen.

"Okay, what did we get from George and Mel?" asked Buck.

Paul turned his laptop so Buck and the sheriff could see. Buck read the text and email exchanges George and Mel had highlighted. Several of them seemed sarcastic, and several seemed to ridicule Dan Pearson's theories about the location of the treasure. Paul scrolled to the next page, and Buck sat forward. He read the page.

"Now, those are different," said Buck. "Do we know who this person is?"

The sheriff read the text exchange and sat back. "Definitely sounds like motive to me." He pointed to one post.

Aztecguide47: YOU SOB. YOU STOLE MY LOCATION DATA. I AM GOING TO MAKE YOU PAY.

Dan had replied: WHY WOULD I WANT YOUR DATA? YOU CAN'T FIND YOUR OWN ASS WITH BOTH HANDS, YOU DIPSHIT.

Aztecguide47: THE NEXT TIME I SEE YOU WILL BE THE LAST TIME. YOU CAN TAKE THAT TO THE BANK.

Dan replied: THE ONLY THING I'M TAKING TO THE BANK, ASSHOLE, IS A BIG PILE OF TREASURE.

The final post on the list caught their attention.

Aztecguide47: WHEN I CATCH UP WITH YOU, I AM GOING TO FUCK UP YOUR WHOLE WORLD. YOU ARE A DEADMAN.

Buck looked at Paul. "When was that posted?"

"The day before Dan Pearson died. Mel is chasing the IP address and thinks she'll have an address for us in a couple of hours. What do you think?"

Their breakfasts arrived, and they set everything aside to focus on the meal. Both Maria and Carlos stopped by the table to make sure everything was good. They finished breakfast, and Paul opened another folder from George and Mel.

"Did you request some photos?" asked Paul.

Buck nodded. "It was a hunch. I wondered if Dan Pearson kept track of what was going on at his various sites by using trail cameras."

Bax looked at him. "What made you think of that?"

"Last night, I searched Pearson's truck and found some photos that might have come from a trail cam. I had hoped that if he had some trail cams, they would be the type that uploaded to the cloud."

Bax laughed. "Look at you talking about the cloud." She tapped Paul on the shoulder. "I knew sooner or later we would rub off on him."

Buck laughed. "So, any luck?"

Paul tapped a couple of keys. "You hit it right on the head. George found feeds from four cameras. Based on the geo-markers from the cameras, this one"—he turned his laptop so the sheriff and Buck could see—"came from the same area where we found the body."

Buck and the sheriff focused on the video. The time stamp indicated it was from the afternoon that Dan Pearson died.

The sheriff pointed to the figure on the screen. "That looks like Dan Pearson."

The next time stamp was an hour later. Bax was standing behind Buck. She pointed to the screen at a figure wearing camo. "That is not Pearson," she said.

Buck hit the pause button and pointed to the figure's hand. "That's a pistol. We need to find out who this is. Any chance George can enhance the video?"

"Unlikely," said Bax. "Those cameras don't have a lot of range to them."

The sheriff was staring at the still picture on the screen. He pushed the pause button again, and the video moved ahead until the figure was out of sight. He sat back and rubbed his chin.

"Do you know that person?" asked Buck.

The sheriff asked Paul to rerun the video, and he rubbed his chin. "I can't be a hundred percent sure, but that could be Melvin Gross."

"Who's Melvin Gross?" asked Bax.

"He's a miner. Lives back in the hills off Boreas Pass. He's kind of a loner. No family that I'm aware of. Comes to town once in a while for supplies but mostly keeps to himself. Anytime I've seen him around, he's wearing this old camo jacket. Rumor is, he came back from Iraq all screwed up."

Buck pulled out his phone and dialed a number.

"Hey, Buck," said Mel. "What's up?"

"Hi, Mel. Can you run a background check on a guy named Melvin Gross? Lives in Park County and might be the guy in the video you guys retrieved off Dan Pearson's cloud thingy."

Bax laughed. "Forget what I said about us rubbing off on him. He's still a dinosaur."

Everyone laughed, and Buck disconnected the call. Sheriff Toomey's phone rang, and he looked at the number. "Denver area code. Might be the pathologist," he said, and he answered the call.

"Toomey."

"Hi, Sheriff. Dr. Meredith Austin at Denver General. Do you have a minute?"

He looked around at the now-empty restaurant, put the phone on speaker and turned down the volume. "Yes, Doctor. I have you on speaker, and I am here with the folks from CBI."

"Excellent," said Dr. Austin. "I just finished the autopsy of Dan Pearson. What I am going to tell you is still preliminary. We are waiting on the tox screens, which the CDC has put a rush on and expects to have back later today."

"Please proceed, Doctor," said the sheriff.

"Mr. Pearson was fifty-two years old and in excellent health. The preliminary cause of death is massive blood loss caused by two bullets. Bullet number one was found embedded in the chest wall and had nicked an artery. He would have bled to death within minutes. Bullet number two entered just above his nose and caused significant brain trauma. It exited out of the back of his head. I believe that was the fatal shot."

"Doctor, this is Buck Taylor, CBI. Anything unusual besides the two bullet wounds?"

"No, Agent Taylor. The doctor from the CDC who assisted asked the same thing. Due to the circumstances under which the body was found, we took numerous tissue, blood and saliva samples. The CDC did some rapid tests to rule out certain infectious diseases and chemical toxins. Biological toxins will take a little longer. We can say with certainty that we did not find anything unusual in his nasal passages, throat samples, on his skin or clothes, and his lungs were clear and normal. In my professional opinion, and until the CDC finishes with the bio screen, this man was not exposed to any kind of toxin. We still have the body in the containment area until the results are back, but I think this body is in the clear. We are about to start on victim number two, William Clark. I will keep you apprised."

Buck thanked the doctor and asked her to forward the final report to him when the results were in. The sheriff disconnected the call. "The bullets, I understand," he said, "but no exposure. That's odd."

Buck thought for a minute. "Maybe it's like a firestorm. We've all seen it. The wildfire tears through an area and burns everything in its path except one house that, for some reason, was spared. Nobody can explain it; they just marvel at it."

Chapter Twenty-Three

Buck's phone chimed. He looked at the number, answered the call and put the phone on speaker. "Hey, Max. What's up?"

"Hi, Buck," said Max Clinton. "I've got some preliminary information on the samples we got from the hazmat team and from Franklin."

"Great, Max. We're all here; let's have it."

"The bullet Franklin found buried in the dirt under the body of the brand inspector was nine millimeter. It was damaged, but we believe it came from a Glock. That's the best we can do until we get the other bullet if it's in better shape. The team also worked all night on the samples from the cows. We have ruled out chemical poisoning. We believe it was a biotoxin, but we are having trouble identifying it. Our tests indicate that it might have been manipulated. It also has a strange characteristic."

"What's that, Max?" asked Buck.

"After about four hours, the toxin became inert."

Everyone looked at Buck, since this was the same thing Buck had realized when he entered the field the night before.

"Hi, Max, it's Bax. So, based on your tests, this product, for lack of a better word, is deadly, and then once exposed, dies after four hours."

"Hi, Bax. Close. The product is still very deadly, but it is no longer transmittable by air. To be completely unscientific, it's like, after four hours, it goes to sleep. We have no idea if there is something that reactivates it, but right now, all the samples we have run are just sitting there. It's the strangest thing my team has ever seen."

"Max," said Buck. "What's our next step?"

"I've sent the information to an expert in the field and have also sent our test results to the CDC to see if they can explain it."

Buck wondered if Max had sent the test results to his visitor from last night. He figured he'd hear from the general before the day was out. He asked Max if there was anything else.

"Not at this time, Buck. We'll keep running tests to see if we can find out more, but for now, that's what we've got. Wish we could have found out some more information for you."

"Thanks, Max. Please thank the team for me. You guys did great."

"You're a good man, Buck Taylor," said Max. "God will watch over you. Call if you need anything else."

Buck disconnected the call. "Well, that's interesting, a

virus that goes to sleep after killing. Sounds like something out of a science fiction movie."

Buck's phone chimed again, and Buck answered it and put it on speaker.

"Hey, Buck."

"Hi, Mel. What have you got?"

"We did some quick background on Melvin Gross. He's fifty-two years old and has been on full disability from the military since nineteen ninety-one. We tried to get his medical records, but the military has a lid on that information that we can't get through. Based on his pay information, George thinks he might have been a Green Beret. The disability pension would indicate he was wounded while fighting in Desert Shield. We found a bank account in his name at a bank in Park County, but he never writes checks on it. Best guess, he uses cash for purchases. He lives on a sixty-acre parcel that was paid for in full, sixty grand, thirty-two years ago."

"Anything to indicate where the money came from?" asked Paul.

"Nothing we could find," said Mel. "He also has quite a social media presence. We found him everywhere, but he's like two different people. Lots of conspiracy theory stuff, and he spends a lot of time ranting about everything under the sun, but then he spends as much time on treasure-hunting websites. He is not a fan of Dan Pearson. He is convinced that Dan stole his data about the lost Aztec treasure. We discovered he is Aztecguide47. He is not shy about his hatred for Dan Pearson."

Buck looked around the table. "Mel, have we ever done a firearms background check on this guy?"

Buck could hear keys clicking in the background.

"We did one background check back in twenty seventeen. Purchase was for a Glock 19 chambered in nine millimeter. You should be aware there are numerous pictures on Facebook of Gross at several outdoor rifle ranges, and he is using different rifles. We have no way of knowing if they are his or rentals, and there's no information on the ranges that we can find."

"Thanks, Mel. Nice job. I'm going to upload some files from a USB drive. Take a look and let me know if you find anything interesting." He disconnected the call.

Buck took the USB drive from his pocket and inserted it into his laptop. He opened the investigation file and started the download. He noticed everyone at the table watching him. When the download was completed, he pulled the drive and put it back in his pocket. He didn't comment on the drive.

"Looks like we need to visit Melvin Gross and see where he was Saturday night. Sheriff, why don't you and I do that? Bax, you and Paul go visit Mrs. Halverson and see if she can figure out why someone would target her and her husband."

Everyone packed up their laptops, and Paul and Bax headed out of the door. Buck found Carlos and paid the breakfast bill, and he and Sheriff Toomey headed for his Jeep in the parking lot. Sheriff Toomey had on his ballistic vest as part of his uniform, and Buck pulled his out of the back of the Jeep and put it on. He put on a black nylon windbreaker and black ball cap, both with CBI in big white letters. They slid into Buck's Jeep, and he pulled out onto Highway 285 and headed north.

He turned left onto Boreas Pass Road and passed through

the small town of Como. After about five miles, the sheriff told Buck to turn left onto Road 801. They followed Road 801 for two miles, and the sheriff pointed towards a small dirt road on the right side, which Buck turned onto and stopped at a locked metal gate.

They slid out of the Jeep, and the sheriff climbed over the gate while Buck looked at the numerous no trespassing signs that surrounded the gate. Seeing no means of communicating with Melvin Gross, Buck followed the sheriff. A quarter mile up the drive, they spotted a small cabin with smoke billowing out of the stone chimney. The sheriff stopped and indicated for Buck to do the same.

"Melvin Gross," said the sheriff at the top of his voice. "Park County Sheriff's Office. We'd like a word. Please step out onto the porch."

There was no response from the cabin, so the sheriff, motioning for Buck to stay where he was, walked forward and repeated the same words.

The bullet hit the sheriff in the left arm a microsecond before Buck heard the crack. The sheriff spun around, and he dove for the bushes. Buck jumped behind a tree as a second bullet whizzed past his head, so close he could hear it split the air as it blew by. Buck pulled out his phone just as he heard the sheriff click the mic on his radio.

"Dispatch, sheriff one. Shots fired, officer down. Need backup and an ambulance. Road 801 off Boreas Pass Road, Melvin Gross's cabin."

"Affirmative, Sheriff. Troops on the way."

Another bullet slammed into the tree that Buck was behind, and the next shot was directed towards where the sheriff had fallen. Buck took a chance, raced across the drive-way and dove behind the tree, next to the sheriff, just as a bullet hit the tree.

The sheriff looked pale and sweat beads had formed on his forehead. Buck moved his hand away from his left arm and looked at the blood that was flowing down his arm. He pulled out his pocketknife and cut the sleeve, revealing a dime-sized hole in the sheriff's upper arm.

"I'm gonna need to put on a tourniquet."

The sheriff shifted sideways and said, "Med kit on my belt."

Buck opened the med kit and pulled out a tampon-shaped plug and a rubber strap. He pushed the tampon into the bullet hole, and the sheriff let out a yell. Buck wrapped the tourniquet around his upper arm and pulled the strap, which tightened, slowing the flow of blood.

"Okay?" asked Buck.

The sheriff nodded as a bullet hit the ground next to his leg. He pulled in tighter to the tree.

"Can you shoot?" asked Buck.

The sheriff pulled out his pistol. "Yeah. I'm good."

More bullets hit the tree, and Buck raised his pistol and fired several rounds towards the cabin, resulting in rapid-fire return from the cabin.

"We need to stop him," said the sheriff.

Buck nodded. "Keep him busy. I'm gonna try to work my way around to the back of the cabin."

The sheriff nodded and changed positions with Buck. "Be careful," said the sheriff, but Buck had already faded into the trees. The sheriff aimed around the tree and fired five rounds at the cabin. The return fire was withering, and the sheriff tucked in closer to the tree. He could hear sirens approaching in the distance. He looked around for Buck but couldn't see him, and he reached around and fired five more times. He dropped the empty magazine. He couldn't use his left arm to pull another clip from his belt, so he set the pistol down and used his right arm to grab the clip and ram it into the pistol. He fired five more rounds during a lull in the fire from the cabin.

His radio crackled. "Sheriff, it's Rivers. What's your situation?"

He keyed his mic. "I've been hit. Buck is trying to get around the cabin. Suspect is using an automatic weapon. Break through the gate and park your unit. Make your way through the woods and stay low."

The sheriff heard a loud crash behind him as Deputy Rivers crashed her SUV into the gate, tearing it off its hinges. He keyed his mic. "Rivers, stay north of the driveway and head around the trees to the left side of the cabin. Who's with you?"

"McDonald and Stinson, CBI is right behind us."

"Okay, fan out and move towards the cabin. Be careful. Buck is circling around to come in behind the cabin."

| 24 |

Chapter Twenty-Four

The shots from the cabin shifted from the sheriff to the left. Return fire came from the trees from several AR-style rifles. The sheriff was about to return fire when Paul came out of the trees and crawled to his position.

"You okay?" asked Paul.

"Yeah. Buck's out there somewhere trying to get to the cabin." They could hear more sirens approaching.

"I'll find him," said Paul, and he crawled a few feet, jumped up and ran into the woods. The sheriff was surprised a big man like that could move that quick. He raised his pistol and joined his deputies in firing towards the cabin.

Paul moved through the trees, following a shallow ravine. He found Buck at the back right corner of the cabin and moved up next to him.

Buck heard something behind him and turned, raising his pistol at the same time. Paul stopped and held up his hands. He moved next to Buck.

"You got a plan, boss?" asked Paul.

More gunfire came from the cabin, and Buck knew they needed to move fast.

"There's a back door. I'm gonna throw a log through that side window." Buck pointed to the window. "When I do, you hit the back door. I'd like to take him alive, if possible, but do what you need to do."

Paul nodded and moved towards the back door. He waved to Buck that he was ready. Buck moved towards the cabin until he got to a spot where he could see where he and the sheriff had taken cover. He pulled out a white hand-kerchief from his pocket and waved it. He hoped someone would see it.

There was a break in the gunfire from the cabin, and Buck ran towards the firewood stack next to the cabin wall, picked up a big chunk of wood and threw it at the window. The log smashed through the window, and at the same time, he heard Paul hit the back door. The back door didn't give, and the gunfire from inside the cabin was now directed at the back door.

Buck stood in front of the window, spotted the gunman, raised his pistol and fired, hitting the gunman in his right shoulder. The rifle flew from his hands, and the gunman slammed into the cabin wall. Buck climbed through the win-dow, with his gun leading the way, kicking a handgun and another rifle out of the way as he approached the gunman lying on the floor.

Melvin Gross held his left hand over the wound. "Damn, that hurts." He looked at Buck. "What the hell, dude?"

"Dude, you shot the sheriff," said Buck.

After making sure the gunman had no more weapons, he flipped him onto his stomach and slapped his handcuffs on his wrists. The gunman started to object; Buck looked at him.

"You have the right to remain silent, so shut the fuck up."

He walked over, pushed the large file cabinet away from the back door and opened the door for Paul, putting his pistol back into his holster.

Buck walked to the front of the cabin and opened the door just as three sheriff's department SUVs, two state police cars and two ambulances pulled up to the cabin. The back door of one of the ambulances opened, and Sheriff Toomey stepped out. He looked at Buck and stepped into the cabin, where Melvin Gross was being looked at by one of the paramedics.

He looked down at Melvin. "Melvin, what the hell is wrong with you? We just wanted to talk."

Melvin looked up at the sheriff and then at the white bandage on the sheriff's arm. "I'm sorry, Sheriff. I thought you were coming to confiscate my treasure."

The sheriff shook his head and tapped the paramedic. "Get this idiot to the hospital and then bring him to jail."

The sheriff's legs wobbled, and he grabbed hold of a table to steady himself. Buck grabbed his good arm. "Time for you to get back in that ambulance and head to the hospital. We'll finish up here," said Buck.

Another paramedic led the sheriff to the ambulance, placed him on the gurney in the back and headed down the driveway. The second ambulance, containing Melvin Gross and Deputy Stinson, followed the first and they disappeared in a cloud of dust.

Buck walked over to Paul. "You okay?"

Paul was rubbing his upper right arm. "Yeah. Surprised the crap out of me when I hit the door and it didn't move. Luckily, he was aiming too high. Good shooting."

Buck smiled and turned as Bax stepped up carrying a black pistol in a plastic evidence bag. She held it up to Buck. "Glock 19. I'll get this to the lab right away, and then we're going to visit Mrs. Halverson." She walked away, followed by Deputy Rivers, and Buck pulled out his phone.

"Hi, Buck. What's up?" asked Director Jackson.

Buck filled him in on the shoot-out, making note that the sheriff and the suspect were both shot during the altercation.

"Sir, can you get me a forensic team from Denver to go through the cabin?"

"You got it, Buck. Interesting way to start your day."

The director hung up, and Buck stepped over to Paul. "Go through the cabin and see if there's anything here and keep your eye out for treasure. Once forensics arrives, meet me back at the sheriff's office."

Paul nodded, and Buck exited the cabin and spotted another sheriff's SUV stop in front of the cabin. The front door opened, and a tall man with a muscular build and shaved head slid out of the SUV and walked up. He wore the same uniform the sheriff wore, except where the sheriff had four stars on his collar, this guy had three stars. He stepped up to Buck and Paul.

"Agent Taylor, Commander Mark Walsch." He reached out his hand, and Buck shook it and introduced him to Paul. "Sorry I missed all the excitement. The wife and I had just arrived home from Cancun when I heard the assist call. Is the sheriff okay?"

Buck filled him in on what happened. Commander Walsch listened and shook his head. "Man, I missed a lot while I was gone." He looked at Buck. "What can I do to help?"

"We need a search warrant for the cabin and all electronics. Do you have a judge you can call?" asked Buck.

"Yes, sir. I'll get right on that." He stepped away and unclipped his phone from his belt.

Buck and Paul walked back into the cabin. Buck thanked the two troopers and released them to return to their patrols. He and Paul and Deputy McDonald started looking through the cabin. Paul sat at the small wooden desk and opened the laptop. He clicked a couple of buttons and sat back.

"You know, for all that guy's paranoia, he didn't password-protect his laptop," he said.

He started clicking buttons and looking at files. He called Buck over and pointed to the screen.

"This guy has been selling Native American artifacts online. He has his own website. Most of it appears to be simple stuff: arrowheads and some bead jewelry. Nothing on here looks like it's worth much. If this is his treasure . . ." Paul shook his head.

"Agent Taylor," came a voice from outside.

Buck turned and walked out the back door to where Deputy McDonald stood next to a small shed. He held open the door, and Buck stepped inside. The shelves were lined with arrowheads, beads and leather strips. Buck looked at the small workbench on which lay an unfinished necklace.

"He's making his own artifacts," said Deputy McDonald.

"Yeah, we found a website on his laptop. Quite the con man."

Buck stepped outside. "Keep looking around, Deputy. And when the forensic team from Denver arrives, hang out with them until they are done."

The deputy nodded and headed for the cabin.

"Warrant's on my phone," said Commander Walsch. "You are good to go."

Buck thanked the commander and tapped Paul on the shoulder. "Paul, you and McDonald stick around until forensics gets here. Meet me back in town later today."

"If it's okay with you, Agent Taylor," said Commander Walsch. "I'm going to head back to the office. Looks like I'm in charge for a bit." They shook hands, and the commander left.

Buck headed for his Jeep, parked by the gate at the end of the driveway. His phone rang, and he looked at the unknown number.

"Taylor," he said.

"Agent Taylor, General Culpeper. We need to meet."

Buck listened, suggested a private spot, disconnected the call and walked to where his Jeep was. A hell of a way to start the day is right.

| 25 |

Chapter Twenty-Five

Lizzy Clark parked her F-250 pickup truck in front of the Halverson house and climbed out of the truck. She walked around the truck and spotted Mrs. Halverson stepping out of the barn. Mrs. Halverson watched her approach. She spotted the pistol clipped to Lizzy's belt.

"I told your brother, I have no idea what he was talking about."

Lizzy stepped up almost nose to nose with Mrs. Halverson. "You are costing my family a lot of money, and you stand to make a lot of money yourselves. So, what the hell are you waiting for? Sign the damn papers."

"I told you. I don't know what papers you're talking about. My husband is in the hospital. Why can't you leave me alone?" She turned and walked into the barn.

Lizzy Clark followed her, grabbed her by the arm and swung her around. She slapped Mrs. Halverson across the face and grabbed her by the collar.

"You listen to me, you old bitch. I'm not as easygoing as my brother. I will not treat you with respect and dignity. You've got twenty-four hours to get those papers signed. If they're not signed when I return, I'm gonna gut you like a fish."

Lizzy shoved Mrs. Halverson, who fell to the ground. Through her tears, she said, "Just leave me alone. I don't know what papers you want signed, so I can't help you. Now get off my property before I call the sheriff."

Lizzy walked over, kneeled next to Mrs. Halverson, pulled her pistol and stuck it under Mrs. Halverson's chin. Mrs. Halverson's eyes got as big as saucers. Lizzy pulled the hammer back.

"Don't think for one minute I won't kill you, and the sheriff won't do a damn thing if I do. We run this county, not the sheriff. You get those papers signed, or you'll regret it."

A voice came from the barn door. "Mom. What's going on?" June ran to her mother's side and shoved Lizzy Clark out of the way. "Are you okay?" she asked her mom. She glared at Lizzy Clark. "What the hell do you think you're doing?"

Lizzy pointed her pistol at June. "You ever talk to me like that again, and I'll kill you."

Lizzy stood up, holstered her pistol and wiped the dust off her jeans. "If your mother doesn't have those papers signed when I get back, I'll kill your whole family."

Lizzy Clark walked out of the barn and climbed into her truck. She threw up a cloud of dust and gravel and tore down the driveway.

June helped her mom stand up and dusted her off. "You sure you're okay?"

"I'm fine," said Mrs. Halverson, and she started to walk away.

June stood there staring at her. "Mom, Lizzy Clark just assaulted you and threatened you. We need to call the sheriff."

June pulled out her phone, but Mrs. Halverson turned and walked back to her before she could dial and slapped the phone out of her daughter's hand.

"You call the sheriff, and there is no telling what that crazy woman will do. Leave it alone."

June was startled, and she picked up her phone. Her mother continued. "You, of all people, should know what she can do."

Lizzy Clark and June Halverson were in the same classes in the small elementary school in Fairplay. When they were in seventh grade, June Halverson scored a goal during a soccer game after she took the ball from Lizzy, who was battling two defenders. Lizzy was so pissed that June scored her goal that after the game, she attacked June in the school parking lot while they waited for their parents to pick them up. When the fight was over, June spent two weeks in the hospital with a concussion, a broken leg and other assorted scrapes and cuts. Her friends told Mrs. Halverson that Lizzy was out of control.

When Edith Clark arrived at the school and saw her daughter sitting in the deputy's patrol car, she went ballistic. She walked up to the car, glared at the deputy, opened the back door and pulled Lizzy out. She looked at her daughter, who had a couple of scratches on her face and arms, and yelled at her. Not for hurting June Halverson, but for getting hurt doing it. She walked up to June, lying on a gurney at the back of the ambulance, and Mrs. Clark stuck her finger in Mrs. Halverson's face and said, "Look at what that little bitch did to my girl. If your daughter ever goes near my Lizzy again, I will kill her."

She grabbed Lizzy by the arm and dragged her to her truck. As they pulled out of the parking lot, Lizzy looked out the window and smiled.

"You know they can get away with whatever they want," said Mrs. Halverson. "Your father is in the hospital, and I don't need anything else to happen to our family. So just let it go."

"But Mom. She put a gun to your head, and what is she talking about signing papers? What are you not telling me?"

"Just let it go," said Mrs. Halverson as she walked away, wiping blood from her nose with the back of her hand. "We need to get to the hospital, so get the kids, and let's go." She stopped and turned. "Not a word of this to anyone. Do you understand?"

June nodded and followed her mother into the house. She had no idea what was going on or if it was related to whatever happened to her father, but she wondered what her parents had gotten themselves into.

| 26 |

Chapter Twenty-Six

Buck was almost back to Como when his phone chimed. He pushed the green button.

"Hey, George. What's up?"

"Hi, Buck." George hesitated for a couple of seconds. "Buck, where did you get the files you asked Mel to look at?"

"Why? Something wrong?" said Buck.

"I'm not sure," said George.

"George. What's going on?"

"Sorry, Buck. The files that you uploaded. Those files are all black flagged."

"Okay. So, what does that mean? Is that a problem?"

"Black-flagged files are at the top of the security clearance list. There is something like four people in the entire country that have access to these files. How did you get them?"

"They were given to me early this morning by a general. Right now, that's all I can tell you. What's in them?"

"They're the personnel files of twelve people who work

154

in biological and chemical engineering at what I assume is a secret lab someplace. So why do we have them?"

"There's a possibility that one of those files belongs to someone who is working a side deal with a bad actor. I don't know anything more than that, but with what Max's team has learned so far, I would guess that someone is not playing nice in a secret government sandbox and is looking to make some serious money that could negatively affect this country."

Buck could hear George laugh on the other end of the phone. "Fuck, Buck, you sound like a politician. You and the general think one of these guys is selling a bioterror weapon to one of our enemies, and he might have tried it on those cows."

Buck laughed. He turned onto Highway 285 and headed towards the crime scene.

"Okay," said George. "Now I know what to look for. We'll take these guys' lives apart. Call you later."

The call disconnected, and Buck laughed again. "If they only knew," he said to no one.

He turned onto the dirt road heading towards the crime scene, and about a half mile from the scene, he was stopped by a couple of black SUVs blocking the road. A stern-looking man in a dark suit approached his Jeep.

"Sorry, sir, you'll need to turn around. This road is closed."

Buck held up his badge. "That's my crime scene. Who authorized you to shut off access, and what are you doing up there?"

The man looked at Buck's ID and wrote a note on his clipboard.

"Sorry, Agent Taylor. You'll have to talk to the SAIC, but he is unavailable. So please turn around and leave the area."

Buck turned his Jeep around under the watchful eye of the stern-looking FBI agent. He parked just before the turn, pulled his phone from his belt and dialed a number.

"Hi, Buck," said Hank Clancy. "What's up?"

Hank Clancy was the special agent in charge of the Denver Field Office of the FBI and one of Buck's closest friends. Hank had been a deputy director until earlier in the year when he fell on his sword and took the blame for a rogue FBI agent. The agent, while working out of the Denver Field Office and fighting Buck at every turn during the investigation of several Christmas Day bombings, caused the deaths of several FBI agents and serious injuries to several others.

Buck had asked the Colorado governor to intervene on Hank's behalf, and as a result, they were able to save his job, but they couldn't prevent the demotion. Hank had a long career with the FBI, and he was involved in many high-profile cases, and even though his wife wanted him to retire, Hank refused to end his career with a black eye.

"Hank, what the hell is going on? I was just turned away from my crime scene by one of your people."

"Sorry, Buck. It was out of my control. The CDC went right to the top and created a task force to deal with a potential terrorist attack, and all I could do was send my people to help the CDC and to investigate."

"You couldn't give me a heads-up?" asked Buck.

"I told you it was in the works," said Hank, "but once it happened, it happened fast. Besides, the agent in charge of the detail was supposed to meet with you and Sheriff Toomey and ask for your help. I'm guessing that didn't happen?"

"No, it didn't. Instead, we spent the morning having a shoot-out with a deranged treasure hunter who might be involved in this case. Your agent could have called me."

"Okay, Buck. I'll deal with him. The task force will want access to your lab results. I would appreciate your help with that."

Buck laughed. "You've got some nerve, buddy. First, you walk all over my crime scene, and then you want my help with your investigation."

"Look," said Hank. "I know it's a lot to ask, but I'm asking you to help in whatever way you see fit."

"I'll do what I can, Hank, but you tell your agents to stay the hell out of my way."

They spent the next few minutes catching up, and Buck disconnected the call. He saw the black SUV with the Colorado plates turn up the road, and he rolled down his window and flagged it down.

General Culpeper rolled down his window. "Sorry, general, change of plans. Seems the FBI and the CDC have taken over my crime scene. Follow me down the road to a turnoff next to the creek about a mile from here."

Buck turned onto Tarryall Road and followed it south along the creek until he reached a wide spot with a small picnic table. He pulled in and stopped his Jeep. The general pulled in behind him. The sound of the creek was nice background noise, and a slight breeze helped ensure that no one could listen to their conversation.

Buck slid out of his Jeep and walked over to the picnic table. The general walked up and sat opposite him.

"Nice spot," said the general. "Thanks for meeting me."

The general was quiet for a minute. Deep in thought. "Agent Taylor, what do you know about botulinum toxin?"

"Isn't that what Botox is made from?" asked Buck.

"That and much more," said General Culpeper. "We tested the samples that Maxine Clinton sent to us. Her team was on the right track; they couldn't quite get there. What screwed them up was that the botulinum had been manipulated."

"Is that what killed all the cattle, and the two kids?" asked Buck.

"Yes. We are one hundred percent certain, and that's what's so scary. Agent Taylor, whoever manipulated this toxin was able to do what we haven't been able to do, and that person made a weapon that could kill every person and animal on earth."

| **27** |

Chapter Twenty-Seven

Deputy Rivers turned her SUV at the Halverson mailbox, followed by Bax, and they headed towards the old house. They parked in front of the barn and noticed a new Ford Explorer with temporary Colorado plates parked by the front door. They headed that way just as the front door opened, and three young kids ran towards the SUV. Mrs. Halverson came out the door, followed by a younger version of herself.

The younger version looked at Bax. "Can I help you?"

"Ashley Baxter, CBI, we would like to have a quick word with Mrs. Halverson."

"We're on our way to Denver to the hospital. Can this wait?"

"It's okay, June. This will only take a minute," said Mrs. Halverson.

June looked disgusted, walked over, opened the door and loaded the kids in the back seat. Mrs. Halverson walked to the barn and turned to face Bax.

"Any idea what is killing my husband?" she asked.

"No, ma'am, but there are a lot of people working on this. We'll figure it out."

"So, what can I help you with?" asked Mrs. Halverson.

"The first thing you can do is tell me what happened to your face?" asked Bax.

Mrs. Halverson looked nervous and looked down at the ground. She had hoped the makeup her daughter put on her face would hide the palm print.

"Nothing," said Mrs. Halverson. "I think it's an allergic reaction to something or maybe a beesting."

"Look, Mrs. Halverson. We're trying to help you out here. That's a palm print on your face, so why don't we try this again? What happened to your face?"

Mrs. Halverson stayed quiet. She twisted her hands together, never once looking at Bax.

"Ma'am did someone threaten you?" asked Deputy Rivers. "Why don't you tell us what's going on? We really do want to help."

Mrs. Halverson walked a few paces to the left and then back. "It's nothing. Someone came by today looking for my husband, and they weren't happy that he wasn't here."

"Who came by, Mrs. Halverson?"

"I . . . I don't want any trouble. I've got enough going on with Gun in the hospital. Now I need to go."

"Mrs. Halverson, your husband was targeted, and I need to know why," said Bax.

"Mom, tell them, for god's sake." June stepped up and stood next to her mother. "My mother was attacked."

"June, that's enough," said Mrs. Halverson.

Mrs. Halverson stepped towards the barn door. June watched her walk away and hesitated for a moment.

"Lizzy Clark slapped her and held a gun to her chin."

"Any idea why?" asked Bax.

"She was yelling something about getting my dad to sign some papers. Mom didn't seem to know what she was talking about. They have nothing except this land, and now that the herd is dead, I'm not sure what will happen to them. We've been here for almost two hundred years. What could my parents have that she could want?"

Bax walked over to Mrs. Halverson. "Ma'am, do you know what papers she was looking for?"

Mrs. Halverson wiped the tears from her eyes. "I have no idea. Look around, Agent Baxter. The herd was everything we had except for each other."

"Is it possible that Mr. Halverson was selling something to Lizzy, something of value?"

"We have nothing but the ranch. We have minimal savings, and other than the land, we are what they used to call property rich and penny poor. My husband has nothing to sell." Tears flowed down her cheeks.

June took her by the arm and led her to the Explorer. Bax looked at Deputy Rivers. "Where can we find Lizzy Clark?"

"You sure you want to go there? Lizzy's nuts."

"Is that why everyone in this county, including you guys, is scared of her and her family?"

Bax was pissed. "These people break the law at will, and no one does a damn thing to stop them. What the fuck is with you people?" Bax caught herself before she said anything else. "Sorry, Kat. It can't be easy watching them break the law."

"It's not, Bax, but they have everyone in this county scared. The whole family is crazy. Do you know that the restaurants and stores around here add a Clark tax to recoup some of what they steal? I've seen them walk into the grocery store, fill up bags with groceries and walk out the door. No one says a word, and no matter what we do, we can't change that."

Bax looked into her eyes. "You want to do something about it?"

"Sure, but what can we do?" asked Deputy Rivers.

"Where can we find Lizzy?"

Deputy Rivers thought for a minute and looked at her watch. "She's probably at the Longhorn Lounge, holding court with all the single and some of the married guys in the county."

Bax smiled and headed for her Jeep. Deputy Rivers was right behind her, and they raced down the driveway and turned onto Highway 285. The Longhorn Lounge was a mile down the highway, and Bax pulled in and stopped in front of the door. Deputy Rivers pulled in behind her. They slid out of their SUVs and walked to the front door.

"Do we have a plan?" asked Deputy Rivers.

"Yeah, we're going to arrest Lizzy Clark and anyone who gets in the way."

Deputy Rivers did not doubt that Bax was ready for war. She was scared and excited, but she was ready to follow Bax into hell if that's where it took her. They pulled open the doors and stepped into the lounge.

Lizzy Clark was sitting on a tabletop in the middle of the room, surrounded by eight or nine men of varying ages. They were laughing at whatever Lizzy was saying until they noticed

Bax and Deputy Rivers at the door, then they started going quiet as Bax and Deputy Rivers walked towards the table.

Deputy Rivers looked at the male bartender standing with his hands on the bar. He kept looking down towards his feet. "Barry, if you know what's good, you'll keep those hands on the bar top." Barry, the bartender, nodded but didn't look happy.

"Lizzy Clark. You're under arrest for assault. Please stand up, turn around and keep your hands where I can see them."

Lizzy didn't move, but several men stood up and formed a wall between Lizzy and Bax. Bax stepped forward, and the men tightened their group. A big bear of a man with long gray hair and a full beard puffed out his chest. "You don't belong here, cop."

Lizzy laughed and turned to look at Bax. Then she looked at Katrina. "You should know better, Kat. I guess you don't like your job or living in this county. You'll never be safe here again, and you know I can make that happen." The men all laughed and nodded.

Bax turned to Deputy Rivers. "Kat, how many ambulances does the county have?"

Kat looked at her. "Five or six."

"Good," said Bax. She looked back at the men, who didn't look amused. "Deputy, please radio dispatch and tell them we are going to need all the ambulances and to put the hospital in Frisco on notice to expect numerous injured individuals."

The men laughed but with much less enthusiasm than before. Several of them backed a few feet away from the group and looked around nervously. They looked like they wanted to escape, but they also didn't want to lose faith in front of Lizzy Clark. They hesitated.

Deputy Rivers clicked off her mic and moved next to Bax, her hand on her pistol.

Bax stepped forward. "Lizzy Clark, I'm not going to tell you again. Stand up and turn around, hands where I can see them."

"Whom was I supposed to have assaulted?" asked Lizzy Clark.

"Mrs. Halverson," said Bax.

Lizzy laughed. "That bitch will never file charges. She knows what my family will do to her and her old man." Lizzy laughed, and the men laughed a little harder.

Bax knew she needed to end this now. She reached into her back pocket, pulled out a collapsible metal baton and snapped it open. Several of the men jumped back at the sound. Bax moved forward. She glanced sideways and saw that Deputy Rivers had pulled her pistol and held it with two hands at low ready.

The big guy with the beard stepped up with his fists hard and ready. There was a sudden flash of movement, and the big man slammed against a table and landed on his back on the floor. He moaned and grabbed his back. Sirens could be heard in the distance. The rest of the men separated, and Bax walked up to Lizzy Clark.

Lizzy spun off the table and threw a punch towards Bax's head. Bax blocked the punch, grabbed Lizzy by the collar and, using her own momentum, flipped her over another table, crashing through beer bottles and dirty plates and landing on the floor. Bax stuck her knee in Lizzy's back, snapped on the cuffs and pulled the pistol from her belt. "You can tell your brother I kicked your ass too," said Bax.

Commander Walsch and Deputy McDonald came through the door and looked at the mess. They noticed that Deputy Rivers had her pistol pointed at Barry, the bartender, who had his hands raised to his shoulders. Deputy McDonald stepped behind the bar, pushed Barry aside and picked up a large revolver that was lying on the shelf under the bar.

Commander Walsch stepped up to Bax, who was lifting Lizzy Clark to her feet. "Charge?" he asked.

Bax explained the assault on Mrs. Halverson and the assault on her. He looked at the big guy still lying on the floor, moaning. He kneeled next to him. "Jerry, you're an idiot." He pulled his arms behind him, pulled out his cuffs and cuffed him. He pulled him to his feet. "McDonald, please take Jerry to the jail and book him for assaulting a police officer."

He stepped up to Lizzy. "That bitch attacked me for no reason, and I have a bar full of witnesses. I want her arrested." She went into a tirade about her rights, and everything else that came to her mind came out of her mouth.

Walsch looked around the bar at all the men who were now sitting at their tables. "Anyone see what happened here?" he asked.

The men in the room became interested in their drinks and their food. He smiled at Lizzy Clark. "You're all dead, you miserable fucks," she said at the top of her voice. "When my family gets through with you, you'll all regret it. I know where you all live."

Walsch took her by the arm and led her out the door, still yelling at the top of her voice. Deputy Rivers walked up and looked around. "I never even saw you move on the big guy," she said.

Bax laughed. "The bigger they are, the harder they fall. You didn't call for the ambulances?" said Bax.

"I thought you were joking, so I called for backup. You stood up to those guys and didn't flinch. You are a badass, Agent Baxter."

Bax laughed again. "Let's go. We have a bunch of paperwork to file."

They headed out the door and slid into their SUVs. Behind them, several people grabbed their phones. This day was about to get more interesting.

| 28 |

Chapter Twenty-Eight

Edmund Clark was not happy when he walked into Tom's kitchen. He stormed over to the refrigerator, opened the door and pulled out a bottle of beer. He popped off the cap against the edge of the counter and swallowed the whole thing in one big gulp. He threw the bottle in the trash and wiped his mouth on his sleeve. No one in the kitchen dared move a muscle.

He looked at his wife. "Did you and Claire get everyone fed?"

Claire nodded, wiping tears from her eyes. She covered her mouth with a kitchen towel to hide the sobs. He looked at Edith, who lowered her head and looked at the floor. "What?" he asked.

"One of the women might be going into labor. Tom called Dr. Sparks, who will be here as soon as he can."

Edmund Clark's neck turned a bright shade of red. "That's

all we need. My grandson is dead, my son is missing and now this. What the hell else can go wrong?"

Tom stepped up to his father. "Dad, any sign of Tucker? I've looked in all his usual haunts, but no one has seen him."

"I let the sheriff know, but they won't do anything to help us. Where the hell could he be? There isn't even any sign of his truck. What the hell is going on around here?"

"You don't think the sheriff has him, do you?" asked Tom Clark.

Edmund Clark looked frustrated. "Why the fuck would the sheriff have him? He hasn't done anything wrong."

"Maybe the cops got wind that we were putting the squeeze on old man Halverson."

Edmund Clark glared at Tom. "What? Do you think your brother had something to do with what happened to Halverson's herd? Don't be an idiot."

"The internet says the cattle were poisoned by the government, and Halverson got too close and had to be taken out," said Edith.

"Jesus Christ, Edith. Stop listening to all that conspiracy shit on the internet and start living in the real world. We've got bigger problems to deal with."

He grabbed another beer, opened it, walked out of the kitchen and stood in the backyard. What Tom had said had somehow taken hold of his brain, and he couldn't shake it. Even if Tucker had something to do with the cattle, where the hell would he have gotten a chemical potent enough to kill them? He wanted to stop the thought, but his brain wouldn't let him. If that were true, then Tucker could have been responsible for the death of his grandson.

He shook his head to try to get rid of the thought. He headed towards the barn and almost ran into James Clark.

"Shit, Dad, you startled me."

"You looked deep in thought, son. What's going on?"

"Too much shit for one day, Dad. With everything that's been happening, now I can't find Tucker."

His dad took him by the arm and led him towards the barn. "Have we gotten anywhere with Mrs. Halverson? Unfortunately, we do not have a lot of time left."

"I sent Lizzy to talk to her. She's a lot tougher than Tucker when it comes to getting stuff done." He looked at his watch. "Speaking of Lizzy. I wonder where she is. She should have been back a while ago."

He grabbed for his phone in his pocket when it rang. "Bet that's her now." He answered without looking at the number.

"Yeah," he said.

"Mr. Clark. It's Barry from the Longhorn. Listen, Lizzy just got arrested. Cops just hauled her out of here."

"What the hell did they arrest her for? She get in a fight with someone?"

"No, sir. Not with anyone in the bar. I heard the lady CBI cop tell her she was under arrest for assaulting Mrs. Halverson, then Lizzy jumped at the cop. She got put down hard. Dragged her out kicking and screaming."

"Thanks, Barry. I'll remember this."

He disconnected the call and threw his beer, smashing it against the barn wall. "Fuck," he said. "Fuck, fuck, fuck." He looked at James Clark.

"Lizzy got arrested for assaulting Halverson's wife."

"So, what's the problem?" asked James. "She won't talk. She knows what will happen if she does."

"Yeah, well, that's not all of it," said Edmund. "She attacked one of the state cops. It sounds like the cop got the better of her."

"Those state cops are gonna be trouble," said James Clark. "We need to clear this place out as soon as possible. Let me make some calls and see how soon we can move the product. Find that idiot son of yours and figure out how to get Lizzy out of jail."

"What about Halverson? It doesn't sound like Lizzy made any progress either."

James Clark turned and faced Edmund. "If she won't cooperate, kill her."

He turned and walked away, and Edmund headed for his truck. Before he got to his truck, he received three more calls from guys who were at the bar and wanted to tell him that Lizzy got arrested. Everyone wanted to be on Edmund Clark's good side. He climbed into his truck and drove out of the yard. He didn't know where he was going, but he needed to go someplace quiet to think.

| 29 |

Chapter Twenty-Nine

General Culpeper looked like he hadn't slept in days, and Buck could see the concern written all over his face. The general stood and walked to the edge of Tarryall Creek. He stood looking out over the water, trying to gather his thoughts. He walked back to the picnic table and sat down.

"Botulinum toxin is one of the deadliest substances on earth," he said. "I could go into a lot of scientific details, but I want to keep this as simple as possible. So, I apologize in advance if you think I am talking down to you. This stuff can get very complicated."

Buck nodded. He had learned, over years of doing interrogations, not to interrupt people once they started to talk.

"There are eight different strains of botulinum toxin. A, B, C1, C2, D, E, F and G. A, B, E and F affect humans, and D primarily affects animals. C1 and C2 are less common, and G has never been known to affect humans. The toxin is a natural substance commonly found in soils and dust, and on food products. People infected with the toxin usually get it from wounds that come in contact with infected soil or ingestion: eating poorly prepared and cleaned foods.

"You already know it is used in cosmetics and commonly called Botox. What you may not be aware of is that it is also used to treat migraines, depression and a whole host of other medical conditions. Used properly, it can alleviate the symptoms of these ailments. Used improperly, it can be deadly.

"Had you been on-site when the brand inspector and the two young boys were infected, you would have noticed paralysis, muscle weakness, trouble swallowing and trouble breathing. Because botulinum is a neurotoxin, it blocks the nerves that control respiration and heart function. Typically, once infected, it can take several days for the symptoms to manifest themselves. However, because this toxin was aerosolized, it appears to work much faster. We will need to study this a lot more to see just how much faster this works.

"One of the issues we have is that no one has successfully aerosolized botulinum, so we have had very little chance to study the effects. For example, in the nineteen nineties, a terrorist cult in Japan called Aum Shinrikyo staged an aerosolized attack on downtown Tokyo. There were no fatalities because they used an ineffective subtype of the toxin."

Buck interrupted. "Isn't that the same group that staged a sarin gas attack on a subway in Tokyo that killed a couple of hundred people and sickened several hundred more?"

"Correct, Agent Taylor. Had the botulinum attack been successful, thousands could have died. It is estimated that one gram—that's a gram of aerosolized botulinum toxin—could kill one and a half million people if evenly distributed.

Luckily wind and weather would also be a factor, but you can see why this is on the wish list of every terrorist group in the world. And keeps people like me up at night.

"Two other historical notes for context. During the D-Day invasion, the government issued all the Allied troops an antitoxin to be used if they were exposed to what at the time was called Agent-X, which we know today was crystallized botulinum toxin. The troops were told that the German army had Agent-X and would likely use it on the battlefield. However, it was speculated that the troops were given the antitoxin because we were prepared to use Agent-X on the German positions, not the other way around.

"At the end of the Gulf War, we were told that Iraq had over nineteen thousand liters of botulinum toxin in storage. I was part of the team that was sent in to locate the supply; however, like all the WMDs we were told were there, we didn't find anything. So, as you can see, botulinum toxin has been at the forefront of weaponization for a long time.

"Thankfully, the toxin is easy to get but hard to weaponize. Making an aerosolized form requires binding the toxin to ultrafine powdered material such as bentonite or silica. Until now, no one has found an effective way to do this.

"Our fear is that the death of the cattle was a proof-of-concept test. That whoever created the product was showing potential buyers that the product could work. I had the lab run a warfare simulation, and we believe, because of the topography and the weather conditions at the time, that the two young boys were infected as the wind and the slope of the land funneled the toxin directly towards them."

Buck stopped him. "Why didn't it kill the deputy and the old rancher? Why just the two boys?"

"That's what's so ingenious about this product," said the general. "Whoever produced this manipulated the toxin and built in a kill switch. From what we can determine, the toxin becomes inert after a period of time. It goes dormant and is no longer infectious. We are not sure how it was done, but by the time the deputy and the rancher arrived on the scene, the product was already shutting down. Until we can study it further, our best guess is they received a small dose of the toxin, which made them sick, but it was not fatal."

"You said there is an antitoxin available? Can we use it on the deputy and the rancher?" asked Buck.

"I have already been in contact with the CDC doctors at Denver General Hospital and have made available several of the antitoxins. Unfortunately, because of the length of exposure and how the toxin was manipulated, we have no idea if the antitoxin will be effective. All we can do at this point is try."

"Can the toxin be killed?" asked Buck.

"The short answer is yes. Temps below four point four degrees Celsius will slow the growth of the spores. High heat, above eighty-five degrees Celsius, high salt levels and low pH levels can also affect the toxin. The spores, however, are heat resistant and, as such, are difficult to kill."

"What's our next step, General? People around here are scared."

"I have already directed the CDC and the military to collect all the cows from the field. They will be relocated to a secure facility and incinerated. Because of the kill switch, we believe the field is no longer hazardous. However, we will set up several discreet air monitoring stations around the field to collect and analyze samples."

"What about the bodies?" asked Buck.

"Once the autopsies are complete, the bodies can be returned to the families for burial or cremation."

The general hesitated a minute. "Have you had any luck with the files I gave you? We need to find the person responsible before he can sell this product to a bad actor."

Buck pulled out his phone and dialed a number.

"Hey, Buck. I was going to call you," said George.

"Hi, George. Is this about the files?"

"Yeah."

"Hold just a minute, George. I'm going to put you on speaker. I am here with the person who provided the files."

Buck clicked a button on his phone. "Okay, George, go ahead."

"We've eliminated ten of the twelve people whose files were sent to us. Their backgrounds are clean, and we don't get any red flags. The other two files we are still looking at. One of them—I'll call them suspects for lack of a better word—has some holes in his background. We are having trouble digging into their educational, financial and residency information. One of the suspects appears to be from California, but we hit a couple of walls. The other one is a local boy, born and raised in Park County. We need to dig deeper into these two but can't get through the encryption."

The general slid Buck's phone closer. "Can you tell me the names of the two people you are looking at?"

Buck leaned over. "It's okay, George. Go ahead."

"Yes, sir. The local boy is Dr. Brian Cole, and the other person is Dr. Simon Lee."

The general stepped away from the table and pulled out his phone. Buck watched him have an animated conversation with someone on the other end of the phone. He disconnected the call and walked back to the table.

"Agent Peterman, you will be receiving an encryption key in a secure email. Use that key wisely, sir, and then forget you ever saw it. The consequences for you and I will be dire if you fail to follow my request."

"Understood," said George. "Thanks."

George hung up, and Buck wondered how the general knew George's last name. He didn't ask. The general looked at Buck. "We need to move quickly, Agent Taylor. Please let me know if there is anything else you require."

The general walked to his SUV, slid inside and drove away from the picnic area, leaving Buck with a lot of information and few answers. He stood up, walked to his Jeep, slid in and headed towards Fairplay. Things were sure getting interesting.

Chapter Thirty

Buck was about to turn into the Park County Sheriff's Office parking lot when he was almost run off the road by a black F-250 pickup that came fishtailing out of the parking lot and onto the highway. The big diesel engine screamed as the truck drove by. Buck recognized Edmund Clark behind the wheel and wondered what that was all about.

He parked his Jeep, grabbed his backpack and headed inside, checking in with the deputy at the front desk, who unlatched the door to the office area. He spotted Bax and Deputy Rivers talking to Commander Walsch, who was leaning against a desk while Bax typed on her laptop. Buck walked up to the trio.

"I almost got run off the road by Edmund Clark. What's got him all twisted up?" he asked.

"We arrested his daughter for assaulting Mrs. Halverson and Agent Baxter," said Commander Walsch. "We were just getting ready to question her. We are also getting lots of calls from people who have heard about the dead cattle. They're concerned about their safety, and I'm not sure what to tell them. The county commissioners are pissed that they've been kept out of the loop."

Buck shook his head and looked at Bax with concern. She nodded, indicating that she was okay. "Let me see if I can get the governor to make a statement. That might calm folks down a little. In the meantime, go ahead and interview Lizzy Clark," he said. "I'll watch on the monitor. I have some phone calls to make." He placed his backpack on an empty desk and pulled out his laptop. Bax and Commander Walsch headed for the interrogation room to see if Lizzy Clark had calmed down enough to talk.

As soon as they opened the door, the cursing and yelling started, followed by the same threats she had made earlier. They closed the door and walked back to Buck, who had pulled out his phone and was dialing a number.

"Hi, Buck," said Director Jackson. "What's going on?"

"We've confirmed that the toxin was botulinum toxin. The bad news is it looks like it's been aerosolized, which makes it a hell of a lot more potent. The good news is that it also seems to have a kill switch that makes it inert after a couple of hours."

Buck spent the next twenty minutes filling in the director on what General Culpeper told him earlier in the day. He didn't tell him where the information came from, and the director knew better than to ask.

"That's some scary shit, Buck. Are you any closer to figuring out who did this?"

"I've got George and Mel working on some files we got

from a source—people with the qualifications and ability to work with this stuff. We're also trying to figure out how the Halversons fit into the picture. Right now, I feel like we're missing something."

"Buck, this sounds like terrorism. What do you think?"

"Can't say for sure yet, sir. We're looking at that angle as well."

"Okay, Buck," said the director. "What do you need from me?"

"I think we need the governor to put out a statement. Since this stuff is natural, he could downplay the terrorism angle and maybe talk about potency or something. The people in the county are scared, and that might reassure them."

"I'll run it by him and his PR people and see what he thinks. One more question, Buck. Does this have anything to do with some secret government lab in Park County? It's all over the internet."

Buck was silent for a minute. He was standing in the middle of the sheriff's office, and he needed to be careful what he said.

"We've heard the same thing here, sir. But, right now, we can't find any connection to any lab, secret or otherwise."

"Okay, Buck. Keep me posted and let me know if you need anything."

Bax, Deputy Rivers and Commander Walsch looked at Buck as he disconnected the call.

"Botulinum toxin," said Bax. "You said it's confirmed?"

"Yeah," said Buck. "I just got the word. CDC has an anti-toxin they are going to try on the deputy and Halverson."

"So, what are we thinking?" asked Commander Walsch. "Was this a terrorist act or what?"

"It looks like it might have been what they are calling a proof-of-concept attack. If it worked, then they go to their buyers, show them the proof and negotiate a price."

"Do we have any thoughts on a buyer?" asked Bax.

"No. George is running background on a couple of guys who had access," said Buck.

Bax laughed. "Did this come from your midnight visitor?"

Walsch looked confused and wondered what was going on. Buck walked to the small refrigerator in the corner and pulled out a can of Coke. He popped the top and took a long drink. He turned and faced Bax and the others.

"Last night, I had a visit from a general who works for US-AMRIID. He was sent here by people above him to see if the cattle attack was a terrorist attack. He was given the samples we sent to the State Crime Lab and had the CDC confirm the toxin. Now we need to take that information and figure out what's going on."

"Shit, Buck. Is the government trying to cover its ass because of the stories about some secret lab?"

Buck didn't hesitate. "No. He's scared, and so are his bosses. There's a lot of crazy shit out there in the world, but this stuff can kill a lot of people. He's trying to keep access to the information confined to a small group to avoid a panic, so it's up to us to figure this out."

They looked at each other and then back to Buck. Bax had seen Buck face many things in their investigations, but she could see that this case weighed heavy on his mind.

"Buck?" she asked. "What next?"

"We need to interview Lizzy Clark, and we need to interview Melvin Gross. I think there's more going on here, and I think the cattle attack was only a part of it. Let's go talk to Lizzy."

Bax grabbed her laptop, opened the recording app and followed Buck into the interview room. Lizzy started screaming about police brutality and false arrest, making threats against everyone and everything. Buck stood against the wall with his back to the observation window while Bax sat at the end of the table, set her laptop down and hit the record button. Buck stood there and stared at Lizzy, not saying a word.

Lizzy squirmed in her seat and pulled against the handcuffs that were welded to a bolt attached to the table. She started running out of steam, and after a few minutes, the obscenities slowed down, and her voice lowered. She watched Buck.

Bax read her the Miranda warning off the card and asked Lizzy if she understood her rights. After a few more curses, she said she understood. "Are you willing to talk to us without a lawyer present?" asked Bax.

Lizzy looked at her and back to Buck. "Sure, why not."

Bax pulled a paper from a manila folder and slid it across the table. Lizzy looked at it, and Buck slid over a pen and had her sign it. Lizzy slid the paper and pen back to Bax, never taking her eyes off Buck.

"Lizzy," said Bax. "You were arrested for assaulting Mrs. Halverson and putting a pistol to her head. Can you tell us why?"

"I didn't," said Lizzy, watching Buck.

"Lizzy, we have a witness who saw the whole thing," said Bax.

"Who? That stupid bitch, June? You know I kicked her ass in grade school. Put her in the hospital. Nothing happened to me then, just like nothing's going to happen to me now."

"In case you haven't noticed, you're in custody, in handcuffs," said Bax.

Lizzy Clark laughed. "You have no idea what my family is capable of. I'll be out of here by morning, which you can count on. Then you'll find out what will happen next." Her eyes never left Buck.

"So why are you threatening Mrs. Halverson? What's the deal with the papers you want signed?"

"None of your fucking business, bitch. I'm done talking to you. Get my lawyer."

Buck stepped up to the table, leaned across and looked deep into Lizzy's eyes. "Let me explain something to you," said Buck.

"I said I want my lawyer, dipshit, and you can't talk to me anymore." She pulled back as far as she could go and smiled.

Buck laughed. "No, what I can't do is ask you any questions. Nothing prevents me from talking to you, so let's try this. You just sit and listen. You assaulted Mrs. Halverson to get her to sign some papers that her husband didn't or couldn't sign. Mr. Halverson was sickened by something that killed all his cattle and killed your nephew and his friend. We are going to assume that what happened to the cattle was because Halverson wouldn't sign the papers. We have determined that what killed the cattle and the boys and sickened Halverson was airborne botulinum toxin, which the government believes was a terrorist attack. So, you will remain in jail while we investigate, and when we determine that it was, in fact, terrorism, the government will send you to prison for the rest of your life. You need to decide if you want to get ahead of this thing before it gets totally out of your control."

Buck stood up and headed for the door, followed by Bax. Lizzy stared after him, still defiant, but once the door closed and latched, she couldn't stop her hands from shaking, and her eyes filled with tears. For the first time in her life, Lizzy Clark was scared.

| 31 |

Chapter Thirty-One

Commander Walsch was watching Lizzy through the interrogation room one-way glass as Buck and Bax walked up and stood next to him.

"You sure took the wind out of her sails with that terrorism threat," said Walsch. "I've never seen that woman look that scared in as long as I've known her. I also just found out from dispatch that the sheriff had a visit from Edmund Clark earlier this morning. It seems his son Tucker is missing. I've put out a BOLO for him and his truck."

"What do you think that's about?" asked Buck.

"No idea. He just lost his son. Maybe he just needed some time alone," said Walsch.

Buck thought for a minute. "Or maybe I wasn't too far off when I told Lizzy that the dead cattle and the papers Halverson was supposed to sign were connected. Is it possible that Tucker had anything to do with the dead cattle?"

"I don't see how that's possible. I've known that family

for a long time," said Walsch. "Tucker barely graduated high school. I don't see him becoming a chemistry wiz."

Bax's phone chimed, and she stepped away to answer it.

"What about someone he knows, a friend, a relative?" asked Buck.

Before Walsch could answer, Buck pulled out his phone and called George and Mel.

"Hi, Buck," said Mel. "What's up?"

"Hey, Mel. Have you guys finished running background on the Clark family?"

"Yes, sir. Uploaded it to the investigation file an hour or so ago."

"What's the bottom line?" asked Buck.

"Both James Clark and his son Edmund have spent time in prison, but that was early in their lives. Most of the family have been arrested at least once, but nothing ever came of the arrests. Nothing in the last five years that we could find."

"Kind of unusual that they haven't committed any crime in the last five years. Maybe they found religion," said Buck. He looked sideways at Commander Walsch.

"Their social media is full of rants about the government and politics, and they have some questionable contacts, but nothing that we could nail them with. They come back clean, for the most part."

"Speaking of their associates. Anyone jumps out at you?" asked Buck.

"We're running several neo-Nazis and a couple of white supremacists through NCIC and ViCAP, but so far, nothing earth-shattering. You looking for something specific?" asked Mel.

"I'm wondering if Tucker Clark has any friends or associates who might have the talent or expertise to work with biological substances. Someone online or maybe someone he went to school with."

"Give me a little bit, and I'll see what I can find. Hang on a minute. George wants you."

George came on the line. "Hey, Buck. I'm going to upload some info on Dr. Simon Lee. Take a look when you get a minute and let me know your thoughts. This guy throws up a lot of red flags when you look beyond what's on his resume. I'm running him through some of my old contacts in the intelligence field. Just starting on Dr. Brian Cole. I'll send you what I can."

"Thanks, George."

Buck disconnected the call as Bax walked up. "That was the Denver police ballistics lab. The bullets from Melvin Gross's Glock are not a match for the bullets the medical examiner took out of Dan Pearson."

"We need to talk to Melvin Gross. Can you . . ."

"Already did," said Bax. "He's out of surgery and resting comfortably at the hospital. The bullet shattered his clavicle. The doctor says we won't be able to question him until sometime tomorrow. He's under sedation. Sheriff Toomey is resting comfortably. The bullet was through and through and didn't hit anything vital. They expect he'll be released tomorrow."

Buck heard what Bax said but was thinking about something else. He looked around the office to make sure no one was listening. The questioning running around in his head was directed at Commander Walsch.

"The Clark family have been in crime in this county for years, yet they haven't been arrested or even accused of a crime in the last five years. I find it hard to believe they just got out of the crime business. Why is that?"

Commander Walsch looked uncomfortable and didn't answer right away. He collected his thoughts.

"We've gone after them several times for various crimes that have happened in the county. The problem is that we can't get anyone to testify against them," said Commander Walsch. "The last time we arrested one of the Clarks was for selling drugs. Somehow, they identified our snitch. Two weeks later, there was a fire, and his wife and young son died. Since then, things have tightened up even more. I know how this looks, but we are doing our job."

Buck looked at Bax. She had seen that look before. It was a look that told her they were going after the Clarks with everything they had, and nothing would get in their way.

They all looked up as the entrance door opened, and Paul walked in, followed by Deputy McDonald. He did not look happy.

"Well, we tore the cabin and the various sheds apart and didn't find anything to indicate that Gross was the one who killed Dan Pearson."

"That's okay," said Buck. "Bax just got a call from the ballistics lab. The Glock we took from the cabin was not the murder weapon. So, we're back to square one on who shot Pearson. Did you find anything regarding the treasure?"

"Nah. We went through his computer and phone, and there's nothing to indicate that Dan Pearson stole any location information from him. From what we could find, he doesn't like Pearson and hates that he's searching for the same thing Gross is, but otherwise, he's just disgruntled. I doubt he would ever act on his threats."

"Then what the hell was he doing on the mountain?" asked Bax. "We have pictures of him from the trail cams carrying a pistol."

"We'll have to ask him tomorrow once the sedatives wear off. Bax, why don't you coordinate some time with the doctor and head over there tomorrow and interview him? Then arrest him for shooting the sheriff and being a public nuisance."

"Anything else, Paul?" asked Buck.

"He has a healthy online business selling genuine Native American jewelry and arrowheads. Of course, it's all stuff he makes in his shop behind the cabin, but he sells it as ancient artifacts. I had George shut the site down."

Buck looked at his watch. "Okay, folks. We've been going hard all day, and I don't know about you, but I missed lunch. Let's grab some dinner and figure out the next steps. Why don't you guys head over and grab a table? I have a call I need to make."

They gathered up their gear just as Buck's phone chimed. He didn't recognize the number.

"Taylor," he said.

"Hi, Agent Taylor, this is Dr. Meredith Austin from the Denver Medical Examiner's Office."

"Hi, Doctor. What can I do for you?"

"I have been trying to reach Sheriff Toomey, but I keep getting his voice mail. I wanted to give him the results of the autopsies on William Clark and Marcus Wells."

"Sorry, Doctor. Sheriff Toomey needed to take some time off. What can you tell me?"

"Both boys were in excellent health prior to death," said Dr. Austin. "Cause of death was asphyxiation. The causative factor was a toxin that was present in the lungs. This toxin caused paralysis, causing the lungs to stop working. Death would have been quick. I don't think either boy realized what was happening. The CDC doctor who assisted me said the toxin was determined to be botulinum toxin, which entered the boys' lungs as an aerosol. He also indicated that the lab tests show that the toxin became inert sometime after death."

"Thank you, Doctor. That squares with what we have learned about the toxin. Can you tell me when the bodies will be released?"

"My office has contacted the Barker Funeral Home in Fairplay. They are arranging to have the bodies picked up tonight. They will contact the parents to make further arrangements."

"Thanks, Doctor. I know it's been a long day, and we appreciate your efforts. Please get some rest, and thanks again."

| 32 |

Chapter Thirty-Two

Buck dialed another number as the others left the office. The phone rang on the other end, and Buck hung up. He sat down in one of the desk chairs and waited. Within five minutes his phone rang with an unknown number. He clicked the green button.

"Taylor."

"It's been a while," said the gruff voice on the other end. "What can I do for ya?"

Buck hadn't seen Frank DiNardo in almost twenty years, but he had files dating back that far, and DiNardo's name was all over them. He thought back to the first time he'd arrested him.

Frank DiNardo was the "godfather" of the western United States. He had his fingers in everything—drugs, prostitution, gambling and protection—that went on in Colorado and a good chunk of Utah and Wyoming. He was a cousin of Vincent Scapelli, the mafia boss who controlled everything from Kansas City to Reno, a guy who ruled his kingdom with an iron fist.

When Buck first joined CBI, he was assigned to a task force investigating the Scapelli crime family. It was a region-wide federal and local task force whose sole purpose was to break up the family. They never succeeded. Buck never got all the details, but one day they were running an investigation; the next, they were told to clear out their desks and leave all the evidence and documents with the FBI. He wasn't sure what had changed, but he had never heard another word about the investigation. As far as he knew, no one associated with the Scapelli family ever went to jail because of that investigation.

Over the years, he'd encountered Frank DiNardo during several investigations, but there was never enough evidence to make a case stick. Which, frustrating as it was, helped Buck. Frank DiNardo could be as charming as he was ruthless, and for some reason Buck never understood, Frank had taken a liking to him. He was never a confidential informant, but over the years, Frank had reached out to Buck with information about potential crimes that were occurring around Colorado.

Buck had also reached out to Frank when he needed information he couldn't get from another source. They were never friends, more like adversaries with a vested interest. Frank DiNardo knew enough about Buck that he understood that if Buck ever found enough evidence, he would arrest him in an instant. Still, Frank also knew it was good business to pass along information to Buck that might get one of his rivals arrested.

Buck would have liked nothing better than to put Frank DiNardo in jail and throw away the key, and he always vowed he would. As far as Buck was concerned, this guy was as dirty and ruthless as they come, but he was also careful.

"What can you tell me about the Clark family in Park County?"

There was a long silence on the other end as Frank DiNardo gathered his thoughts. "The whole family is nuts. They are single-handedly responsible for almost all the crime that happens in the central mountains. If they disappeared tomorrow, the world would be better off."

"What's their primary business?" asked Buck.

"They're into everything: drugs, guns, prostitution; you name it. They've been untouchable for years because they are not afraid to intimidate or make witnesses disappear."

Buck sensed something underlying in Frank's answers. "What are you not telling me?"

Frank hesitated again. "Have you ever heard of baby farming?"

"I'm familiar with the term," said Buck.

"Good. Edmund Clark got into baby farming a few years back when he branched out of human trafficking. He is the way station for human trafficking rings from all over the world. Traffickers bring in victims from the Philippines, Vietnam and South America, among other locations. They ship them to Colorado, and the Clarks take care of them until arrangements can be made to ship them elsewhere in the country. The Clarks now, almost exclusively, take pregnant women who are shipped out within days of their arrival. Once the babies are born, they are taken from their mothers and shipped elsewhere. What happens to the mothers? I can't say. I've heard they are either impregnated again and again until they are all used up or they disappear. These people are the lowest of the low, and the thought of what they are involved in makes me sick."

"You sound pretty passionate about this."

"Damn straight," said Frank DiNardo. "You may not like some of the things I may or may not have been accused of over the years, but bottom-feeders like the Clarks should be taken out in a field and shot, and their bodies left for the buzzards. Kids and mothers are sacred."

"Do the Clarks run this thing, or is someone else pulling the strings?"

"I've heard that some ex-doctor, a real scum sucker, runs the program. And before you ask, I don't have a name for him. That's your job."

"Thanks, this has been helpful."

"Hey. If you decide to go after these people, give me a call. I'll have twenty guys there in a heartbeat."

The line went dead, and Buck looked at the phone. He'd known Frank a long time, and this was the first time Buck had heard him sound like he could take out the Clarks single-handedly. Buck was surprised. Instead of the hardened criminal, tonight, the Italian family man showed up.

Buck grabbed his backpack and left through the front entrance. The wind had let up, and the sun was a few minutes from setting. Buck stopped in the parking lot to look at the alpine glow, the pink and orange colors on the face of the eastern mountains. He loved this state and most of the people in it. But after talking to Frank DiNardo, Buck was now mad.

He wasn't Italian, but family was more important to him than anything in this world, and he made a vow to the spirits all around him that he was going to put the Clarks out of business. He slid into his Jeep and headed for the Azteca Mexican Café. He had a feeling this was going to be a long night. He pulled out of the parking lot, heading for what, he had no idea, but the bug in his brain told him the end was close.

| 33 |

Chapter Thirty-Three

The Clark farm was buzzing with activity. Word had come from Dr. Sparks that he would be there in a couple of hours and that he intended to move all the women tonight. He didn't like the idea that state cops were looking at the family. He also didn't like that one of the family was now in jail, and another was missing. Too many things had gone south to take any chances.

Edmund and James were concerned. They wanted to get the women moved as soon as possible, but the speed with which Dr. Sparks had set everything up made them nervous, and James wondered if they would live to see morning. Edmund called the family together, and they all gathered in James Clark's cavernous living room.

"We need to get all the women ready to travel tonight," Edmund said to the gathered family members.

Claire leaned forward. "We've got fifty women here and

one going into labor. We've never moved that many before. Are you sure about this?"

Edmund looked at each family member. "Right now, I'm not sure of anything. We were told to get the women ready to travel, and that's what we're going to do."

He looked at Tom. "Tom, we're short Lizzy and Tucker. Call some of our friends, and let's get a few more bodies here."

"Are you expecting trouble, Dad?"

"I don't know what to expect. Sparks has never moved this fast, and I don't like that he's coming himself to make sure everything goes well. He was not happy when Dad talked to him," said Edmund.

James Clark stood up and paced in front of the group. "We've never let these folks down, and I don't intend to start tonight. But, just in case things go south, I want everyone armed until the transfers are over. We get paid good money to make sure things go smoothly, and that's what I expect tonight."

James and Edmund walked out of the room and made their way to the kitchen. James poured himself a cup of coffee and held up the pot. Edmund shook his head.

"Anything new on Halverson?" asked James. He looked at his watch. "We've got less than twelve hours to deliver the shares, or we are in deep shit. I've talked to our partners, and they are unhappy."

"When I spoke to Lizzy at the jail, she told me that Mrs. Halverson played dumb like she had no idea what Lizzy was talking about."

"You think Halverson would have kept it from her? We know we're not the only ones chasing shares and that

Halverson had turned down some serious money to sell his. We had a plan, and it all went to shit."

"What's the latest on Billy's body?" asked James.

"The funeral parlor called Claire. They are picking up the body tonight. We can go in tomorrow morning and make the final arrangements. This sucks. If I find out who did this, I'll kill them myself." He wiped some tears from his eyes and turned away from his father.

James walked over to him and wrapped his arms around him. "You won't be alone if you do find out. I'll be right there with you."

Edmund stepped away and looked at James. "Something's been bothering me."

James sat at the long kitchen table and pointed to the chair beside him. "What's going on?"

"The lawyer called me. He spoke with Lizzy before they put her in jail. The state cops told her they were going to charge her with terrorism. They told her she could get a life sentence."

James sat back in his chair and took a sip of coffee.

"I thought they arrested her for hitting Mrs. Halverson. Where the hell did this come from?"

"According to the lawyer, they think this is connected to the dead cattle. It seems they think the cattle were killed to pressure Halverson into signing the papers, and then Lizzy assaults the old lady to get them signed. It turns out the cattle were killed with Botox or some such shit. They're calling it a terrorist attack, and they want to lock up my little girl for the rest of her life."

James walked to the sink, opened the upper cabinet and

took down a bottle of bourbon. He took two glasses down, filled them halfway and brought them to the table, placing one in front of Edmund.

"Botulinum toxin, and they think it was a terrorist attack," said a voice from the doorway.

They turned to see Edith Clark standing there, tears in her eyes.

"It's all over the internet. The governor just put out a press release. He said that botulinum toxin is naturally occurring and can be found all over the area. He said the situation is under control, and there is no threat to the public."

She slid her laptop onto the table, and James read what was on the screen. "There's nothing in his statement that says anything about terrorism," said James.

"Of course. It wasn't terrorism. It came from that lab in the mountains." She stopped talking, and her body shook.

"Oh my god," she said. "Did Tucker have something to do with this?"

She glared at Edmund. "You put so much pressure on him to get Halverson to sign the shares. Did you push him to do something drastic?" Tears now flowed down her face. "My god, Tucker killed his own son because you wouldn't let up. You son of a bitch! You murdered my grandson!"

Edmund jumped up and wrapped his arms around her, but she pushed away and hit him with a tight fist across the cheek. "You stay away from me, you bastard. I'll kill you if you come near me."

She grabbed her laptop off the table and ran out the back door. Edmund started to go after her, but James called him back. "Let her go and cool off." He looked into Edmund's eyes. "Could she be right?"

Edmund sat back down and finished the glass of bourbon. "I don't know what to think, Dad. I started to wonder the same thing myself earlier today, but where would he get the stuff? You can't just buy it off the internet."

James leaned forward. "Let's keep this from the rest of the family. We've got enough to worry about right now. For now, this stays quiet until after the women are moved."

Edmund nodded, and James slapped him on the shoulder. "Good, I'll talk to Edith. You get everyone armed up and get those women ready to travel."

Edmund Clark stood up, wiped his eyes and left the kitchen. James watched him leave and then pulled out his phone. He dialed a number and waited.

"Yes, sir," said the voice on the other end of the phone.

"Get the jet ready to fly."

"Yes, sir. Where are you headed?"

"Bogotá," said James.

He hung up and went to find Connie. It was time to pack.

Chapter Thirty-Four

Buck pulled out the chair at the end of the corner table and sat down. Carlos set a cold glass of Coke in front of him and told him it was good to see him. He then headed to the front door to seat some more guests. As with the night before, no one had menus, knowing that Maria would take good care of them.

Buck leaned forward, lowered his voice and looked at Paul. "You have your gear?" he asked.

Paul nodded. "What do you need?"

Buck pointed to Bax's laptop, and she slid it over to him. He opened Google Maps and entered the address for the Clark ranch. They all got closer.

Buck pointed to the ranch house area and the multiple homes on the property. Next, he pointed to a series of what looked like metal containers at one end of the area near a large barn.

"We need to get eyes on this area," said Buck.

Paul slid the laptop over to get a better look and zoomed out. He studied the map for a minute and then leaned in to Commander Walsch. "You familiar with this area?"

Walsch looked at the map. "Yeah. There's a forest service road that leads to a big field. Good hunting up that way."

"Good," said Paul. He pointed to a spot on the satellite view. "How long to get from this point on the road to here?"

Walsch thought about it for a minute. "Probably twenty minutes." He looked at Buck. "What's going on?" asked Walsch.

"The Clarks are involved in baby farming, and we're going to shut them down."

"Baby farming. Are you sure?" asked Bax.

"Yeah. I wish I weren't, but there's no doubt," said Buck.

Bax smiled at Buck. She knew where Buck had gotten his information, and she knew the information was good.

Commander Walsch leaned back in his chair. "How is that possible? We don't harass them, but how could they do that right under our noses and we not know about it? Are you sure your information is good?"

"There's no doubt about the information. My source has never been wrong," said Buck.

"So, what's the plan?" asked Bax.

"Paul is going to get as close as possible and get eyes on the compound. We need photos of everyone on the ranch, so we know who we are dealing with. We also need video of everything going on." He looked at Commander Walsch. "Can you get Paul to the spot on the road?"

"Sure. Do you want me to go with him?"

"No. Paul can move faster on his own," said Buck. "Besides, I need you to coordinate things down here."

He looked at Paul. "We need to make sure the women are there, or this is all for naught."

"No worries, Buck," said Paul.

Maria stepped up to the table and started setting plates of burritos down. The smell was overwhelming. She noticed the map on the laptop screen and called Carlos over. She leaned in to the table. "Carlos knows this area very well," she whispered.

Carlos walked up to the table, and Maria said something to him in Spanish that Buck didn't catch. He looked at the map and then at Buck. "It is true, Señor Buck. I know this area very well. Maria says you need to get close to these containers. I can show you a faster way than coming in from up here. No one will know you are there." He pointed to the road Paul had pointed out.

Buck and the others looked shocked. "How did she know?" Buck asked.

Carlos laughed. "My Maria. She knows what I am going to do before I even think about doing it. Sometimes it is no fun, but sometimes, *muy bueno*." Everyone laughed. "I will help you find the way to the trailers."

"Carlos," said Buck. "I can't ask you to do this. It could be dangerous."

Carlos looked serious. "If you are going to help our little town, how can I not help."

Buck looked at Paul and then at Commander Walsch. No

one objected. "Okay, Commander, looks like you have two passengers. Let's eat up and get moving."

They were just finishing up dinner when Walsch's phone rang. He answered, listened for a minute, disconnected the call and looked at Buck. "That was dispatch. There's a guy at the office who wants to talk to you. Wouldn't tell the deputy what it was about."

Buck stood. "Bax, why don't you come with me? Paul, gear up and stay in constant contact. Good luck."

Buck was concerned about Carlos going with Paul, but he needed the local knowledge. He knew he didn't need to tell Paul to take care of Carlos. He knew Paul would protect Carlos with his life. Everyone dropped some money on the table, and they stood and headed for the door.

Bax slid into her Jeep and followed Buck to the sheriff's office. They parked next to a silver Mercedes and walked through the public entrance. An older man with a full head of silver hair and a silver mustache stood up as they entered. He was as tall as Buck and wore jeans and a flannel shirt. He held a leather briefcase. The deputy nodded towards the man.

Buck held out his hand. "Buck Taylor, CBI." He pointed to Bax. "Ashley Baxter, CBI, and you are?"

They shook hands, and the man handed Buck a business card. "Martin Comstock, attorney," he said.

Buck looked at the card. He looked up. "Water law?" asked Buck.

"Is there someplace quiet we can talk?" asked Martin Comstock.

Buck nodded to the deputy, who unlatched the door to the office area. He held open the door, and Bax, followed by Martin Comstock, walked through. Buck stepped around them and led the way to the small conference room next to the sheriff's private office. Buck took a seat and pointed to the other chairs. Bax and Martin Comstock sat down. Comstock set his briefcase on the floor next to the chair.

Buck set the business card on the table. "How can we help you, Mr. Comstock?"

"Hopefully, I can help you, Agent Taylor. As you saw on my card, my practice involves water law. As you probably know, water law in Colorado is very complicated, and I am not going to attempt to make you understand it. I've been practicing for thirty years, and there are still facets of the laws that confuse the crap out of me, to be perfectly blunt.

"Agent Taylor, I've just come from Denver General Hospital, where I spoke with Mrs. Irene Halverson. Irene and Gunther Halverson have been clients and friends for as long as I can remember. After speaking with Irene, I knew I needed to contact you as soon as possible. I would have been here sooner, but I only heard about what happened to Gunther a couple of hours ago."

He picked up his briefcase, opened it and pulled out a manila folder. He closed the briefcase and placed it back on the floor.

He opened the folder and slid a document over to Buck. He gave Buck a minute to review the document, and then Buck slid it over to Bax. Bax read it and let out a low whistle.

"Yes. Agent Baxter. The number you are looking at is real," said Martin Comstock. "Gunther's ancestors were the first white people to settle in the South Park valley. They struggled against the cold, the wind and the Native Americans who inhabited the valley. One of the things Soren Halverson did once civilization arrived was to lay claim to all the land that surrounded the headwaters of the North and South Platte Rivers and record the claims at the state capital for posterity. Over the years, the family sold off much of the land, but they always kept the water rights, allowing other settlers to use those rights but never own them. Basically, the family shared those rights at no cost to the settlers.

"As you can imagine, over the years, the ownership information became muddied, but the rights to the water were recorded forever. This brings us to today. A consortium of developers is planning to build a massive development between Castle Rock and Monument. We are talking housing for a hundred thousand people and millions of square feet of office and retail space. This project is more extensive than anything ever developed in Colorado. The project is reportedly worth several billion dollars and will take twenty years to build out. The thing standing in their way is water. For the most part, they have none."

He stopped for a minute and looked at Buck and Bax. Since they didn't ask any questions, he continued.

"This project will require massive quantities of water. Now, the developers could piecemeal the project and attempt to buy water shares on the open market or even through some private sales, but it would take them years to accumulate what they need before they could get permission to build, and they would never be able to buy enough. Since they have already invested millions in the planning and development process, this is unacceptable to them. This is where the Halversons come in. As you can see from that document, the

Halversons could supply all the water rights needed for this development out of what they own. It would take every bit, but they could do it. The problem is the Halversons are not interested in selling their water rights, for if they did, it would affect almost everyone in the valley. If you look around the valley, everyone you see is sharing the Halversons' water.

"That document you just looked at is the latest offer my clients have received for the rights. Gunther Halverson refused this offer on Saturday, much to the dismay of the developer's attorneys. At this point, you are wondering how this affects you and what happened over the weekend that brought you all here. For the past couple of weeks, the Halversons have been under pressure to sell the rights to a local family. Unfortunately, it seems that some of the developers that are part of this group are willing to go to any length to get those rights, including threatening the Halversons, or worse."

"Let me guess," said Buck. "That family would be the Clark family."

"Correct, Agent Taylor. When the threats began, I asked one of our investigators to look into it. Our understanding is that a large sum of money was given to James Clark and his son Edmund to procure those rights and for significantly less than the developers were willing to pay. Tucker Clark was the one who first approached the Halversons. But, you see, there was a catch. The county commissioners gave the developers until this coming Thursday to secure the rights, or they would kill the deal. Several of the commissioners and their constituents were not happy with the deal anyway, but a lot of money was at stake for everyone involved, so this was their way out. They, of course, had no idea the amount of water Gunther Halverson and his wife owned."

"So?" asked Bax. "You think the attack on the Halversons' cattle herd was a last-ditch effort to force them to sell the water rights?"

"Precisely," said Martin Comstock. "Mrs. Halverson believes that the Clarks thought that if they killed the herd, it would force them to face bankruptcy, and that would make them sell the rights. They didn't understand the circumstances and misjudged the Halversons' cash situation. Believe me when I tell you Gunther Halverson raises cattle because he enjoys it. He will never be able to spend all the money he has in a dozen lifetimes."

Bax looked surprised. "I've been to their ranch. Their house is lucky to be standing. They look like they're on their last dime."

"They never wanted their neighbors in the valley to understand their situation or make people feel beholden for using the water, which has never been revealed to anyone. The ranch is just to keep up appearances. Just between us. The Halversons own a cattle ranch in Costa Rica that is twice the size of their property here."

"Can you protect the Halversons and their family until we can wrap this up?" asked Buck.

"Arrangements have already been made to keep them secure," said Martin Comstock.

He returned the document to the folder, picked up his briefcase, inserted the file and stood. "I hope this helps your investigation. If I read between the lines of the governor's statement tonight, I think my client is lucky to be alive."

They shook hands, and Bax escorted Martin Comstock to the front entry. She stepped back into the conference room. Buck looked at her. "I think we just found the missing piece to the puzzle."

"But," said Bax, "Billy Clark was killed during the attack on the cattle. Do you think they would kill their own family? That's sick."

"I think that was an accident. We need to find Tucker Clark."

| **35** |

Chapter Thirty-Five

Paul opened the back of his Jeep and slid on his camo coveralls and camo jacket. He put a camo boonie cap on his head. Then, unlocking the secure gun safe, he pulled out a black rifle bag and carried it to Commander Walsch's unmarked SUV. He loaded it in the back. Carlos stepped out of the back door to the restaurant, dressed the same way as Paul, except he had a large revolver in a holster that crossed his chest.

Paul walked back to his Jeep, grabbed his backpack that contained his camera gear and they climbed into the SUV. Walsch pulled out of the parking lot, and Carlos gave him directions on where to go. They followed Highway 9 north until Carlos pointed to a small dirt road that headed east. Walsch took the turn and followed the dirt road for several miles before Carlos pointed to an even smaller dirt road. They followed that road for about ten minutes when Carlos told Walsch to stop.

"From here, we go on foot," he said.

They slid out of the SUV, grabbed their gear from the back and loaded up. Paul opened the rifle case, assembled the long rifle, attached the scope and slung the rifle over his shoulder. He checked the battery on his sat phone, and they shook hands with Walsch and headed into the woods. Walsch headed back to town.

The route Carlos had taken was rugged and looked barely used. They stayed tight to the trees, and after fifteen minutes, Carlos raised his fist and indicated to stop. Paul stopped and kneeled next to Carlos. Carlos pointed to a small game trail.

"Once we go through here, we are on Clark property. We need to be very quiet. About half a mile, and we will come to a rock outcrop. This will give us a good view of the ranch."

Paul nodded, and Carlos headed out, ducking under some low branches that Paul had difficulty navigating. By the time they reached the rock outcrop, it was almost full dark. Paul looked down and had a perfect view of the compound. He set his rifle against the rocks and pulled a camera out of his back-pack. He connected a long lens to the camera and sighted in on the barn. He panned around the area and grew concerned. There were a lot of people moving about, and they were all armed. Paul snapped pictures of the people that automatically loaded to a cloud file that Buck had access to.

He and Carlos ducked behind the rocks as headlights from several SUVs approached the compound. They stopped, and several more armed men and women exited the SUVs, followed by a tall, thin, gray-haired man who wore a suit jacket and jeans. He gave orders to the people who had arrived with him and shook hands with James and Edmund, and they headed for the barn. Paul got a good front-facing picture of the newcomer and the others who came with him. He sent a secure text to Buck.

Two women who had just arrived opened one of the trailers and stepped inside. The door was open wide enough that Paul could see several women inside. The two women came out, leading a very pregnant Asian woman between them. The Asian woman looked to be in a great deal of pain. Paul selected video mode and filmed the action below. The door to the trailer was closed and latched.

Paul watched as they led the Asian woman into the barn and disappeared inside. Two men with AR-style rifles took positions on either side of the door.

Paul continued to take pictures of the people below and got some good video of an older woman and a younger woman, not dressed like the newcomers in tactical gear and T-shirts, carrying baskets of food into the trailers. The two women were about to enter the third trailer when they stopped and looked towards the barn. Carlos tapped Paul on the shoulder, touched his ear and pointed towards the barn. Paul heard it too. The sound of a baby crying. He focused his camera on the barn and waited.

A few minutes later, the gray-haired newcomer came out of the barn wiping his hands on a towel. He handed the towel to one of the men by the door to the barn and rolled down his sleeves. He spoke to James and Edmund Clark, who nodded, and they headed for the largest house on the compound.

Paul signaled for Carlos to follow and, crouching, worked his way back from the rocks and into the trees. Once clear of the edge of the trees, he pulled out the sat phone and called Buck.

"Hey, Paul. You guys good?" asked Buck.

"Yeah. The pictures are on the cloud. Take a look at the gray-haired guy coming out of the barn. I think he's a doctor. He also seems to be in charge, giving a lot of orders to everyone around. There's a lot of activity going on. A bunch of people with guns. And I think this guy I mentioned just delivered a baby."

"What about the other women, Paul?"

"We spotted some when they opened the trailer to get the woman we think was in labor. Saw whom we believe to be Edith and Claire Clark carrying baskets of food into the trailers. I get the feeling they are getting ready to move these women."

"Great work, Paul. Is Carlos okay?" asked Buck.

Carlos leaned in. "I am good, Señor Buck. We did good, no?"

"You did good, Carlos. Paul, stay low, but stay on-site and let me know if anything changes."

Paul disconnected, and they worked their way back to the rocks, where they settled in for a long night.

| **36** |

Chapter Thirty-Six

Dr. Eugene Sparks finished wiping down the baby and handed her to one of the women who had brought in the pregnant Asian woman. She placed the baby in a warm incubator and covered her with a blanket. Dr. Sparks came over, did a quick check of the infant and pronounced her in good condition.

He returned to the delivery table and looked down at the mother. The cut on her abdomen from the C-section was still open, and blood pooled under her back. She asked the doctor something in a language that he did not appear to understand, and he just nodded his head.

He lifted a syringe off the table next to the woman and filled it from a small vial he pulled from the medical cabinet next to the delivery table. The woman started to shake, and Dr. Sparks leaned next to her and made soft shushing sounds. He inserted the needle into her arm and pressed the plunger. The woman's eyelids closed, and her breathing slowed. He held his position next to her until her breathing stopped. He pulled out the needle, picked up a stethoscope and checked her heart and lungs. He set the stethoscope down on the table and stepped away.

He walked over, washed his hands in the sink, picked up a clean towel and dried them. He left the barn and handed the towel to one of the two men standing guard. He walked over to James and Edmund.

"We've got a healthy baby girl. Should bring a nice price. Lungs sounded good and healthy."

"What about the mother?" asked Edmund.

"She was hemorrhaging too badly, and I couldn't stop the bleeding. She died on the table. You got anything to drink around here?"

They headed towards James's house and settled in the living room. The doctor looked around. "James, I think I pay you too much. Your home is beautiful. Almost better than mine, but not quite." He laughed and accepted the drink from James. They toasted to their success.

"I couldn't help but notice," said the doctor, "that every one of your people is armed. Are you expecting trouble?"

James sat in the armchair and sipped his drink. "We can never be too careful with CBI crawling all over the county."

"Of course," said the doctor. "Any word on the whereabouts of Tucker? I understand he's been missing since yesterday."

"Not yet. Hopefully, he's just drunk on someone's couch or, heaven forbid, shacked up with some woman he met in a bar. He'll show up sooner or later."

James did not feel the need to share that Lizzy had been

arrested. He figured what the doctor didn't know wouldn't hurt him.

"So?" asked Edmund. "What's the plan for tonight? This was all very sudden."

The doctor set his glass down on the side table. "I was able to secure six vans and drivers." He looked at his watch. "I expect the first to arrive in a couple of hours. I'd like to have all the women on the road before first light."

He got a serious look on his face. "My clients are not happy about this. They are concerned that maybe we are losing our touch, but I've assured them that we have the best setup to handle their needs and that your missing son and your daughter's arrest are only minor setbacks. Ah, I can see by the look on your faces that you did not think I was aware of Lizzy's arrest."

Edmund struggled for words until James stepped in. "We knew you would hear about that, but since it is not related to our work, we didn't want to bother you with it. We have it all under control."

"I'm glad to hear that, James. You realize, though, that because of these minor glitches, we will have to make other arrangements to house the women. Just for a short time, until things cool off a bit. As a sign of goodwill, I will ensure you are compensated through that whole period."

"That's very generous, Eugene," said James Clark. "You know you'll never find a better team than mine to meet your needs, and I assure you we will get everything worked out as quickly as possible."

They all picked up their glasses, clinked them and drank. Dr. Sparks stood up.

"I need to check on my people to make sure they are getting everything ready for the arrival of the vans. Please excuse me, gentlemen."

Sparks left the house, and James looked at Edmund. "Well?"

"I think we're screwed. Did you see how many people he brought with him? It's like a fucking army."

"Okay. Spread the word to all our people to be on high alert," said James.

He stood up and walked out of the room, leaving Edmund to wonder what was going to happen next.

Chapter Thirty-Seven

Buck opened his laptop and pulled up the pictures on the cloud. He and Bax were looking through them when Commander Walsch walked into the conference room. He turned the laptop so Walsch could see the pictures and flipped to the picture of the gray-haired man.

"You know this guy?" Buck asked. "Any possibility he's local?"

Walsch studied the picture. "Nope. Doesn't look like anyone I know. Who is he?"

"We're not sure, but we think he's a doctor, and he seems to be giving a lot of orders. Paul said he just delivered a baby."

Walsch looked at the video and the rest of the still pictures. "There are a lot of guns on the Clark ranch right now."

"Yeah. How many SWAT officers do you have?" asked Buck.

Walsch thought for a minute. "If I call in mutual aid, I can have six or eight here in a couple of hours."

"Call them in. No lights or sirens."

Buck pulled out his phone and dialed a number.

"Evening, Deputy Taylor. How can I help you?" asked Harriet.

"Hi. I'm going to send you a picture of a suspected human trafficker. I'd like to see if you can identify him."

"Okay," said Harriet. "I'm ready to receive."

Buck opened the gallery on his phone, pulled the picture of the gray-haired man out of the cloud and hit send.

"Thank you, Deputy. I will call you back once we have an identity."

Buck disconnected the call. Bax looked up from her laptop. "Did you get the information on the Clarks from your Italian godfather?"

Buck laughed. "Yeah. He is not a big fan and even offered to send some of his friends to help us."

Now it was Bax who laughed. "Wow, he must really not like the Clarks. Should we call Hank Clancy and let him know what's going on? He may still have agents working with the CDC up on the mountain."

"Let's wait and see what Harriet says."

Commander Walsch returned after letting dispatch know to call in the SWAT officers.

"Do you know where Tucker Clark hangs out?" Buck asked him.

"Yeah. Where everyone else hangs out. The Longhorn Lounge. Why?"

"We need to find him and figure out his part in all this," said Buck.

Buck filled the commander in on the conversation he

and Bax had with the lawyer, Martin Comstock. Walsch just stood there and listened. When Buck finished, Walsch sat down and rubbed his temples.

"I can't believe it. Everyone who knows Gunther and Irene thinks they are on their last legs, and here they've been making sure everyone in the valley has water. Shit. So, you think somehow Tucker got involved with someone who could provide the toxin and used it to try to bankrupt them? That's incredible."

He stopped and looked from Buck to Bax. "If that's true, then he also killed his own son. No wonder he disappeared. If his wife doesn't kill him, his father or grandfather will. They loved that kid."

"You wait here for the SWAT guys," said Buck. "Bax and I will head over to the Longhorn and see what folks there have to say."

Buck and Bax grabbed their backpacks and headed for the parking lot. They slid into Buck's Jeep for the half-mile drive to the lounge. The parking lot was full, and they found a space in the grass next door to the parking lot. They slid out of the Jeep and headed for the door. Loud music filled their ears as they stepped into the bar.

They walked up to the bar, and Bax noticed that several of the regulars who were there when Lizzy Clark was arrested pulled down their hats or turned their chairs to face the other way. Bax smiled. It seemed she'd made quite an impression on the locals.

They walked up to the bar, and Buck called over the bartender. "Hi. What'll you have?" she asked.

Buck held up his badge. "Taylor and Baxter, CBI."

She held out her hand. "Lacy Marks. How can I help you?"

"We're wondering if you've seen Tucker Clark?" asked Bax.

Lacy Marks looked from side to side and leaned into the bar. "He hasn't been in since Friday night, which is unusual. You the guys busted Lizzy?"

Bax nodded, and the bartender smiled. "Heard you took her down in one move. Good for you," said Lacy Marks.

"Is it unusual for him not to come in for a couple of days?" asked Buck.

"Yeah." Lacy wiped down the bar top in front of them and dropped the rag behind the counter. "Tucker does most of his business in here."

"Do you remember who he was in here with on Friday?" asked Buck.

"Yeah, his buddy, Brian. Those two are always scheming something."

"This Brian got a last name?" asked Buck.

"Yep. Cole. He's some kind of doctor. He was a whiz kid in high school. I graduated with both of them. They were inseparable."

Buck looked at Bax. She could see his brain working, and she knew exactly what he was thinking. Someone down the end of the bar called Lacy, and she told him to hold on a minute. "Anything else? This place is jumping, and the natives are getting restless," she said.

"One more thing," said Buck. "Any idea what they were talking about?"

"Not sure," she said. "Tucker was in here all depressed, and then Brian came in, they talked for a while, then they left, and Tucker was smiling. I heard him say something about his dad bustin' his ass because he didn't get something done. Now I've got to go, okay?"

Buck and Bax walked out of the bar into the parking lot, and Buck pulled out his phone.

"Hey, Buck," said Mel. "What's up?"

"Tucker Clark went to high school with Brian Cole, one of the names from the file I sent George."

"Hold on, we just downloaded the yearbook for the year Brian Cole graduated."

He could hear Mel clicking keys, and then she stopped. "Son of a bitch. You hit that one right on the head."

"Okay. Pull out all the stops and go deep on Brian Cole. I want to know everything about him and see if you can get his address."

"Will do, Buck. Call you back."

Mel disconnected, and Buck clipped his phone to his belt. He looked at Bax and was about to say something when the phone rang again.

"Taylor."

"Deputy Taylor, it's Harriet. I am sending you a file. We've identified the picture you sent as being Dr. Eugene Sparks. He is wanted on federal human trafficking charges. I am sending you a copy of the arrest warrant, and I also have two teams on standby."

"Why two teams?" asked Buck.

"After we identified him, I went into your cloud file. The other pictures are of his entourage, and there are at least a half dozen outstanding federal warrants for members of his group. He is a real whacko, and we've been looking for him for a long time."

Buck didn't hesitate. "Roll the teams. I'll call you with a meetup location."

"Will do," said Harriet, and the call disconnected.

Bax started to say something, and Buck held up a finger. He pulled up a number from his contact list and dialed. The phone was answered on the second ring.

"Buck Taylor, it's been a while. How are you, my son?"

Buck always laughed when Sister Agnes called him "son" since she was twenty years his junior. Sister Agnes was the mother superior of a small convent just off Highway 285 and just before the north fork of the South Platte River branched off and headed north. It was one of Buck's favorite places to fish. And even though Buck was not religious, the sisters appreciated his visits.

"I'm fine, sister," said Buck. "I have a favor to ask."

"Are you looking to come by and do a little fishing?" she asked.

"I wish I had time, sister. This is a professional favor."

"I see," she said. "How can I help?"

"I need to meet some people, and we need to keep it quiet. So, I was wondering if you could open the gate to the north parking area and give us permission to stage there?"

"Of course. I know I shouldn't ask, but you know how we love a little gossip around here. Will you be going after some bad people?"

"Yes, ma'am," said Buck.

"Oh, wonderful. Perhaps the next time you come up, you can regale the sisters with a tale of your derring-do?"

"It would be my pleasure," said Buck.

"Wonderful. I will run over now and unlock the gate. And

Buck. You and your people, be careful. I will say a prayer for your success."

Buck thanked her, and Bax looked at him with a crooked grin. "Holy crap. You really do know everyone in Colorado." They both laughed. It had always been an inside joke at CBI that there wasn't anyone in the state that Buck didn't know, yet it always surprised his associates when it proved to be true.

"Someday, you'll have to tell me how you came to know a nun in the middle of the Colorado mountains."

"Someday," he said.

He dialed another number and gave Harriet the address of the convent. She told him the team was about forty minutes out.

The little bug in his brain was jumping up and down, and he felt like they were getting a handle on the events of the past few days.

They jumped into Buck's Jeep and headed east on Highway 285 to a small convent in the mountains.

| **38** |

Chapter Thirty-Eight

Halfway up Kenosha Pass on Highway 285, Buck's phone rang. He looked at the number and hit the green button.

"Yes, sir," said Buck.

"Buck, what's going on?" asked Director Jackson. "I'm hearing that some things are falling into place."

"Yes, sir. We identified the doctor running the baby farming operation, and he is on-site now. I have a copy of a federal warrant on my phone."

"Buck. What baby farming ring?"

"Sorry, sir. Things have been moving pretty fast up here. We discovered that besides drugs, guns, human trafficking and just being a general criminal nuisance, the Clark family is also involved in baby farming. They get paid to take the pregnant women who are smuggled into the country, keep them safe and healthy until they are ready to be delivered to their final destination and then ship them out. Paul is sitting on the ranch right now, and he said it looks like they are getting ready to move the women tonight."

"And you identified this doctor as being connected to this operation?" asked Director Jackson.

"Yes, sir. Dr. Eugene Sparks. I haven't had a chance to look at his file, but the Marshals Service identified him from pictures Paul took of him and the people he brought with him, several of whom have outstanding federal warrants."

"Any connection to the dead cattle and the botulinum toxin?" asked the director.

"Yes, sir, but it's kind of convoluted," said Buck. "The cases are related because some of the same players are involved, but one is not part of the other."

"How does that work?" asked the director.

"The Clark family runs the baby farming operation out of their ranch here in Park County. The guy running the whole operation is this Dr. Eugene Sparks. The Feds have been onto him for a while, but they haven't been able to touch him. He's very secretive and surrounded by a small army. So that's one piece of the puzzle. The second piece is kind of wild. It seems the Clarks were also trying to force a local rancher to sell them thousands of shares of water rights, so they could sell them to a group of developers who want to build this huge development between Castle Rock and Colorado Springs. The lawyer we spoke to represents the owners of those shares and says this could be worth upwards of a hundred million dollars."

"Canyon Creek," said the director. "We've been investigating several of the developers involved in this plan. We received several complaints about strong-arm tactics being used to force people to sell their land at rock-bottom prices. Our white-collar crimes division is putting the case together, and they are supposed to present it to a state grand jury in two weeks. Do you think this doctor is the one who modified the toxin?"

"No, sir," said Bax. "I'm looking at his file right now. He lost his medical license seven years ago after too many malpractice complaints. He was just a medical doctor, and other than being a general scumbag, it doesn't look like he would have the expertise to pull this off."

"Thanks, Bax," said the director. "So, besides the family's regular crime operations, they had also branched out into securing water shares for questionable developers?"

"Yes, sir," said Buck. "With the potential of making millions of dollars for their efforts."

"Fuck, Buck. How do you always find these convoluted cases? Just once, I'd like you to tell me you have a simple case that's easy to solve." The director laughed, as did Buck and Bax.

"Someday, sir," said Buck. "By the way, please thank the governor for the press release. It helped to calm some people down."

"No problem, Buck, but I will tell you that the governor is concerned that there might be a federal government lab in his state that he is unaware of. Is this going to come back and bite him or me in the ass?"

"I'm not sure I can answer that, sir," said Buck, "and if I do answer it, then you might be forced to have to tell the governor, and you know how he gets when it comes to the federal government."

Colorado Governor Richard J. Kennedy was a multimillionaire businessman and a seasoned politician, having spent twenty years in the state legislature before running for governor. Having just been reelected to his second term by another landslide victory, the governor was riding a huge wave of popularity, and one of the things that made him popular with the citizens of Colorado was his take-no-prisoners attitude when it came to dealing with the people in Washington.

The governor had little tolerance for stupidity and even less for politicians who spent more time bickering than getting anything done. And he hated it when he found out that the federal government was involved in some activity in his state that he was unaware of.

During his first term in office, he went after the federal government several times after Buck and his team cracked a case and exposed some government program he was unaware of. He didn't trust the federal government, but he trusted Buck without question. Buck and his team had closed several high-profile cases over the last few years that made the governor look good.

Buck never got involved in politics, and because of that and his record, the governor occasionally asked Buck and his team to take on cases that might be sensitive. He knew Buck would always follow a case to wherever the evidence led him, no matter what.

It was because of that respect that had grown between the governor and Buck that Buck felt bad not giving the director the answer he should have, but the director also knew that Buck would never set up either him or the governor to be embarrassed.

"Okay, Buck. Enough said. What's the plan?"

"We are on our way to meet with the US Marshals' door kickers, and we have the sheriff's office pulling together a SWAT team. I would expect we will hit the ranch within the hour."

"What do you need from me?"

"At this time, we are good, sir. I'll call you when it's over."

"All right, Buck. Good luck, and stay safe. I don't want to lose any of you."

Buck looked at Bax, and she smiled. "You think you'll ever tell him?"

"Hopefully not," he said, and they headed into the darkness.

| 39 |

Chapter Thirty-Nine

Buck turned his Jeep onto a small dirt road and passed through the green gate. Bax smiled as they passed the wooden sign at the gated driveway that read: the little convent in the wilderness. She couldn't see the building in the distance except for a small yellow light over what looked like the front porch. There were no other lights to be seen. She wondered how Buck had come to know this place and the sisters within.

They followed the dirt road for a third of a mile and parked in a grass lot surrounded by a split-rail wooden fence. Bax could hear the river flowing on the other side of the fence, although it was too dark to see. Buck parked along the fence where two black SUVs with government plates were parked. Standing next to the vehicles were three people familiar to Buck and Bax and three people they didn't know. All were dressed in black tactical pants and black T-shirts, and all carried a sidearm strapped to their thighs.

Buck killed his lights and pulled up next to the first SUV. He and Bax exited the Jeep and approached the group.

Vicky Dorsett was about five foot seven and had a muscular physique, which was accented by the black T-shirt she wore. She had short black hair and dark eyes.

Ari Schoenberger set down his backpack. He wore a black T-shirt. He was bald and stood a shade over Dorsett. His arms were covered in tattoos, and Buck noticed that the tats appeared to be the story of his military career. Buck was impressed.

Dorsett started to say something, but all eyes fell on the third member of team Able, who stepped around the front of Buck's Jeep and extended his hand. The team got the same reaction wherever they went.

Chicago was six foot eight or nine and weighed three hundred and fifty pounds. He had shoulder-length dark hair and a scraggly beard, and the muscles under his T-shirt had muscles of their own. He was a mountain of a man.

When they had first met, Paul had asked why they called him Chicago. Dorsett, who'd said the same thing several hundred times, explained. "He was born in Chicago into a Russian family. His family had a tradition, and he was named after his two great-grandfathers, who had unpronounceable names. Couple that with the fact that no human can pronounce his last name. It's just easier to call him Chicago."

The last time Buck and Bax had seen this team, they had just rescued a bunch of FBI agents who had walked into an ambush set up by a mad bomber. Buck could still remember Chicago, standing next to them, holding the bomber by the back of the neck with blood dripping down his arm, where the bomber had shot him.

"Hey, Vicky," said Buck. He shook hands with Chicago, Schoenberger, and then Vicky. "How's the arm, Chicago?"

Chicago flexed his muscle. "Never better, Agent Taylor."

He looked at the next group. "Who do we have here?" he asked.

Vicky made the introductions. "Tanya Juarez, Vinny Castiglio, Brad French, meet Buck Taylor and Ashley Baxter." They all shook hands.

Tanya Juarez was five feet four inches of solid muscle. She had long dark hair tied back in a ponytail. Vinny Castiglio was six-foot and weighed one eighty. He had a strong New York accent when he spoke. Brad French looked more like a high school teacher than a deputy US Marshal. He was five foot nine, thin and wiry, wore wire-rimmed glasses and had medium-length blond hair.

"Okay," said Vicky. "We didn't get told a lot, so what have we got?"

Bax pulled her laptop out of her backpack and opened it, pulling up a satellite view of the Clark ranch. She also pulled up the mug shot of Dr. Eugene Sparks.

"This guy is wanted on federal charges of human trafficking. Worse, we discovered just a little while ago that he is running a baby farming operation out of the ranch you see on the screen. That ranch is about twenty miles from here. The people inside, the Clark family, and the people that this doctor brought with him are all heavily armed. There is also an unknown number of pregnant women in several metal containers. We believe the doctor is here to oversee the shipping of the women to their final destinations."

"Is the Clark family part of this baby farming ring?" asked Juarez.

Buck nodded. "Yes. They are involved in multiple criminal enterprises and are to be considered hostile. That includes the women and several teenagers. Our number one priority is to save the pregnant women. Our number two priority is to all go home today. So do not sacrifice number two for number one."

Bax placed her laptop on the hood of the Jeep, and the team gathered around it.

"Not going to be easy in the dark," said Schoenberger. "Not a lot of cover."

"Maybe we should just come through the front door in a blitz attack," said French. "Might be easier."

Vicky looked at Vinny and pointed to the treed areas on each side of the main compound. "Vinny, what about coming in from both sides? We could run two skirmish lines. Come in low and dark." She looked at Buck.

"What's our support like?" she asked.

"The sheriff's office is bringing in six to eight SWAT officers from around the area." He pointed to a rock outcropping. "Paul is up here, somewhere, with a long rifle. He's our overwatch."

Vinny looked closer at the satellite view and zoomed in on several places. He pointed to a spot east of where Paul was situated.

"What if we bring the SWAT guys in from back here, and

we come in from both sides like you were thinking? Might be able to take them by surprise."

"I like it," said Vicky. "Buck, Bax, whataya think?"

Buck and Bax looked at Vicky. "Looks good," said Buck; Bax agreed.

"Okay. Buck, do you want to coordinate with the SWAT team?"

Buck nodded and pulled out his phone, but before he could dial, Bax's phone rang.

"Ashley Baxter."

"Agent Baxter, It's Mark Walsch. We've got eight SWAT officers geared up and ready to go, but that's not why I'm calling. Lizzy Clark sent a request through her lawyer that she wanted to talk to you. I sent Deputy Rivers over to the jail to talk with her. She wants to work a deal, and she's in right now talking to a lawyer from the district attorney's office, but she told Rivers that if you are planning a raid, behind the containers where the pregnant women are, two escape paths lead up into the mountains."

"That's great info, Commander. I'll pass that along to the team. Buck needs to talk to you; please hold on."

She handed her phone to Buck, who asked the commander to open the map of the ranch. He pointed out where they wanted the SWAT team to stage.

"Can you get in there without being seen?" Buck asked.

"The SWAT lead is standing right next to me. He says it shouldn't be a problem. We'll also cover those two escape routes that Lizzy Clark mentioned. Give us twenty minutes to get into position."

Buck explained the rest of the plan, and everyone agreed.

"We're gearing up now," said Buck. "We'll coordinate as we get closer."

Vicky pointed to the top of her radio. Buck nodded.

"Put everyone on channel four, Commander."

Buck disconnected the call and clipped his phone to his belt. Buck and Bax grabbed their ballistics vests from the back of Buck's Jeep and put them on, adding a couple of ceramic plates to strategic pockets. Buck unlocked the gun vault in the back and removed two AR-style rifles. They each grabbed several extra magazines and put on dark blue CBI wind-breakers. Each team member checked another team member, and they loaded up and headed for the highway and whatever storm was coming their way.

| 40 |

Chapter Forty

Five white Econoline vans turned off the highway onto the ranch road and headed for the gate. Each van had been converted and now had four rows of seats. None of the vans had windows on the sides or the back. Inside each were two armed members of Dr. Sparks's team, all on high alert.

The vans crossed through the gate and parked next to the barn. Dr. Sparks checked with each team and gave them directions to their final destinations. One van was heading to Chicago, one to Boston, one to Atlanta, one to Canada and one to Dallas. The sixth van was running late due to a flat tire and, once loaded, would be heading to Phoenix. The van teams all understood their jobs, and they were well paid.

Edith and Claire brought out supplies and food and loaded the backs of each van. Although bathroom breaks were inevitable, the vans would not have to stop for food, which gave the women less opportunity to contact someone. In all the trips they had made, none of the van teams had ever lost one woman. It was quite an accomplishment.

The van teams hung out in the barn while the women loaded the food and supplies. They would have a small window of time to rest before the long journeys began. They each found a quiet spot in the barn and crashed until it was time to leave.

Edmund Clark had spent his time wandering around the yard, noting the location of every member of the doctor's team. He was hoping his gut feeling was wrong, but he wanted to make sure, if there was a fight, that his guys came out on top. So, he quietly repositioned his family and the men that Tom had brought in so they were all near a member of the doctor's team.

He thought he was in good shape until the vans showed up and the drivers exited the vehicles, and all were armed. This was unusual, and Edmund couldn't remember a time when the drivers carried their weapons with them.

Tom stepped up to his dad. "What's with all the drivers being armed? They've never done that before."

"Yeah," said Edmund. "I was just wondering about that myself. If this goes bad, make sure your mom and your family get out of here safely."

Tom nodded and walked away.

At the same time, James and his wife, Connie, were loading up their carry-ons.

"Remember," said James. "Pack only what you need. We can buy everything else when we get to Colombia."

"Did you call the property service?" she asked.

"Yes. Everything will be ready for us. The refrigerator will be stocked, and there will be clean sheets on the bed."

She looked up at James.

"I am still worried about leaving the rest of the family," she said. She started to cry.

James walked over and wrapped his arms around her. "It will be all right. We've been taking care of them long enough. It's time we took care of ourselves before we are too old to enjoy life. They know where we will be, and they can visit anytime they want."

James heard the vans arrive and looked out the bedroom window. When the teams exited the vans, and they were all armed, James was confident he had made the right decision. He didn't want any of his family to die, but he and Connie had saved for a long time to have the life they expected to have in Colombia, and no one was going to take that away from them.

James left Connie to finish packing and headed to the living room, where he ran into Dr. Sparks.

"James," said Sparks. "Where have you been? We missed you. The vans have arrived, and we should be loading the women in the next half hour. Where is that lovely wife of yours? I haven't seen her all evening."

"Connie has a headache. She took something for it and is lying down. She will be down before you leave."

"Perhaps I should go up and see her. After all, I am a doctor."

James hesitated. "She'll be okay. Happens a couple of times a month. She does what her doctor tells her to do, and she'll be fine. What do you say we grab a drink before you leave? I just got a wonderful bourbon that I'm looking to try. Please, join me."

James Clark and Dr. Sparks walked over to the bar on the opposite side of the room. James reached under the counter and grabbed the unopened bottle of bourbon. He looked at the pistol next to it but took the bottle instead. Taking two glasses off the shelf, he poured two fingers into each. He handed the glass to Dr. Sparks and led him to a round table in the middle of the floor. Dr. Sparks sat, took a sip of the bourbon and smiled.

"Very smooth," he said.

"It's made right here in Colorado. A friend of mine has a small distillery up near Steamboat Springs. This is some of the best bourbon I've ever tasted." He took a sip.

"There's something I'd like to talk to you about," said James Clark. "I'd like to increase our role in your operation. I think we can increase the number of women we can handle by another twenty percent."

Dr. Sparks looked stoic. "You would, huh? I could see that happening, but I'm wondering how that fits with all your other endeavors?"

James Clark looked bewildered. "I'm sorry, Gene. I'm not sure what you're talking about. You get a taste of everything we have going: the guns, the drugs, the prostitutes."

"That's true," said Dr. Sparks. "But you didn't bother to tell me about the water shares you were negotiating."

James Clark was stunned. He'd believed that no one outside the family knew about this. Hell, he hadn't even told Edith or Claire the full extent of what they were working on. So how the hell did this guy figure it out?

"I can see by the stunned look on your face that you are wondering how I knew about it. Believe me, James. I know everything that goes on."

James Clark stuttered. "I . . . I . . . was going to tell you once the deal was done. Didn't want to jinx it by having too many people involved. I was going to cut you in for your usual fifteen percent."

Dr. Sparks smiled. It was a smile James did not like the look of. "No worries, James. You've been one of my most trusted earners." He picked up James's glass and stood. "Let me get you another drink, and you can tell me all about the deal."

Dr. Sparks walked behind the bar, picked up the bottle and refilled both glasses. He walked around the bar holding the two glasses in his left hand. James Clark didn't notice the silenced pistol until Dr. Sparks raised it and fired a shot into James's chest, forcing him deeper into the leather chair.

James looked on in disbelief. "Poor James," said Dr. Sparks. "You were going to screw me, and then you managed to screw up the deal. It's sad that you won't be able to make that trip to Bogotá you were planning."

Dr. Sparks raised the pistol and shot James Clark in the forehead. He finished his bourbon and headed for the stairs.

Connie Clark saw the shadow out of the corner of her eye. She was zipping the suitcase. "I'll be ready in just a minute, James. Just need to grab my pills."

She turned and was shocked to see Dr. Sparks standing in the doorway. "Hello, Connie. I'm afraid that you aren't going to be making that trip to Bogotá." He stepped into the room and looked around. "You have a wonderful eye for design.

I'm sure if the house in Colombia is as nicely decorated as this one, I will be very comfortable there."

He raised the pistol, shot Connie twice in the chest and watched her fall between the bed and the nightstand. He walked over, checked for a pulse, stood and left the room. He pulled the walkie-talkie from his belt, pushed the talk button and spoke. "Kill them all. Try to keep it quiet."

| 41 |

Chapter Forty-One

Buck called Paul while heading to the Clark ranch, filling him in on the plan. Since Paul and Carlos were already in position, Paul would remain where he was. He tried to talk Carlos into going back to the restaurant, but Carlos was having none of that. He promised Buck he would be careful, but he was going to stay with Paul in case he needed backup. Buck admired the man's spunk. He also hoped that spunk wouldn't get him killed.

The first SUV, containing Juarez, Castiglio, French and Bax, turned onto a dirt forest service road and headed back into the trees. With their lights off, Castiglio almost drove off the road twice before they reached their destination. He parked the SUV, and they got out and opened the back of the SUV. They each grabbed their helmets with night vision capability and checked their weapons one last time. They headed into the trees towards the field they would have to cross.

Buck pulled his Jeep onto a forest service road on the other side of the ranch, followed by the other SUV. They drove with their lights off, and Buck continued through the trees until they reached a slight rise in the road. From the rise, Buck could see the ranch compound. He was concerned because once clear of the trees, the people in the compound would have a good view of them as well. The one thing in their favor was that the sky was cloudy, which blocked all the moonlight.

Donning their helmets, Dorsett, Schoenberger and Chicago stood next to him as he surveyed the area.

"I wish we had a way to knock out those lights," said Vicky Dorsett. "Once we hit that circle of light, we will be seriously exposed."

Buck pulled out his phone and dialed Paul.

"Hey," said Paul, barely above a whisper.

"Paul . . . once we move, can you take out some of the lights around the compound?"

There was silence for a minute, and Buck thought he had lost the connection. Then, finally, Paul came back on the line. "Carlos says, no problem, Señor Buck. We will take out the lights."

Buck disconnected the call and laughed. The others looked at him. "Who is Carlos?" asked Vicky.

"A guy whose wife makes the best burritos I've ever eaten."

They stared at him for a minute and then turned back towards the compound. Vicky Dorsett, who was in tactical command of the operation, checked her watch and keyed her mic.

"SWAT leader. You in position?"

"This is SWAT leader. We are behind and above the containers. There are four white vans parked near the barn and a shitload of people with guns. We are locked and loaded."

"Okay, SWAT leader. Stay frosty until we engage. Team Baker, are you ready?"

"Affirmative," said French.

"On my mark. Stay low and move quick. I want to hit them before they know what's happening. Move!"

Both teams, with members side by side and spaced ten feet apart, moved out. They left the safety of the woods and moved towards the ranch compound. Fifty yards from the compound and the circle of light, gunfire erupted. The sound reverberated across the valley as it echoed from mountain to mountain. Lights across the valley were coming on as the residents wondered what was happening. It sounded like war had come to South Park.

"Shots fire, multiple shooters," said Paul. "Engaging."

"All teams," said Vicky Dorsett. "Engage. Chicago, flank left. French, break towards the barn. SWAT leader, I need two SWAT to back up French at the barn. The rest of your team, protect the pregnant women."

Edmund Clark was sitting at his kitchen table drinking a cup of coffee, trying to stay awake, when the first bullets broke the silence.

"Shit," he said as he stood, pulling his pistol from his belt. He pushed open the back door and spotted two black-clad figures running towards his house. They spotted Edmund, raised their rifles and fired as they ran. Bullets took chunks out of the doorframe surrounding Edmund. He raised his pistol and shot both. He didn't hesitate and raced towards Tom's house, firing as he ran and reloading on the run.

Edith Clark was sitting in her living room reading a magazine when the bullets started to fly. She heard her husband race out the back door and engage several shooters. She jumped up, grabbed her shotgun behind the kitchen door and stepped onto the back porch. She spotted the two bodies in the yard and looked around, not sure what to do or where to go. She spotted more shooters near her house.

Both Marshals teams broke into a run as more weapons opened up. Paul aimed and took out two barnyard lights, which diminished the light circle. Vicky's team hit the light circle and immediately engaged two shooters dressed in black tactical gear. They took them out.

"US Marshals," she yelled at the top of her voice. "Lower your weapons." The other members of her team yelled the same thing throughout the compound.

Tom Clark had been loading one of the vans with supplies for the trip when he spotted several black-clad people who had arrived with Dr. Sparks tap their throat mics and disengage the safeties on their weapons. Tom didn't wait, and as the woman standing ten feet away from him raised her rifle, Tom shot her in the side of the head. He dove out of the way as two people opened fire on his position.

Two of the guys he had called in for the evening took out both shooters and then died as bullets riddled their bodies. Tom crawled along the side of the nearest van and moved towards his house. He needed to get to his kids. He spotted a shooter sneaking towards his back door, jumped up and raced towards him. The shooter reacted faster than Tom realized, and Tom took two rounds in his right thigh. He collapsed next to the door.

Tom's three teenagers, one girl and two boys and all armed with pistols, pushed open the back door and dragged their father into the kitchen. His fifteen-year-old daughter, Sarah grabbed a kitchen towel, wrapped it around his thigh and tied it tight. He pulled his oldest son, James, closer.

"Take your brother and sister and head for the path behind the barn," he said. "Don't stop for anything and don't look back. Get to safety and wait for us. I love you guys."

He gave them each a hug and watched as they ran out the back door. He propped himself up against a cabinet and tried to stand, but his leg wouldn't hold his weight. He dropped the clip from his pistol and rammed home a new one. The creaky first step leading up to the porch indicated someone approaching, and he raised his pistol and aimed at the door.

Edmund Clark stood next to the back door with his pistol pointing forward. He lowered his voice. "Tom," he said. "It's Dad, you in there?"

He waited a moment and heard Tom's voice. "Yeah."

Edmund opened the door and ducked inside. He spotted Tom sitting on the floor and slid over, staying low. He looked at the tourniquet on Tom's leg. "Where are the kids?"

"I sent them to the escape path behind the barn."

Edmund dropped another clip into Tom's lap. "I'll be back." He moved towards the back door, peeked outside, stood and ran out the door. He headed for his father's house. He hadn't seen his father since the shooting started.

Buck heard Chicago's shotgun boom multiple times as he took cover behind one of the vans. He looked around the van and shot one of the tactical guys. He turned around and spotted Edith Clark step out onto the front porch. She leveled the shotgun she held and fired both rounds at two of the van drivers. One went down hard, the other one opened fire at Edith, and Buck watched the bullets tear through her torso, and she flew back into the kitchen. Buck dropped the shooter.

Juarez circled the house and saw Edmund Clark run out the back door shooting at several black-clad shooters hiding behind his truck that was parked behind his son's house. She cut down two shooters, and a third shooter surrendered. She kicked him to the ground, cuffed his hands and cuffed him to the ring under the back bumper of the truck. She broke his rifle against the bumper and threw the broken gun up on the roof of the ranch house.

She looked around and spotted three armed young people darting from behind the SUVs and heading towards the barn. They veered right at the barn and, in a low run, headed for the back of the barn. She ran across the compound, circled the barn and spotted the teens moving up an almost hidden trail.

Juarez moved into the trees and sprinted, coming out ahead of the teens, and she raised her rifle.

"Freeze. US Marshal," she said at the top of her voice.

The teens stopped as a group and stared. The horrified look on their faces said it all.

"Drop your weapons," said Juarez. The oldest teen started to raise his pistol. His brother and sister froze.

"Don't be stupid, kid. I would prefer not to kill a kid today." She looked at him, and he must have believed her because he put down his pistol, followed by the others. They kicked their guns off the trail, and Juarez flex-cuffed them.

She heard someone coming up the trail, and she told the teens to move off the trail and stay down. She slipped in next to them and waited. Two black-clad bad guys moved up the trail, rifles extended in front of them. They were talking about three people they had seen head up the trail. They weren't sure where they went.

Once they were about ten feet up the trail, Juarez stepped out onto the trail with her rifle raised to her shoulder.

"US Marshal, freeze."

They both spun at the sound of her voice, one pulling the trigger as he turned. Juarez let off several three-round bursts, and the shooters both fell back into the trees. She walked up to them with her rifle still raised and kicked their rifles out of the way. One of the shooters was obviously dead. The other took a final breath while she looked at him.

She turned and called the teens out, who looked up the trail. Luckily the men weren't visible from where they stood. Juarez led them down the trail, and when they broke through the clearing, she headed for the largest house on the property.

Chapter Forty-Two

The SWAT team had positioned themselves in front of the containers. They were behind a black pickup truck taking heavy fire. "SWAT leader, we are taking heavy fire at the containers. Need backup."

Carlos peeked over the rocks and tapped Paul on the shoulder. Bullets pinged off the rocks. He pointed to the containers, and Paul nodded. Carlos aimed around the side of the rocks and popped off a couple of rounds, allowing Paul to find the shooters at the containers and drop two of them. The SWAT team dropped two more black-clad shooters as they ran towards the containers.

Bax was pinned behind one of the vans, had already dropped two of the van drivers and was taking heavy fire. Castiglio came up behind her. She held up two fingers and pointed. He moved to the other end of the van and opened fire. One of the shooters stepped out from behind another van to change his aim to the front of the van, and Bax shot him in the head. The other shooter popped up at the front of the van, and Castiglio dropped him.

Brenda Clark stood next to the operating table and looked at the dead Asian woman. She wrapped the baby in a blue blanket and placed the newborn in the incubator next to the operating table. She hated that Dr. Sparks had allowed the woman to die an undignified death and hated even more that he had helped her along with a syringe full of morphine.

She watched as the young black-clad woman standing on the other side of the operating table touched her ear and flicked the safety off her rifle. Without even thinking about it, Brenda grabbed the bloody scalpel off the table and reached across the table, slashing the young woman across the throat. Blood splattered the front of her blue scrubs as she watched the life drain from the woman's astonished eyes. The young woman bounced off the table and hit the floor.

Brenda Clark walked around the table just as gunfire erupted on the other side of the door. She pulled the woman's pistol from the holster on her thigh, pushed the incubator into the farthest corner from the door, made sure the baby was covered by the blanket and positioned herself in front of the incubator, pistol raised.

French and the two SWAT officers dashed into the barn and encountered three guys in T-shirts and jeans who spun around and fired wildly at the barn door. They took all three out and searched the barn for more shooters.

They spotted the side door and approached it. French twisted the knob and pushed open the door, and a bullet slammed into the side jamb. They pulled back.

"US Marshal, drop your weapon," said French in as calm

a voice as he could manage. He pulled his badge from his belt and held it at the edge of the door, visible to anyone inside the door. He glanced around the doorjamb, spotted a woman in blood-splattered blue scrubs, holding a pistol, and pulled back.

"Lady, we don't want to hurt you. Please drop your weapon and get on your knees," said French.

He nodded to the two SWAT officers, lowered his rifle and stepped into the doorway, the words us marshal in bright white letters across his chest.

"C'mon, lady. Please put down the gun."

Brenda Clark stared at the words emblazoned on his vest. She hesitated for a second, then dropped the pistol and got down on her knees. The two SWAT officers moved around French, kicked the gun into the corner, pushed her to her stomach and handcuffed the woman. They rolled her over and pushed her against a stainless steel cabinet.

Brenda Clark looked at the officers with disdain. "Can you give us your name, ma'am?" asked French. She looked him in the eyes. "Lawyer" was all she said.

French checked the baby, who was still sleeping, and turned towards the table. The site of the dead Asian woman with her abdomen cut open disgusted him. One of the SWAT officers checked the body of the young woman on the floor and shook his head. French looked away and clicked his mic.

Vicky Dorsett took out three shooters who had blockaded themselves inside one of the houses. She and Chicago blew through the door and fanned out as best they could. She found Claire Clark lying on the floor, bleeding from multiple chest wounds. They moved through the house and cleared the space.

The gunfire was starting to dwindle, and she keyed her mic. "All teams. Let's round up the stragglers."

She and Chicago left the house and headed for the large house at the end of the compound. Halfway there, two shots rang out.

Edmund Clark entered his dad's house through the sliding door off the back deck. He had his pistol out ahead of him and scanned the room. He spotted a body sitting in a chair by the bar and walked over. The shock of seeing his father with a bullet hole in his chest and his forehead hit him hard, and he put his hand up to his mouth to keep from crying out. He wiped the tears from his eyes and raced up the stairs.

He stopped before he entered the master bedroom and leaned against the doorjamb. The sight of his mother lying bloody on the floor shook him to his core. He heard a noise downstairs and slowly descended the stairs.

Dr. Eugene Sparks stepped around the bar with a drink in his hand and stopped short. "Ah, Edmund. I was expecting you." He looked at the gun in Edmund's hand. "I wanted to discuss our future plans and the role I want you to play in those plans."

Edmund was dumbfounded. "You murdered my parents, and you expect us to work together?"

Eugene Sparks smiled. "Your mother and father were going to run out on your family. They were planning to catch a plane to Bogotá tonight. I bet you didn't know that?"

Edmund Clark remembered seeing a suitcase on his parents' bed, but he hadn't thought anything about it. Eugene

Sparks had gradually walked away from the bar and got closer to the table that held his pistol.

"Your father," said Sparks, "and his greed created a problem for our partners. We can spin this so you come out smelling like a rose. With my plans, we will make even more money than before."

The gunfire outside had all but stopped, but a fire raged in Edmund Clark. "You wiped out my entire organization, and god knows how many of my family you killed. You are a sick fuck."

Eugene Sparks threw his drink across the room, but Edmund Clark was focused on him and never flinched. As Sparks reached for the pistol on the table, Edmund fired twice, both rounds hitting Sparks in the chest and knocking him to the floor. Edmund stepped next to the body, ready to fire a round into Sparks's head, but he saw it wasn't necessary.

Vicky Dorsett and Chicago raced up the front porch, and Chicago hit the doors with all his bulk. The doors blew off their hinges, and Chicago hit the floor, rolled onto his knees and raised his shotgun.

Vicky ran in behind him and aimed her pistol at the man standing in the middle of what appeared to be a large living room. He was standing over a body on the floor.

"US Marshal. Drop your weapon!"

The man hesitated for a minute and then threw the pistol onto the couch next to him. He raised his hands and turned towards Vicky and Chicago, who nodded at Vicky, shouldered his shotgun and shoved the man down on the floor. He applied the flex-cuffs and pulled the man to his feet. Looking around, they noticed the other body sitting in a chair by a large, well-stocked bar. There was blood all over his chest and a bloody hole in his forehead. Juarez came in through the sliding door, and Vicky looked at her. "You good?"

"Yeah, found three teenagers trying to escape up the trail. Castiglio has them out by the barn. They want to know if their mom and dad are okay. Said their dad was shot in the thigh and was bleeding badly. I sent two SWAT guys to the house they indicated to see if they could locate him. Don't know anything about the mom?"

"Let's clear the rest of the house. Chicago, you got him?" asked Vicky.

He nodded, and Vicky and Juarez headed in different directions. Vicky took the stairs and cleared the bedrooms. She called down the stairs.

"Juarez, up here."

Juarez finished clearing the ground floor and raced up the stairs. She found Vicky standing at the entrance to a lavish master bedroom.

"We've got another body." She pointed to the dead woman lying between the bed and the nightstand.

They left the room and headed downstairs, where they ran into Buck and Bax. Buck walked over and looked at the body of James Clark in the chair and then at the body on the floor. Dr. Eugene Sparks had two holes in his chest. He walked up to Edmund Clark.

"Did you kill him?"

Edmund didn't hesitate. "He killed my mother and father. What would you have done?"

Vicky led Buck upstairs, and he looked at the other body

on the floor. He shook his head, turned and headed down-stairs.

"Vicky," came a voice over the radio. "We need you in the barn."

Buck and Vicky headed for the barn while Juarez and Chicago read the prisoner his Miranda rights. As they walked, Vicky keyed her mic.

"SWAT leader, status."

"This is SWAT leader; we are rounding up the stragglers. Several are in custody. The women are safe, and we have a couple of teenagers who were hiding in the woods."

"Any casualties, SWAT leader?"

"One officer down shot in the thigh. Medic is working on him now. One officer was shot in the shoulder, through and through. He's resting comfortably."

Bax, Paul and Carlos stood outside the barn door talking to French. Buck slapped Carlos on the back. "Did you call Maria and let her know you are okay?"

"Sí, Senor Buck. She is very happy." He smiled.

Buck heard the sirens in the distance and saw the flashing red-and-blue lights coming up the ranch road. Three Colorado State Patrol SUVs, followed by three Park County Sheriff's Office SUVs and six ambulances, entered the compound and parked wherever they could find a space.

Sheriff Toomey, with his arm in a sling, slid out of the passenger seat of the first PCSO SUV. He looked at the carnage that used to be the ranch compound and shook his head. He headed towards Buck.

"Sheriff, good to see you up and around," said Buck.

"Looks like I missed a hell of a party. Our people good?"

Commander Walsch, wearing his SWAT uniform, walked up to the group. He shook hands all around.

"Two injured, John. Medics are on them," he said to the sheriff.

Bax spotted more flashing lights heading down Kenosha Pass and tapped Buck, who looked where she was pointing.

"Looks like the Feds are arriving," she said.

Everyone looked. Nothing was said, and Buck and Vicky walked into the barn.

| 43 |

Chapter Forty-Three

Deputy French and the two SWAT officers met Buck, Bax and Vicky at the door to the barn.

"You're gonna want to see this," said French, and he led them through the barn past the bodies of two dead bad guys in jeans and T-shirts and one guy lying handcuffed on the floor with blood dripping down his arm. He pulled open a door at the side of the barn, and they entered a room that looked like it had come straight out of a hospital.

"This is a whole surgical suite," said Vicky.

The room was full of stainless steel hospital equipment that could match a surgical suite in any hospital. There was also an incubator in one corner. The small bundle wrapped in the blue blanket moved, and Vicky walked over and picked the baby up. "I'm gonna take this to the EMTs."

Lying on the surgical table in a pool of blood was the body of an Asian woman. The saline drip was still attached to her arm, and her abdomen was cut wide open. Her pale skin said it was too late to save her, but Bax checked for a pulse anyway. She shook her head.

Bax checked the body lying on the floor next to the table and noticed the slice across the throat and the scalpel lying on the floor next to the body.

Buck put on a pair of Nitrile gloves and picked up the syringe lying on the operating table next to the body. He looked around and spotted a small vial on a table full of surgical instruments.

He held up the bottle. "Morphine. The son of a bitch killed her after he took her baby." He pulled an evidence bag out of his pocket, dropped the vial and the syringe in and sealed the bag.

He walked over to the woman in the blue scrubs sitting on the floor and held up the evidence bag. "Your handiwork?" he asked.

The woman glared at him but remained quiet. Vicky Dorsett, who had reentered the room, tried a different approach.

"Are you Mrs. Clark? We have three teenagers who are looking for their mother. Should I let them know you're okay?"

Brenda Clark lost all her bravado, and tears fell from her eyes. "Please. Are they all right?"

"Yes. They are safe," said Vicky.

"What about Tom, my husband?"

"We have reports of an injured man in your house. We've sent a couple of SWAT officers to see if they can locate him," said Vicky.

"Fuck, Buck. What the hell did you get involved in this time?" asked a voice from the door.

Buck recognized the voice and turned around. Hank Clancy, special agent in charge of the FBI's Denver Field Office, stepped into the room. He was dressed in jeans, boots and a navy-blue FBI golf shirt instead of his usual dark suit, white shirt and, as Buck liked to call it, his government-issue red-white-and-blue-striped tie.

Hank looked at the dead woman on the operating table. "You froze me out," he said without looking at Buck. "Your director called me."

"It wasn't on purpose, Hank. Things just moved at lightning speed, and we needed to keep it small so we could adapt."

"And so, of course, you called your friends at the Marshals Service."

Vicky walked into the room and stepped up to Hank. "Special Agent Clancy. How nice to see you again."

"Deputy Dorsett," said Hank. "Somehow, I figured you would be in the middle of all this carnage."

Vicky Dorsett laughed. "Just helping a friend. Buck, Edmund Clark would like a word."

Buck, Vicky and Hank left the barn and headed for the big house. Hank looked at the bodies, the injured and those in handcuffs. "Do you have a count, Buck?"

"The only one that matters right now. We saved forty-seven pregnant women and one newborn baby from lives of servitude and death."

"What about Eugene Sparks?" asked Hank.

Buck didn't respond; instead, he walked up the stairs to

the front porch and entered the house. Chicago was standing near Edmund Clark. He nodded as they entered. "He wants to talk to you," he said, stepping aside.

Hank looked at the dead body in the chair and then at the body lying on the floor. He pointed to the one on the floor.

"Dr. Eugene Sparks?" he asked.

Buck nodded and stepped up to where Edmund was sitting. Edmund looked up from his seat on the couch. He was a broken man, and it showed on his face. His whole world had just been shot to hell, and all he cared about now was how many members of his family had survived.

Buck pulled up a chair and placed it in front of Edmund Clark. He waited a few minutes while two EMTs placed the body of James Clark into a black body bag and strapped it to a gurney. Tears formed in Edmund's eyes as he watched them remove his father.

"Before you say a word, I am going to read you your Miranda rights," said Buck. He unclipped his phone, opened a video app and handed the phone to Vicky, who aimed the camera at Edmund.

Buck pulled the Miranda card out of his back pocket and read Edmund his rights. He asked him if he understood them, and he said yes. He then asked him if he was willing to waive his rights and talk to them without a lawyer present.

"Where are my wife and son?" Edmund asked.

"We don't know yet. We arrived late to your little war and are still trying to figure out who all the players are. Are you willing to talk to us without a lawyer?" asked Buck.

"Sure, why not. You caught me standing over the dead

Dr. Sparks with the smoking gun in my hand. What do I have to lose?"

Sheriff Toomey and Commander Walsch joined the group and stood looking at Edmund Clark.

"You want to tell us what happened, Mr. Clark?" asked Buck.

"To be honest, I'm not sure. When Sparks got here earlier tonight, he was concerned that we were being looked at by you folks. We knew something was up. He'd never brought that many people with him, and they were all heavily armed."

"What set this whole thing off tonight?" asked Buck.

"I'm not sure. I was sitting at my kitchen table having coffee when the shooting started."

"Why did you shoot Eugene Sparks?" asked Hank.

"Like I said earlier. He killed my parents."

"Mr. Clark," asked Buck. "Do you know where your son Tucker is?"

Edmund Clark looked up at Buck. "You think he had something to do with whatever killed those cows?"

"We need to ask him some questions. We know you were trying to force Mr. Halverson to sign away his numerous water rights. Did you have anything to do with the death of the cattle?"

Edmund Clark hesitated. "I want a lawyer," he said.

Hank stopped the conversation and arrested Edmund Clark for human trafficking and handed him over to two FBI agents who were standing off to the side. He turned to Buck. "Since you arrested him on a federal warrant, our evidence response team will take over from here."

Buck stepped out onto the back deck. The sun was just

coming over the mountains, and he was running out of steam. Bax and Sheriff Toomey walked up behind him.

"We still need to find Tucker Clark," said Buck.

He pulled his phone off his belt and was about to dial when his phone rang. He looked at the number and answered.

"Don't you guys ever sleep?" he asked.

George laughed. "Look who's answering his phone at five thirty in the morning."

Buck laughed. "Okay. It looks like you got me there. What's up?"

"We have an address for Brian Cole."

| 44 |

Chapter Forty-Four

George gave Buck an address in Alma for Brian Cole. "We've torn his life apart. He was previously assigned to the Plum Island research center. He was reassigned when the new facility opened here in Colorado. We found four off-shore accounts, only one of which we have been able to get into. Mel is applying for warrants right now for the other three. Over the last two weeks, he deposited two hundred grand into the account we could access. Far above his salary, which is fairly impressive in its own right."

"Any idea where the money came from?" asked Bax.

"We're still tracking it; the encryption key is helping, but it's still a slow process. You want us to bring in the FBI?"

"Hank's got his hands full right now. So, let's give it twelve hours and if you can't get in, then go ahead and bring them in. In the meantime, we need to find Brian Cole, and maybe he can lead us to Tucker Clark."

Buck clicked off. "Sheriff, do you know where that address is?"

"Yeah," said Sheriff Toomey. "How do you want to handle it?"

"Why don't you and I go see if Brian Cole is home? Bax, why don't you see if the hospital will let you talk to Melvin Gross? Who knows, maybe we can get something out of him."

He handed his Jeep keys to her. "Take my Jeep back to the sheriff's office to get your Jeep. The sheriff and I will ride with Deputy Rivers."

Buck raised his phone and called Paul. "Hey, Paul."

"Hi, Buck. What's up?"

"Hey, the FBI is going to take over here. Why don't you take Carlos home and grab some shut-eye? Bax is going to see Melvin Gross at the hospital, and the sheriff and I are going to see if we can find Brian Cole. No sense all of us being exhausted."

"No problem, Buck. Call if you need me."

Buck hung up, and they headed in different directions. Buck and the sheriff found Deputy Rivers, and they slid into her SUV. Buck gave her the address, and they squeezed their way down the ranch road through all the emergency vehicles. Buck looked around and was glad Hank and the FBI had taken over. The baby farming case had taken on a life of its own, and the FBI was better suited to handle it at this point.

They pulled onto Highway 285 and were stunned by the number of reporters and TV stations that had vans parked on the sides of the highway. Several reporters tried to stop the SUV, but Deputy Rivers continued driving. They cleared the crowds and headed towards Fairplay.

They turned onto Highway 9 and headed north until they reached Buckskin Street, where Deputy Rivers turned left and then turned right onto N Pine Street. The address was in the middle of the block, and Rivers parked her SUV on a grass strip in front of the house. The house was a small ranch with a detached garage, and Buck wondered why someone who made the kind of money Brian Cole made would live in such a small house.

They slid out of the SUV and approached the front door. The small front porch squeaked as they stepped up to the front door, and Buck knocked first normally and then with the side of his fist in the classic cop knock.

A voice from inside called out, "Coming," and the door opened. The young man wore workout shorts and no shirt and looked like he had just crawled out of bed. When he saw the deputy's uniform, he took a step back.

Buck pushed open the door. "Are you Brian Cole?"

The man wiped the sleep out of his eyes. "Whaaat? No, I'm Philip Ridge. Brian Cole is my landlord. What's this all about?"

"We're looking for Brian Cole. Do you know where he lives?" asked Buck.

"No. I only met him when I picked up the keys."

"How do you pay your rent?" asked Buck.

Philip Ridge tried to shake the cobwebs out of his head. He refocused on Buck. "Sorry. I send it to a PO box in Fairplay."

Buck looked at the sheriff and then back to Philip Ridge.

"Thank you, Mr. Ridge. Can you get us the PO box number, and how long have you been renting this place?"

"Almost two years." Philip Ridge stepped away from the door and, a minute later, returned and handed Buck a slip of paper with an address on it. Buck thanked him, and he closed the door. They headed back to the SUV. Buck pulled out his phone and called George.

"Hey, Buck."

"George, can you track a PO box to a specific address?"

"It's possible."

Buck gave him the number and hung up.

"Let's head back to the office and regroup. Maybe we all need a little sleep." They slid into the SUV and headed back to Fairplay.

They pulled into the parking lot and walked through the front door. The deputy at the desk looked frazzled.

"Sheriff, the phones have been ringing off the hook, and there are reporters all over town. Everyone wants to know about the war they heard this morning."

"Thanks, Rich. I'll issue a statement later this morning."

They'd headed for the sheriff's office when Buck stopped. The sheriff and Deputy Rivers turned to face him. "What's up?" asked the sheriff.

"Tax rolls. We need to see if Brian Cole owns another house."

Deputy Rivers smiled. "I can access the information from here." She sat at one of the desks, fired up the computer and logged in to the county website. She ran Brian Cole's name and came up with nothing; she looked at Buck and the sheriff and then clicked some more keys. She did this for five minutes and sat back, her smile bigger than when she'd started. She turned the screen so Buck and the sheriff could see it.

The building permit application had the name of the general contractor, and below his name was the name of the owner. Brian Cole had built a new house on five acres of land on the east side of Kenosha Pass.

"You up for a drive?" he asked the sheriff and Deputy Rivers. He knew they were both wiped out, but they nodded.

Buck pulled out his phone and dialed a number. Vicky Dorsett answered right away.

"Hiya, Buck. What's up?"

"Hey, Vicky. Can you and your team pull away for a little while?"

"The FBI seems to have everything under control for the moment. I think we can get away. What's going on?"

Buck told her about Brian Cole, his foreign bank accounts and his relationship with Tucker Clark. He told her to keep it low-key and meet them at the base of Kenosha Pass.

He clicked off the call, and they headed for the parking lot. Buck slid into his Jeep and followed Deputy Rivers's SUV, and they headed for Kenosha Pass. As they passed the ranch road, Buck could have sworn that the media crowd along the highway had doubled since they passed by earlier. They drove past and continued to a small turnout at the base of Kenosha Pass, where they pulled in behind the Marshals' SUV.

Buck slid out of his Jeep and walked up to the SUV. Vicky Dorsett rolled down the window, and Buck leaned in. He gave her the address, and she pulled it up on her laptop. The house was a good size and was tucked back in the woods, almost invisible. She nodded, and Buck walked back to his SUV and slid in.

He led the way up Kenosha Pass and, after a few miles, turned onto a dirt road. They headed up the mountain, and he slowed as the house came into view.

Tucker Clark's pickup truck was parked in front of the house. Buck stopped his Jeep and slid out. The others pulled in behind him and did the same.

"Tucker Clark's truck is parked out front." He looked at Sheriff Toomey. "John, can you call a judge and get us an arrest warrant and a search warrant for Tucker Clark and Brian Cole?"

The sheriff nodded, pulled out his phone and stepped away from the group. Buck looked at Deputy Rivers and the marshals. "Let's gear up."

Since they all still had on tactical vests, they pulled their rifles from the back of their vehicles, added loaded clips to their vests and put new clips in their rifles.

Sheriff Toomey disconnected the call and walked back to the group. "The judge will cover us on the warrants. We're good to go."

Chapter Forty-Five

They agreed that Vicky, Schoenberger and Chicago would cover the back of the house, Buck and Sheriff Toomey would go to the front door, and Deputy Rivers would stay behind as cover in case someone decided to run. Vicky and her guys split up and headed around both sides of the house, sticking to the edge of the trees.

Buck and the sheriff approached the front door, paused and pulled their pistols. The front door looked like it had been kicked in and was partially open. The smell was unmistakable, and they looked at each other.

"Vicky to Buck," said a voice in his ear.

"Go ahead."

"We're getting a strong death smell, and it looks like there's a body on the deck."

"We're getting the same thing at the front door, and the door has been kicked in. Let's hit it."

Buck pushed open the front doors and swept his pistol

from side to side. He moved farther into the space, and the sheriff followed. They heard Vicky yell, "Clear," and they spread out, checking the kitchen and dining room before entering the large living room. Vicky was standing next to a leather couch; they could hear the flies buzzing before they got close.

Schoenberger and Chicago joined the group. "We cleared the rest of the house; all good," said Chicago as he holstered his pistol.

They looked down at what was once Brian Cole. Vicky pointed to the bullet holes in his chest. "Five of those are dry. Dude was dead before someone turned him into Swiss cheese."

Buck looked at her. "What about the other body?"

She led him and the sheriff out to the back deck. Tucker Clark sat in the chair with the top of his head blown off. Scavengers had already started on the soft fleshy parts. Buck looked at the sheriff.

"Yep," said the sheriff. "That's Tucker Clark." He pointed to the three empty beer bottles next to the chair. "Looks like he couldn't live with the thought that he killed his son."

Schoenberger stepped out of the sliding glass door. "You're gonna want to see this."

He walked away, and the others followed him through the living room to a door that led to a flight of stairs that descended to the basement. He pushed open a wooden door, and they all stared in amazement.

Behind the door was a better-equipped lab than any of them had ever seen. The stainless steel tables and equipment shined under the LED lighting. The space was immaculate.

"Looks like we found the lab," said Vicky.

Buck held everyone back. "We know how deadly the toxin is; we better wait for the experts. Let's get out of the house. It's now a crime scene."

They exited the house and stood in the driveway.

"What do you think, Buck?" asked the sheriff.

"I think Tucker found out what had happened to his son and had it out with Brian Cole. I think his guilt as a father was unbearable, and he did the only thing he could think of."

Buck stepped away from the group and pulled out his phone. He dialed the number and waited.

"Buck, what's up?" asked Director Jackson.

"Morning, sir."

Buck filled in Director Jackson on the raid from earlier in the morning and told him about what they found at Brian Cole's house.

"This is going to be a jurisdictional nightmare, Buck. It's a local crime involving a weapon of mass destruction, which makes it terrorism. That means we should call the FBI."

"There's also another party that is interested in this case," said Buck.

"Yeah," said Director Jackson. "I figured there was. And I bet they would prefer we not invite the FBI to our little party?"

"Who else is with you?"

Buck told him, and the director did not sound happy. "Shit, Buck. Now we have the Marshals Service involved too."

Vicky stepped up to Buck and leaned in to the phone. "Hi, Director Jackson, Deputy Dorsett, U.S. Marshals Service. If it makes things a little easier, we were never here."

"Thank you, Deputy. That will definitely help, and I appreciate your noninvolvement."

Vicky nodded to Buck. "We're gonna get out of here before you call the troops." She shook Buck's hand and waved to her guys, who headed for their SUV.

As she turned the SUV around, she rolled down the window. "Hey, Taylor. You sure know how to show a girl a good time." She waved and headed down the driveway.

Buck turned back to the phone. "Sorry, sir."

"No worries, Buck. Call your friend. I can buy you six hours before I call Hank, so do what you need to do."

Buck hung up and dialed the number from his recent call list. The general answered right away.

"Agent Taylor."

"We found Brian Cole and Tucker Clark. They're both dead. There is a full lab in the basement of the address I am going to give you. You've got six hours to do whatever you have to do before we call the FBI." He gave the general the address and walked back to the group. He explained what was going to happen, and they all agreed. He didn't tell them about the general.

"Why don't you guys get some rest? I'll stay for a while until forensics shows up."

The sheriff nodded, and he and Deputy Rivers headed back to the SUV. Buck called Paul and gave him the address. He returned to his Jeep, removed his vest, locked up his rifle, sat in the front passenger seat and closed his eyes.

| 46 |

Chapter Forty-Six

Bax, parked in the parking lot of the Centura St. Anthony Summit Hospital in Frisco, slid out of her Jeep and grabbed her backpack. She entered the hospital, flashed her badge and asked the volunteer at the reception desk to page Dr. Harrison. She sat in the waiting area and opened her phone to check messages.

"Agent Baxter?" said a voice behind her.

Bax stood and turned to see a short older man wearing light blue scrubs standing in the doorway. She walked up and stuck out her hand. "Dr. Harrison." They shook hands.

"Nice to meet you, Agent Baxter. If you'll follow me, I'll take you to see Mr. Gross. One word of caution. He's still a little groggy, so if you could keep your time short and not excite him too much, I would appreciate it."

"No worries, Doctor. I appreciate whatever time you can give me."

They passed through a locked door and stepped up to a

security guard sitting outside the room. Bax signed in, and the guard unlocked the door. Bax entered and walked up to the bed.

Melvin Gross was lying in bed with his shoulder wrapped in a large white bandage, and his other hand was handcuffed to the rail on the bed. He looked up as Bax entered.

"Mr. Gross, I'm Ashley Baxter with the Colorado Bureau of Investigation. I would like to ask you some questions, but first, I am going to read you your Miranda rights." She set down her backpack, pulled out her phone, clicked on a video app and positioned it so Melvin Gross was in the frame. She pulled a laminated card from her back pocket and read him his rights.

"Do you understand the rights I have read to you?" she asked.

"Yes," said Melvin Gross.

"Are you willing to waive your right to an attorney and talk to me?"

Melvin Gross hesitated. "Yes," he said.

Bax put the card back in her pocket. "Melvin, can I call you Melvin?" He nodded. "Melvin, we have video of you from a trail cam following Dan Pearson up on North Tarryall Peak the night Dan died. Why were you there?"

"Dan Pearson was a thief and a liar. He stole information about the location of a treasure that was mine."

"Where did you get the information from?"

"I got it around. People told me."

She stared at him. "So, how did Dan Pearson steal this information?"

"I don't know. He just took it. Probably got it from my computer. It was all in there, and now it's not."

Bax tried to process this. "So, Dan not only took information from your computer but also made the information disappear." She gave him a sideways look and rolled her eyes.

"That's right, it was right there, and then it was gone, so I followed Dan that night, and he went right to the place."

"Melvin, did he find any treasure?"

"He didn't look hard enough. It's right there where I told him it was."

"Where you told him it was. I thought he stole your information?"

Melvin stuttered. "He did after I told him where it was."

Bax saw this line of questioning was going nowhere. She needed to change her approach.

"Melvin, why did you kill Dan Pearson?"

Melvin Gross looked shocked. He looked around like he was trying to find a way to escape.

"I don't know what you're talking about."

"C'mon, Melvin. We have a video of you following him, and you have a pistol in your hand. We found that pistol in your cabin when you shot the sheriff. When we get the ballistics back, it's gonna show you shot him. What happened, Melvin?"

"I didn't shoot him. I thought the sheriff was gonna take my treasures, but I didn't shoot Dan. I liked Dan."

"What treasures, Melvin?"

Melvin didn't answer. He stared at Bax, and his eyes darted from side to side.

"Melvin, I'm going to arrest you for shooting the sheriff

and killing Dan Pearson. As soon as you are released from the hospital, you will be arraigned and taken to jail."

Bax picked up her backpack and her phone and turned towards the door. She pulled the door open.

"Wait," said Melvin Gross. "You have the video. Check it."

Bax walked back to the bed. "The video shows you stalking Dan with a gun in your hand. How will that help you?"

"Not the game cam video, the one from my GoPro. It shows the two guys in black suits killing Dan and the cows."

Bax set her backpack down and put her phone back on the table.

"Melvin, you have a video of two men killing the cows? Where is it?"

Melvin looked incredulous. "You guys found it in my cabin. It was on the table. Go look at it. What I told you is true. Go look at it. Dan Pearson was alive when I left him. I headed down the road and spotted a pickup truck and something odd in a field. Two guys in rubber suits and oxygen tanks were spraying something at the cows, and they were falling over like they got hit by a brick. I still had the camera on and watched them from the trees for a while, then Dan came along in his truck and stopped and walked into the field. One of the rubber suit guys walked up to him and just shot him. I kept filming while these guys took off their suits. Got real good video of their faces. Please, ma'am, you have to believe me."

Dr. Harrison walked into the room. "Agent Baxter, I'd like you to end this now and let Mr. Gross rest."

Bax nodded and grabbed her phone and backpack. She

thanked the doctor and ran out of the hospital towards her Jeep. She pulled out her phone and called Paul.

Paul answered and sounded groggy. "Hey, Bax. What's up?"

"Paul, did you guys find a GoPro camera in Melvin Gross's cabin?"

Paul thought for a minute. "Yeah, I think we did. We sent everything to George and Mel. Why?"

Bax told him what Melvin Gross said about the two men and getting video of them killing the cattle and Dan Pearson. Bax told Paul to go back to sleep and she would call Mel. She hung up and dialed Mel's number.

"Hey, Bax. How goes the battle?" asked Mel.

"Good, Mel. Hey, Paul thinks there was a GoPro camera in the evidence they sent you from Melvin Gross's cabin."

"Yeah," said Mel. "We charged it but haven't opened it. What do you need?"

"I'm looking for a video showing two men killing the cattle and shooting Dan Pearson."

"Hold on. Let me hook it up and see what we can find."

Bax heard keys clicking and then silence. She waited patiently even though she wanted to climb through the phone and see what Mel was looking at.

Mel came back on the line. "I'm sending you the clip."

Bax's phone chimed with an incoming message, and she opened the file. She watched the video twice.

"This is just what we need, Mel. One more piece to the puzzle. Thanks."

She hung up, slid into her Jeep and headed back to Fairplay. She was excited. She had just found Dan Pearson's killer;

unfortunately, she had no idea what Buck had found at Brian Cole's house.

| 47 |

Chapter Forty-Seven

Paul arrived at Brian Cole's house and parked next to Buck's Jeep. He looked over at Buck, who was sitting in his passenger seat and was waking up. He looked at Paul, who looked as tired as he felt. Maybe he was getting too old to pull these all-nighters.

Buck shook off the little sleep he had just gotten and slid out of his Jeep. Paul did the same and joined him next to the vehicles.

"You look like I feel. What have we got here?" asked Paul.

Buck laughed. "I was just thinking the same thing. Follow me."

They headed for the stairs when they heard a vehicle—actually, several vehicles approaching. They stopped at the foot of the steps and waited.

General Culpeper's SUV stopped behind Buck's Jeep. Struggling up the dirt driveway behind him was a thirty-foot panel truck with the logo of a regional supermarket on the

278

side. It stopped behind the general, who slid out of his SUV and approached Buck.

He shook Buck's hand and looked at Paul. Buck took the hint.

"General, Paul Webber. CBI. He can be trusted."

The general shook Paul's hand but never introduced himself. He waved over a tall blond woman who climbed out of the passenger seat. She walked over and stood at attention. Her white lab coat had no information printed on it, and the general did not introduce her. The general looked at Buck.

"Where is the lab?" he asked.

"Basement, left through the kitchen, first door on the right. There are two bodies inside."

The general frowned. "I thought I recognized the smell."

"You will confine your people to the basement. The rest of the house is a crime scene, and I would rather the FBI evidence techs not find any indication that you were here. Most important, I would like you to make sure there is no residue of the toxin left in the basement. You have five hours left to do whatever you need to do. At that point, I will be calling the FBI to report the deaths of two terrorists. Any questions, sir."

"Just one, Agent Taylor. Why?"

Buck looked at him.

"Why are you protecting us?"

"Two reasons, General. I believe that what you folks are involved in could one day save a lot of people, and in order to do that, you need to remain anonymous."

"And the second reason?"

"Because I still have one more terrorist to find, and I need everything at your lab to appear perfectly normal until I wrap up this case."

The general nodded and looked at the blond woman behind him. She nodded and returned to the truck where six other people, all with military bearing, were putting on rubber hazmat suits.

Buck and Paul stepped into the house and put on Tyvek booties and Nitrile gloves. Buck's phone rang, and he looked at the number.

"Hi, Bax."

"Hey, Buck. Melvin Gross had a camera with him that night he was following Dan Pearson. We have the murder on camera. You'll never guess who was with the shooter."

"Tucker Clark," said Buck.

"Way to steal a girl's thunder."

"Sorry, Bax. We just found Tucker Clark dead."

He told her what they found at Brian Cole's house, and there was silence on the other end of the phone.

"So, the other guy in the video was Brian Cole?" asked Bax.

"Looks like it. Nice work though, Bax, on the video. If these two guys were still alive, that would help our case. Go get some rest, and we'll meet you at the sheriff's office in a little while."

Buck disconnected and was stepping into the living room when his phone rang. He looked at the number and answered.

"Dr. Jess, how are you?"

"I'm fine, Agent Taylor. Well, no, I'm not fine. I'm pissed. I received a call from the pathologist at Colorado State University. He told me that they misplaced all the samples I sent them and could I send over some more samples. I went back to the field this morning, and all the cattle are gone, and the field is charred. What's going on?"

Buck thought for a minute about how to handle this. He wanted to be honest with her, but he also needed to protect the investigation.

"Doctor, I'm not sure what to tell you. Our investigation came to a head this morning, and we've all been a little busy."

"I heard the gunfire last night. Everyone in the valley did. It's hard to believe something like that could have been going on in our quiet little part of the world, and no one knew. But, Agent Taylor, I have a responsibility to my patients to make sure they are safe. What do I tell people when they ask if whatever happened to Halverson's cattle could happen to theirs?"

"Doctor, all I can tell you at this time is that the threat has been neutralized, and there should be no impact on the other cattle in the valley."

"That's bullshit. How could you know that?" Then she hesitated. "You know what happened, don't you, but you can't tell me?"

"Doctor, I would suggest you tell your patients that there was some kind of poisonous plant in the field and that the field was burned to get rid of the infestation."

"Swear to me, Agent Taylor, that you are absolutely sure there is no threat to the neighboring ranches."

"There is no threat to the neighboring ranches. You have my word," said Buck.

"Thanks for that, Agent Taylor." The phone went dead,

and Buck looked at Paul. "I hated to do that, but what choice do I have?"

Paul smiled. "I know that went against everything you believe in, but better you than me."

Buck nodded. "Yeah, let's get going; we're running out of time."

They separated and went in different directions. They had less than five hours to figure out who was paying for the toxin.

Chapter Forty-Eight

Paul walked out of what looked like an office and called Buck.

"You need to see this."

Buck stepped around the bar he had been searching and walked into the office. Paul was behind the desk, clicking keys on a laptop. His phone was on and sitting next to the laptop.

He looked up from the keyboard. "Thanks, Mel. I'll let you know what I find."

He disconnected the phone call, and Buck stepped behind him. "Brian Cole had a bunch of encrypted videos. Mel helped me get in," said Paul.

He clicked on one video file, and it opened to a night scene. The video showed someone spraying a substance at each cow, and within minutes, they were dropping like flies. They watched for a while, and then the video ended.

"Proof-of-concept video," said Buck. "What's on these other ones?"

Paul clicked on the next file, and the video opened in the office they were sitting in. Buck recognized the chair in front of the desk. Paul raised the volume, and they listened. When the video ended, Buck looked at Paul. He walked out of the office and stopped at the top of the basement stairs.

"General."

The general appeared at the bottom of the stairs and pulled off his mask.

"Could I ask you to come up here for a minute? We need to show you something."

The general spoke to someone behind him and climbed the stairs. His head was covered in sweat, and he had a depression around his mouth where the mask had sealed. He followed Buck into the office.

"That lab is incredible," he said. "He has a small level three containment chamber down there. That's some sophisticated and expensive equipment, and it is all state-of-the-art. It rivals our lab but on a smaller scale. It must have cost Cole a fortune. I wonder where the money came from?"

Buck didn't say anything in response but directed him to stand behind Paul, who reran the video.

"General, do you know those people in the video?" asked Buck.

The general watched and then stood up. "That's Dr. Brian Cole, and the man in front of the desk is Dr. Simon Lee. Dr. Lee works at the lab. He is a virologist."

Paul looked at the general. "Does he work with the deadly viruses?"

The general hesitated. "Yes, he does. Do you think he was involved?"

Paul played the next several videos, and then the general sat down. "It's bad enough to have one traitor in our midst, but to have two. I can't believe it."

"This was his insurance policy, General. Brian Cole knew the people he was dealing with were dangerous, so he recorded all the meetings and all the time they spent in the lab working on the formula."

Paul had been listening to several more videos with his headphones on. He clicked off the video he was watching.

"He didn't tell Lee about the kill switch," said Paul.

The general and Buck looked at him. They stood behind him, and he clicked on the video. "This is the last video he recorded. It's from two nights ago."

The video started with Brian Cole standing in the lab.

"If you are seeing this video, then something terrible has probably happened to me. I want to set the record straight. It was all about the money. Everything Simon Lee and I did was because of the promise of ten million dollars each we would receive from the North Korean government.

"As we got further into the project, I became more and more concerned that the product we were working on would be used against us. I guess I was naïve to think anything else, but we had done something no one else had been able to do. We aerosolized botulinum toxin.

"After I convinced my best friend, Tucker Clark, to use the toxin to persuade old man Halverson to sell him his water rights, and we killed all his cows to test the toxin, I began to realize what we had done. I was sick when I learned that Tucker's young son and his friend had snuck into a ravine below the cattle herd. No one was supposed to get hurt. I don't know if Tucker will ever forgive me.

"I also want you to know that Tucker had nothing to do with killing that brand inspector. That was all me. Please tell his family I am truly sorry.

"Please tell General Culpeper, my boss at the lab, that I am sorry this all got out of hand. When Simon and I first discovered the aerosolization process, we were like two kids in a candy store. Unfortunately, Simon seemed to change, and I went right along with him. So, you can rest easy. The real process is on my computer at the lab. The USB I gave to Simon, the one that was going to earn us the ten million dollars, was a fake. Simon never got the chance to get it to his contact. You will find the USB inside the frame of my parents' picture on the fireplace mantel. Simon you will find in the basement of his house in Bailey.

"Whomever you are. Please let my parents know that in the end, I tried to do the right thing, and I'm sorry. Tell Tucker Clark that I love him like a brother."

The video ended, and there was silence in the room. Paul leaned back in the chair and rubbed his temples. He looked from Buck to the general. "What do we do with this?"

Buck walked behind the desk, and Paul slid aside. Buck unplugged the computer from the power supply and closed the lid. He handed the laptop to General Culpeper.

"Are you sure?" asked the general.

Buck nodded. "If we are going to keep your secret, General, we need to keep it all the way."

He looked at Paul. Paul smiled. "Remember, I'm not even

here." Paul stood up, walked up to the general and held out his hand.

"You're a lucky man, General, whoever you are." They shook hands, and Paul walked out of the office.

The blond in the white lab coat walked into the office. "Sir, we have everything we need."

"Thank you, Major," said the general. "You may clear the area."

The general walked up to Buck. "Your partner is right. I am very lucky to have met you, Buck." They shook hands, and the general headed for the door. He stopped and turned around.

"Please tell whomever you gave the encryption key to that they can keep it with my compliments."

He turned and walked out of the room.

Buck pulled out his phone and dialed the director.

"Is it over?" asked Director Jackson.

"Yes, sir," said Buck.

He filled in the director about the videos, the lab, the Koreans and the botulinum toxin. He didn't leave anything out. After half an hour, he stopped talking.

"Is your friend in high places satisfied?" asked the director.

"Yes, sir. We did everything we could to protect him."

"Then we've done our bit for national security," said Director Jackson. "Wrap it up and head home. Take some time off and tell everyone they did a good job. I'll call Hank Clancy and tell him what you found at the cabin. Once he gets there, our part in all this is over."

Buck disconnected the call, walked out to his Jeep and removed the booties and gloves. He opened the cooler sitting on the back seat of his Jeep and took out a Coke. He walked around, leaned on the hood and took a big gulp. He felt good. He finished his Coke, leaned back and waited for the FBI.

| 49 |

Chapter Forty-Nine

Buck, Bax and Paul spent the rest of the week and the following week wrapping up the events of the past couple of days. The FBI had taken over most of the paperwork and the evidence collection. The final totals from the gunfight at the Clark ranch were staggering.

Besides Dr. Eugene Sparks, seven of the men and women he brought with him were killed, nine were injured and four were arrested. In addition, the FBI found addresses for a dozen drop-off sites in major cities nationwide and were working with local authorities to arrest those involved.

The Clark family suffered terrible losses. Tucker, his son Billy, his wife Claire, James, Connie and Edith were all dead. Edmund and Lizzy were in jail, and Tom Clark had to have his leg amputated because of the damage to his thigh. He was arrested following the surgery. Along with the family, nine men Tom had called in to help were also killed. A week later and the FBI was still working the scene.

Hank Clancy wasn't pleased when he got to Brian Cole's house and found two more bodies. The game cam videos that came from Melvin Gross helped to close the case of the dead cattle and the death of Dan Pearson.

Hank and his team had checked out the lab in the basement but hadn't found any trace of the botulinum toxin. Since the CDC confirmed that the kill switch had worked and they had burned the field and the cattle, there was no threat to the rest of the ranches in the area.

Simon Lee was found dangling from the end of a rope in his basement. He'd been dead a couple of days when the sheriff's office, acting on an anonymous tip and doing a welfare check, found him. His death was ruled a suicide.

Buck sat in Sheriff Toomey's office and finished his Coke. The sheriff read his final report, put the papers on his desk and took off his glasses.

"Hell of a week," he said. "Maybe someday after we're retired, we can meet for a drink, and you can tell me what's not in the report."

Buck laughed. "Don't look a gift horse in the mouth. We helped get rid of the biggest source of crime in the county."

The sheriff laughed.

Bax stepped into the office. "Good news. I just heard from the doctor at Denver General. After four doses of anti-toxin, it looks like Deputy Carmichael is going to recover. Mr. Halverson is recovering but at a slower rate. The doctor thinks it's probably because of his age."

"That's great," said Buck.

"We're all packed up. We've given everything we had to

the FBI. It looks like we're ready to head home. You need anything else before we go?" she asked.

Buck thanked her. "You guys did a great job. Take some time off. I'll see you next week in the office."

Bax shook the sheriff's hand and walked away from the office. Buck stood up and shook the sheriff's hand.

"You need anything, John, you know how to get us. I can't say it's been fun, but it sure was interesting."

They both laughed, and Buck walked out of the office. He said goodbye to Deputy Rivers and Commander Walsch. He followed Bax into the parking lot. She placed her backpack in the back of her Jeep and turned to him.

"You ever going to tell me what happened at Brian Cole's house and what that had to do with your midnight visitor?"

Buck smiled. "Maybe someday I'll sit down and write my memoir, although I probably won't be able to put it in there either."

She gave him a sideways glance and smiled. "You going home?"

"No, I've got something to do before I leave the area; besides, if I'm here, I might as well get some fishing in."

He gave Bax a hug and told her to be safe. Then he stepped aside as she pulled out of the parking lot and headed for Grand Junction.

It was a beautiful evening in the South Park valley with hardly any breeze. Buck decided to walk to the Azteca Mexican Café for dinner.

Carlos was happy to see him. "Señor Buck, I thought you had left without saying goodbye to us"

He led Buck to the table in the back and brought over

a large glass of Coke. "Maria has something special for you tonight."

A few minutes later, Maria walked to the table and set a beautiful rib eye steak and loaded mashed potatoes in front of him. She leaned over and gave him a big hug. The steak was cooked to perfection, and Buck dug in.

When he finished, he called Carlos over. "I have a favor to ask, my friend."

Carlos sat down and listened to Buck, then smiled and nodded. They shook hands, hugged and Buck left several twenties on the table. He headed out into the night.

| **50** |

Epilogue

Buck pulled a small rainbow trout out of his net and held it facing upstream until it was revived enough to swim away. He pulled a bottle of Coke out of the pouch on the side of his waders and took a sip. He looked upstream and watched as Sister Agnes slipped her net under a trout and leaned over to let it go. She stood up and waved to him.

Farther upstream, Carlos taught six kids from the Denver foster care system how to cast. Buck had recruited Carlos that night in the restaurant to help, and Carlos couldn't have been happier.

Buck stepped out of the river and walked towards Sister Agnes. She struggled to climb up the bank and limped towards Buck.

"It still hurts?" he asked.

She straightened up. "The weather still makes it hurt. Today it's the cold water, but I wouldn't miss this for the world." She smiled, and they walked back to the picnic area where several other nuns were cooking burgers. They called for the kids, and Carlos led his troop of fishermen to the tables. He helped them grab plates and fill them with the goodies the nuns had cooked. The chocolate chip cookies were the biggest hit.

He walked over to Buck and Sister Agnes. "The kids are great," he said. "After all the bad we saw last week, it is so good to see children enjoying themselves. Thank you for asking me to come teach them."

He grabbed a plate, filled it with food and sat in the middle of the kids at the table. Their laughter was infectious.

"I heard about the gun battle near Fairplay. I assume the folks you met that night in the field were the good guys, and you all came out okay?"

Buck didn't go into details, only to say that everyone on the side of good was okay. She nodded her head. "After you left, I had the sisters pray for your safety. Perhaps it helped."

Sister Agnes knew how Buck felt about organized religion, and she never pushed him. She enjoyed that after all these years, he was still willing to come up and teach a group of kids how to fish and then share stories with them.

Buck had met Sister Agnes many years ago, and not under good circumstances. Buck had been with CBI for two years when he was called to a hostage situation. When he arrived at the Little Chapel in the Wilderness, he had no idea what he was about to face.

Three dopers, looking to steal gold religious artifacts, had taken over the convent. They had been wanted in connection with thefts of religious objects from several churches, monasteries and convents. They were looking for a quick score that night when an observant Park County deputy spotted them and called it in.

By the time Buck got to the convent, the sheriff at the time, Wade Johnson, was trying to negotiate with them. After several hours, and with the drugs wearing off, the bad guys went on a rampage. The sheriff ordered his men to enter the convent, and when it was over, six nuns had been raped and murdered, and the sheriff had been fatally wounded along with one other deputy. The three bad guys were pronounced dead at the scene. It was a horrible night.

Buck found a young novitiate named Agnes and two nuns hiding in a closet under the stairs. Agnes, who had also been raped, had been shot in the thigh and was losing blood rapidly. A doctor who lived down the highway was able to stop the bleeding, and Buck rode with Agnes in the ambulance all the way to the hospital in Golden and stayed with the frightened young woman.

The doctors were able to save her leg, but she still walked with a bit of a limp. A strong bond developed between Buck and Sister Agnes, and when she became the Mother Superior, she asked Buck to help her put together a program to teach disadvantaged children how to fish. It soon evolved into a full day of activities for the kids and was a huge success.

Over the years, before her death, Buck would bring Lucy with him, and she fell in love with the kids, some of whom still contacted Buck to keep him apprised of what they were up to and to make sure he was doing okay. Lucy was like that. No matter where she went, she would come away with a half dozen new friends.

After dinner and an hour of storytelling, Buck and Carlos

hugged all the kids and the sisters and thanked them for their hospitality. The bus arrived to take the kids back to their foster families, and they waved to them as they left.

Buck helped Carlos pack up all the fly rods and waders and load them into his truck. They thanked all the sisters, and Buck hugged Sister Agnes. Carlos shook Buck's hand and headed home.

She told Buck she would say a prayer for him, and he thanked her and slid into his Jeep. It was time to go home and see his own grandkids. As he pulled out of the convent's driveway and headed west into the setting sun, he knew he was a lucky man.

ACKNOWLEDGMENTS

A special thank you to my daughter Christina J. Morgan, my unofficial collaborator. She devoted a significant amount of time making sure the book was presented as perfectly as possible.

Thanks to my editor, Laura Dragonette, whose efforts helped turn my manuscript into a polished novel. Her help is greatly appreciated. Any mistakes the reader may find are solely the responsibility of the author.

Also, I would like to thank my family for their encouragement. I have been telling them stories since they were little, and I always told them that someone should be writing this stuff down. I decided to write it down myself.

I want to thank my closest friend, Trish Moakler-Herud. She has been encouraging me for years to write my stories down. I hope this will make her proud.

A special thanks to my late wife, Jane. She pushed me for years to become a writer, and my biggest regret is that she didn't live long enough to see it happen. I love her with all my heart and miss her every day. I think she would be pleased.

Finally, thanks to the readers. Without you, none of this would be important.

ABOUT THE AUTHOR

2019 Pacific Book Awards Best Mystery Finalist . . . *Crime Delayed*

2020 Pacific Book Awards Best Mystery Winner . . . *Crime Denied*

2020 Chanticleer International Book Awards: 1st Place Blue Ribbon, CLUE Book Awards for Suspense, Thriller Fiction . . . *Crime Denied*

2021 Chanticleer International Book Awards Finalist, CLUE Book Awards for Suspense, Thriller Fiction . . . *Crime Conspiracy*

2021 Chanticleer International Book Awards Finalist, Book Series, CLUE Book Awards for Suspense, Thriller Fiction . . . Crime Series, The Buck Taylor Novels

2022 Chanticleer International Book Awards Finalist, CLUE Book Awards for Suspense, Thriller Fiction . . . *Crime Exploded*

2022 Chanticleer International Book Awards Final-

ist, CLUE Book Awards for Suspense, Thriller Fiction .
. . *Crime Spree*

Chuck Morgan attended Seton Hall University and Regis College and spent thirty-five years as a construction project manager. He is an avid outdoorsman, an Eagle Scout and a licensed private pilot. He enjoys camping, hiking, mountain biking and fly-fishing.

He is the author of the Crime series, featuring Colorado Bureau of Investigation agent Buck Taylor. The series includes *Crime Interrupted, Crime Delayed, Crime Unsolved, Crime Exposed, Crime Denied, Crime Conspiracy, Crime Unknown, Crime Exploded, and Crime Spree.*

He is also the author of *Her Name Was Jane*, a memoir about his late wife's nine-year battle with breast cancer. He has three children, four grandchildren and a Siberian Husky. He resides in Lone Tree, Colorado.